M000195890

Jonathan Haymaker

By

Sam Ferguson

This is a work of fiction. All of the characters, organizations, and events portrayed in this book are either products of the author's imagination or are used fictitiously.

Jonathan Haymaker

Copyright © 2015 by Sam Ferguson
Published by Dragon Scale Publishing

All Rights Reserved
ISBN: 1943183147
ISBN-13: 978-1943183142

For L.B.

Other Books by Sam Ferguson

Other Dragons Scale Books:

Contents

CHAPTER ONE

An arrow whizzed by Captain Ziegler's head. The whistling shaft plunked deep into a thick, moss-covered tree and quivered violently. The large man grunted, and turned his attention back to the group in front of him. His body was soaked from the heavy rain that had assaulted him and his men all afternoon. Salty sweat mixed with the rain running over his face, stinging his eyes. Another arrow sailed by, this one missing by a wide margin. A flash of lighting tore through the sky above and a deafening thunder rumbled through the forest.

A troll moved into view, coming around a muddy knoll and wielding a spear. This was no lumbering idiot from the caves in the north, it was a swamp troll. It was lean and muscular. It wore leather armor over its groin and torso. A pair of long, curved knives hung from its belt. The spear was made with an iron head, honed to a point so deadly that it could pierce even through chainmail. Ziegler had seen that plenty of times before.

The troll looked up and the two locked eyes. The troll's red, fierce orbs sparkled and the creature snarled to reveal a set of long, bottom teeth curled upward toward its pointy nose. Its blazingly red hair was neatly kept in a short mohawk that ran all the way down the back of its green neck. It snarled and moved toward Captain Ziegler.

The captain leapt over the fallen log that had shielded him from the onslaught of arrows, his sword held firmly in his left hand and a small javelin in his right. He threw the javelin at the beast and charged. His boots squished and sloshed in the watery mud below, but he didn't lose his footing, for his boots were made with iron cleats along the bottom to afford him better purchase in the Murkle Quags, as the area of the trolls was called.

The troll lunged forward, easily avoiding the thrown javelin by ducking under it nimbly. It jabbed its spear toward Ziegler's face. The large man jerked his body to the left and came in with a savage blow of his sword. The sturdy blade tore into the troll's flesh, ripping and tearing through the tough exterior to slice the tender sinew beneath. Brown blood oozed out from the wound and the troll's right arm fell off, severed just a few inches below the shoulder.

The monster howled ferociously, but Ziegler didn't let up. He knew that if he gave the troll more than a few moments of respite, it could easily grow its limb back. He pressed in, reaching up and planting a heavy boot in the troll's stomach, driving the iron cleats through the leather armor and sending the troll flying backward.

The green creature somersaulted backward and came up with a long knife in its left hand. It slashed at Ziegler and then jumped forward, gnashing and biting at him. Ziegler reacted in an instant, gripping the leather-wrapped hilt of his sword and coming up to connect with the troll's jaw. The bone shattered as the crossguard connected. Ziegler cut out to the side and then drove a powerful strike with his left knee into the troll's stomach, knocking the wind out of the creature. It flailed to its back, gasping for breath.

Ziegler came down on the troll's neck with his left boot, letting his cleats pin the troll down as he flipped his sword down and pierced the creature's heart. The troll twitched a few times and then it went still. Ziegler wiped his face, clearing the rain and filth from it before moving on.

A pair of trolls were coming up over the muddy knoll. Water and mud sloshed out from their unshod feet as they charged him. One raised a bow made of wood and bone. It snarled at him, but Ziegler dove behind a thick tree. The arrow bit into the side of the tree and glanced off, separating hunks of bark from the trunk and spinning over Ziegler's leg as he made it to cover. He slid when he hit the ground, carried by the viscous mud out from behind the tree and back into the open.

The second troll had anticipated this, and was already in the air over Ziegler with a heavy axe. Zeigler had more than enough experience with the trolls to know that the troll would have calculated his trajectory. The human captain was more than ready, smiling as he drove the tip of his sword up into the troll's heart.

"Look before you leap, lady," Ziegler advised as he ripped his sword free and clambered back to his feet. The other troll still stood on the knoll, aiming another arrow. Ziegler used his right hand to grip the dead troll by the throat and lift him up as a shield. The dead body jerked as the next arrow bit into its back. Ziegler dropped the dead troll and ran at the troll with the bow.

The troll reached back with blinding speed, pulling another arrow free and bringing it to the bowstring before Ziegler could close the distance. It sneered wickedly and let the arrow fly. Everything slowed for Ziegler then. His senses amplified and time nearly stopped. The plinking sound of raindrops sounded as drums while the arrow shaft slowly ran along the bow, scraping along like a strange fiddle that played only the melody of death. The fletching broke the monotonous sound, raising the pitch and alerting Ziegler that his life was nearly over.

Then everything rushed in all at once. A mighty hammer smashed into the bow, catching the tail end of the arrow and rendering it flightless as its back half splintered off. The bow limbs snapped back, causing the troll to flinch as they pummeled him, providing just the opening Ziegler needed.

The captain rushed in and took the troll's head with one swing. The body went stiff, finally falling backward like a felled pine as the head bounced to the ground some seven feet off to Ziegler's right.

A moment later, Bull was rushing up the knoll to retrieve his hammer. The large, bald headed man bent down and drove a thin dagger into the dead troll's heart. He looked up and winked. "Can't be too careful," he said with a wink. Bull then got up and tugged at his beard. "I reckon that is the last of them," he said. "How many did you kill?" The berserker's brown eyes looked down to Ziegler and the captain smiled.

"Before I got pinned down by the archer, I took maybe a dozen or so," Ziegler said as he spun around and looked at the bodies littering the forest around him. "Plus these three," he added.

"Uh-uh," Bull said with a shake of his head. He thumped his hammer on the headless corpse. "This one's mine."

Captain Ziegler narrowed his eyes on Bull and slowly sheathed his sword. "How do you figure?"

"You may have taken its head, but without my hammer, he would have had you pinned and stuffed on his mantle. He had a bead on you, clear as day." Bull winked and then motioned with his arm for Ziegler to follow him.

Captain Ziegler sighed and let Bull count the headless troll as his kill. There wasn't much point arguing with Bull, Ziegler knew. The crazy oaf would just tell everyone that it was his kill regardless of what Ziegler said. That was his way. Better to let him count it. At least this way he wasn't gloating about saving Ziegler's life.

As if hearing the captain's thoughts, Bull stopped and held a finger in the air. "Does saving the captain's life get me a promotion?" he asked with a wry smile.

Captain Ziegler didn't miss a beat. He slapped the man on the shoulder and nodded. "Sure, you are now promoted from cow-pie to ox-tail. I'd tell you not to spend the extra salary on booze and women, but you won't live long enough to use it anyway."

Bull grunted. "None of us will at this rate," he said.

The two regrouped with the others, hands on their weapons in case there were more trolls nearby.

Captain Ziegler saw Moose first, though that wasn't really a surprise. The giant man stood over seven feet tall. His body was too wide to hide behind any of the trees that grew in the ever damp swamps of the Murkle Quags. Add that to the fact that he always seemed to have a cigar in his mouth and it was fairly easy to spot the smoking mountain of a man anywhere, which probably accounted for the many jagged scars he carried on just about any bit of skin that was visible. The trolls seemed to spot him first also, and almost always started an assault by coming at Moose.

Moose saw the captain and nodded to him. Then he moved to the side and revealed that he was not alone. Bear was walking behind him. Despite Moose being so large, it was no easy feat to eclipse Bear, for he was a large man as well. He stood six feet tall and weighed well over two hundred pounds. Yet, he didn't show any scars. Unlike Moose, Bear was silent and quick. So adept was he as a scout that he could stand on your toes and still you wouldn't be able to see him. Any battle with the trolls that didn't start with them attacking Moose, were initiated when Bear found a group of the nasty creatures to ambush.

Bear moved past Moose and knelt down next to a groaning man lying face down in the mud. Bear was also the group's field surgeon. He slid his right hand down around the fallen soldier's chest and came up with a copious amount of blood in his palm. He looked up and shook his head at Captain Ziegler.

Ziegler had long ago learned not to argue with Bear when it came to medicine. If there was a chance to save someone, Bear would fight the demons of Hammenfein to heal that person. On the other hand, if Bear said that the wounded man wasn't going to make it, then there wasn't anything a mortal could do to save the wretch. With the fighting fierce as it was, they didn't have the medicine or supplies to waste on any who couldn't make it.

Captain Ziegler nodded to Bear and the man rose to his feet, whispering a prayer over the still-groaning soldier on the ground.

Ziegler turned around, realizing that no one else was regrouping with them. "Where are the others?"

Moose shook his head grimly as he cupped his hand and poured the rainwater over his armor and wiped the battle's blood from his armor and body.

"They call us the Ghosts of the Quags for a reason," Bear said.

Ziegler nodded and spun around, looking through the trees. His stoic expression turned to a frowning grimace, and then to an open-mouthed look of dread. "Where is Raven?"

Bear and Moose looked behind them, leaning and peering around the trees. Ziegler turned to Bull, but the bald man merely shrugged.

"Looks like we need a new wizard," Bull said. "It ain't the first time."

Ziegler huffed and kicked the mud at his feet. A bit of brown mud splattered onto a nearby tree and started to slime its way down to the ground.

Just then, the rain let up. The clouds cleared from the forest above them and the sun managed to break through to the forest floor with its warming light.

"No, he's not dead," Ziegler said with a grin.

"Well of course I'm not dead!" Raven called out from twenty yards to the north. "Sorry about the rain gentlemen, but I had a nasty group of trolls to deal with. They sprang up from one of those covered mud-holes and tried to surprise me." The wizard moved easily in the mud, using his staff for balance and smiling as he rejoined the group. "Still haven't met a troll that can best my fire magic."

Ziegler returned the smile and nodded. "Good. I would hate to think that we would have to travel through The Warrens without you."

"Not to worry," Raven said with a flourish of his arm to the sky. "I'll keep the monsoon at bay."

"How many in the group that attacked you?" Bull asked Raven.

"Seven," Raven said smugly.

Bull snorted and waved the wizard off. "Captain bagged fourteen, and I got twenty-six."

Bear laughed and shook his head. "Still counting yesterday's kills are we?" he poked at Bull.

Bull glared and pointed the top of his hammer at Bear. "All freshly killed this afternoon!"

"Easy, Bull, just a jest to lighten the mood," Bear said.

"Unless you got more, keep yer mouth shut!" Bull shouted. There was a time when Captain Ziegler would have stopped such arguments, but as harsh as the words may get, he had come to know that Bull was actually quite fond of Bear. The two were like brothers. They fought all the day long, but if any troll ever came upon the other, they would be the first in line to defend the other.

"I got thirty," Bear said.

"You lie!" Bull shouted.

Bear shrugged. "Doesn't matter," he said as he thumbed in Moose's direction. "He got well over fifty."

"Not possible," Bull replied, though the fire had gone out from his voice now.

Moose smiled and bit down on his damp cigar. He didn't say anything, but he didn't have to. They all knew what he was capable of. Moose walked toward Raven and leaned down. The wizard quickly weaved a spell of fire to dry and then light the cigar. A cloud of gray smoke swirled around Moose as he inhaled and then walked to the north.

Raven coughed and waved his hand in front of his face. "I hate it when he does that," he said quietly when he got closer to the others.

"Why don't you tell him that?" Bear asked with a shrug.

Raven looked at Bear incredulously and shook his head. "Cuz he just killed half a hundred trolls. I am not about to tell him 'no' and risk his wrath if he can't get his cigar."

"Scared of Moose, are ya big wizard?" Bull poked.

"I don't see you rushing to challenge him either," Raven fired back.

Bull nodded and arched a brow as he ceded the point. Then he looked beyond the group and watched Moose. "Where is he going?"

Captain Ziegler broke in then. "North," he said simply. "Everyone else is dead. We can't storm The Warrens with just the five of us. We need to get back to Battlegrym and find some new recruits."

"I think we have run out of fools," Bear said as he looked at the bodies around them.

"There are always fools to be had," Bull said. "Every kingdom is full of 'em, and ours is no different."

"True," Bear agreed. "But other kingdoms don't seem to be killing their fools off as quickly as the trolls are working through ours."

"Come on, let's get moving," Ziegler ordered. As the group made their way to the north through the swampy trees, Ziegler counted the dead and then made a note in a small, leather-bound journal.

"You're going to run out of room soon," Bear commented to Captain Ziegler.

Ziegler nodded and looked down at the skull tattoos on his left arm, then he placed the journal into a small pouch on the back of his belt.

CHAPTER TWO

Jonathan set his left hand to the hay bale, fingers near the base of the arrow shaft protruding from the yellow, dried grass. He squeezed the arrow between his right thumb and forefinger and pulled steadily. The scratchy hay was difficult to pull against at first, but then the arrow loosened and came free. The fourteen-year-old placed the arrow into his leather quiver hanging on his back and then turned around to make the trek back to his firing position.

All of the ground around him was covered with a light dusting of bits of hay and new grass springing up under the freshly cut crop. His bow sat upon a large, flat boulder of gray stone that sat conveniently just over seventy yards away from the bale Jonathan was using for target practice. His boots crunched the bits of chaff as he walked. The air around him was still, perfect for target practice.

He set his quiver down upon the stone, with the open end facing his left thigh so he could easily retrieve the arrows. He took up his bow in his left hand and pulled the first arrow out of the quiver. He set the nock to the string and held the bow loosely, pointed down at the ground as his eyes focused on the bale of hay. He was never allowed to paint the hay, for then it would be useless for the animals, not to mention he would then have to face grandfather's fury. Still, he had to have something to aim for. His eyes scanned for the focal point, the red maple leaf he had wedged into the straw.

His lips curled into a smile when he saw the target. He drew his string back as he inhaled deeply. The back of the arrow just touched the corner of Jonathan's mouth and he held his eyes on the maple leaf. He released his fingers, allowing the string to snap back into place and launch the arrow sailing through the air. It whistled as it spun during its flight. Jonathan's smile widened when he heard the *thabump!* The arrow sank deeply into the hay bale, directly in the center of the red maple leaf. The bottom half of the leaf fell to the ground, but that didn't matter now. Jonathan had a new target.

The young boy retrieved another arrow from the quiver and set it to the string. He breathed out before drawing a deep breath in as he pulled the bowstring back. He concentrated on the back of his first arrow. If not for the goose feathers, he may not have been able to focus in on the arrow. It was an impossibly small target, but that was the point. He let the second arrow fly. For half a second he smiled wide, fully expecting his first arrow to be split in twain by his second shot. He held his arms frozen in position, with his right fingers extended and the bow held directly out in front in the palm of his left hand. His breath stopped, as if any movement he might make now would set the arrow off from its intended course.

The arrow struck just to the right of the first.

Jonathan sighed and his smile disappeared. Another boy might be overjoyed with such a close grouping, but all he could think about was splitting the first arrow. He readied a third shot. It went just to the left of the first arrow. The next shot struck the side of the first arrow, and then glanced upward. Two more did the same thing. With each arrow Jonathan felt his frustration grow.

He set his bow down on the boulder next to him and stared at the hay bale, as if he could find the solution with his mind only. As he watched, he imagined an arrow flying straight into the first and splitting the arrow in two.

The village archery tournament was only a few days away.

Sir Bingham would be there, scouting for new recruits to fight in the war against the trolls.

If Jonathan could prove his talent, then he would surely be offered the chance to go with Sir Bingham. The only problem was that Jonathan knew he stood no chance of winning the tournament unless he could split an arrow, even then it wasn't a guarantee.

He sighed and folded his arms as he stared at the bale of hay. Just then, a gray streak flew just over his head and exploded into his first arrow. The gray arrow hardly quivered as bits of wood and feather fell to the ground from the hay.

Jonathan grunted and kicked the dirt. He didn't have to turn around to know who had accomplished the feat so easily.

"Hello Jason," Jonathan called out without turning around.

"Turn around and look at me," Jason called back. His voice sounded farther away than Jonathan had expected.

Hesitantly, Jonathan glanced over his shoulder. He didn't see anyone. His sour grimace turned into an open mouth and his arms fell to his sides as he turned completely around to see his brother standing more than twenty yards away from him.

Jason slung his bow over his shoulder and started walking toward Jonathan. "How do you like that?" he asked. "Popped it from a hundred yards on the first shot." Jason smiled wide, his immaculate teeth shined in the late afternoon sun.

Great. Jonathan shook his head and turned around to stare at the hay bale again. *Not only did he manage to split my arrow, but he did it from farther away.* There was no way the tournament could be won by anyone else now, Jonathan knew.

"Don't give up," Jason said as he closed the distance between them and clapped Jonathan on the right shoulder. "It takes practice. After all, I am five years older than you." Jason looked down with his happy, deep blue eyes and reached up to smooth his black, windblown hair. "Give it time, you'll get it."

Jonathan feigned anger, drawing his brow together and pointing a finger at Jason's chest. "You shot from behind me, you could have killed me," he accused.

Jason's eyes went wide and he took a step back as he raised his arms. He recovered quickly though, seeing the real reason for Jonathan's frustration. "You and I both know I never miss. I'd only hit you if I *wanted* to, and believe me, if I wanted to, there wouldn't be anything you could do about it."

"I wonder what Pa would think about talk like that?" Jonathan pressed.

Jason shrugged. "Grandfather would probably understand that you were being an annoying, jealous badger and that you deserved it," Jason replied smugly. "Just because someone is better at something doesn't mean they are better than you as a person. Remember what Father always said; there is always someone bigger and better than you at everything you do. Humility and wisdom is better than natural talent."

Jonathan sighed and shook his head. "But why does that person *always* have to be you?" he asked. "I run fast, but you always beat me in races. I am second to almost no one in archery, but you

11

can always outshoot me no matter how hard I train. I'm not even going to talk about swords."

Jason nodded. "Yeah, even Gertrude Vonderden can beat you with a sword," Jason said.

"You aren't helping," Jonathan replied.

Jason slugged Jonathan in the shoulder playfully and gestured out with both of his arms. "There is something you can always claim that I will never have," Jason said.

Jonathan screwed up his face, wondering what Jason could possibly be referring to. Jason was taller, stronger, and better at anything Jonathan ever tried. Even the girls in the village that were Jonathan's age preferred Jason. Jonathan was a blonde haired kid, while Jason had unusually black hair. The girls all fell for that, not to mention Jason's skin was darker and tanned evenly whereas Jonathan was as pasty as any farmer could be, with a mass of freckles dotting his shoulders.

Jonathan shook his head. "I don't need your patronizing compliments," he said. "You've got everything."

Jason shook his head and grabbed Jonathan by the shoulders and looked into his eyes very sternly. "You, are the best little brother in the entire world," Jason said. "I can never be a little brother, and even if I was, I am certain that I wouldn't be as good as you are."

Jonathan grunted in disgust and pushed Jason away. "Thanks a lot, I am sure there are many people who will value that virtue. Why, Sir Bingham himself is probably looking for a little brother right now. Maybe that is how I will get my chance to fight the trolls."

"Well, Sir Bingham can't have you, you're *my* little brother and that's that. Nobody can interfere with that."

Jonathan turned and picked up his bow and quiver. "We should get moving back. Pa will want us home before sundown."

Jason waved it off. "Bah, Grandfather can wait a bit." He slipped his bow off his shoulder and took a firing stance. "Let's practice a bit more. After all, once I leave the village, *you* will be the best archer we have. I can't very well leave without knowing you can hunt efficiently."

"I can hunt enough for everyone," Jonathan said quickly. "But, I want to go with you. I want to be at your side when you fight the trolls. Remember how we used to play?"

Jason nodded. "We used sticks to cut down the tall, dry thistle stocks."

"They weren't thistles," Jonathan corrected. "They were trolls!"

"And giants!" Jason added. Jason reached over then and put his hand on Jonathan's shoulder. "I meant what I said, about being the best little brother in the world. I know if anything ever happened to me, you would be there with a stick and a bow, ready to fight off the trolls and anything else."

Jonathan nodded and ceded the point. "Can you show me how to hit the arrow?"

Jason shrugged. "Well, I can try, but you still won't be as good as *me*. Let's play centers."

"Centers?" Jonathan replied, the obvious dissention pulling his face into a frown as his shoulders slumped. "Every time we do that, I lose all of my arrows," Jonathan said.

Jason shrugged. "How else to learn if not under pressure?"

Jonathan agreed finally and the two took turns firing at the hay bale. Jonathan fired three arrows into three different points on the hay bale. Two times out of three, Jason split Jonathan's arrows. They then cleared the hay bale and started over. This time, Jason fired three arrows first. One to the top center of the hay bale, one to the bottom right, and another dead center. Three times out of three, Jonathan grazed Jason's arrows.

Jason smiled. "That's thirteen points for me and nine for you," he said.

"Round two?" Jonathan asked.

"Aren't you afraid of losing your arrows?" Jason replied with a mocking frown and fake sniffling.

Jonathan shrugged it off and pointed to the hay bale. "You go first this time."

The two continued until Jonathan had only two arrows left that had not been split. A few of Jason's arrows needed new fletching, but none of them had been destroyed. Jonathan dug into the hay bale to retrieve the iron arrowheads he could find. He couldn't recover all of them, but some was better than none.

"Pa is going to be upset," Jonathan said as he looked to

his nearly empty quiver.

Jason smirked. "You should have stopped," he said. "I didn't force you to play the other rounds. I would have stopped after losing the first round."

Jonathan smiled wryly. "Ah, so there is one more thing I am better at than you," he said.

"Oh yeah, what's that, losing?" Jason teased.

"No, persistence," Jonathan said with a self-satisfied smile on his face. "I don't give up." Jason snatched out and pulled Jonathan into a headlock. Next thing Jonathan knew there were sharp knuckles raking over the top of his head.

"Want to give up now?" Jason shouted.

Jonathan dropped his things and wrapped his arms around Jason's waist. Jonathan was young, but he was strong. He drove into the ground with his feet and hoisted Jason up over his shoulder. The problem was, Jason was strong too, and agile. Jason flipped his feet into the air and before Jonathan could understand what had happened, the young boy was on his back on the ground, with Jason smothering him from above. Somehow, Jonathan's nose and face was buried deep into Jason's left armpit.

"Give up!" Jason shouted.

"Nfr!" Jonathan mumbled into Jason's armpit.

"Give up or smell the sweet aroma of a day's work!" Jason yelled. The larger brother pressed Jonathan's face tighter into the sweaty armpit. The stink had been offensive before, but now Jonathan could hardly breathe. His nose was pressed flat and his mouth was stuck right up against Jason's body. He tapped on Jason's back with his left hand.

Jason let him go and Jonathan gasped for breath.

"I think you are back down to one talent," Jason teased. "*I* am more persistent than you."

Jonathan shook his head and rolled over onto all fours and then pressed up. "One day I will be as big as you," Jonathan said. "Then we shall see who the better man is."

Jason laughed and then moved to help Jonathan pick up his things. Afterward, the two set off through the field toward the village.

Holstead was fairly large, for a farming village anyway. The hay fields consisted of several thousand square acres on the west side of Holstead, with Tanglewood Forest to the north. The forest consisted mainly of tall pine trees, but there was the occasional maple, oak, and madrona tree as well. A tangled screen of bushes and vines stretched up from the forest floor to latch onto many of the trees, climbing as far as half-way up the trunks in many places. The mess of thick brush and foliage made traversing the forest nearly impossible, and was the cause for its name as well.

Still, there were some who called the forest home. A nation of elves lived within the emerald forest, and scarcely ventured outside of its borders. Jonathan knew of three major elf cities within the forest. There was Teo near the southwestern border of the forest, sitting upon high cliffs that overlooked the Chamdrian Sea. There was a well-known, and highly prized trading market in the ports below that great city. Jonathan had often dreamed of traveling there one day, as he was fond of the idea of sailing and becoming a merchant upon the high seas, though he knew it was not a likely outcome given his farming background. He knew little of matters of trade, and less of sailing.

In the eastern parts of Tanglewood forest, many hundred miles northeast of Holstead was another coastal elven city called Telward. Jonathan had heard little about that place, except that it was the seat of some sort of order of wizards, grand elven sorcerers who prized their privacy as much as the arts they researched and practiced.

Then there was Tirnog, the closest city which rested in the southeast corner of the forest, roughly one hundred miles north-northeast of Holstead. Given Tirnog's proximity to Holstead, one might have thought there would be some amount of trade facilitated between the two settlements. This was not the case.

Tirnog was close in distance, but there were no roads leading through the forest between the two cities. Even if there were, Jonathan knew that the elves would have little need for anything Holstead could produce. In terms of agriculture, the elves were well-renowned for their abilities and never wanted for grains, fruits, or vegetables. They also saw little value in money, and therefore had no need to sell their surplus. Whatever other crafts Holstead had to offer with their blacksmiths, leather workers, or craftsmen, the elves far surpassed Holstead in terms of skill and experience. Occasionally an elf would wander out from the forest and pass through Holstead, but it was usually only a scholar or messenger on their way to the city of Lehemat, the seat of the human kingdom that lay sandwiched between Tanglewood Forest to the north and the Murkle Quags to the south.

Jonathan wondered then, if the elves had better craftsmen and farmers, whether they had better warriors as well. Why the elves wouldn't lend their skill to King Roan, Jonathan didn't know. Certainly their blades and bows would be a great asset in the ongoing war against the trolls, and that was to say nothing of the elves and their magic.

He continued to ponder the possibilities of an elf army marching south as he and Jason followed the dirt road away from the forest and back to their village. Jonathan imagined rows and columns of finely dressed warriors marching rhythmically, in perfect lock-step, with their spears held upright and chanting in unison. Or maybe they would ride upon the elk that lived in the forest. Surely if the humans had tamed the horses, then perhaps the elves had managed to tame the great elk. Jonathan's imaginary army shifted from marching on foot to loping along on the backs of great elk, holding long scimitars in their hands, and exquisite bows slung over their backs. Such a sight would be certain to turn even the fiercest of trolls in fear, Jonathan thought.

So why hadn't they come? Surely King Roan had asked for help. It was well known that King Roan's father had even sent dispatches to Graebner, the mighty Imperial capitol thousands of miles to the west beyond the desert canyon, mountains, and forested plains that separated them.

No response had ever been received.

King Roan and his people were left to their own devices in fighting the ever relentless war with the trolls. Now with the monsoons growing in intensity, the trolls were gaining power. The lines of battle were pressing deeper into King Roan's territory, and even the people in the northernmost reaches of the kingdom walked as if a weight sat upon their necks. The men of Holstead often cast nervous glances to the south, as if they expected the heavy rains to invade even this far inland and turn their beloved home into the domain of the swamp trolls.

Jonathan shuddered as he thought about it. He wondered

whether Holstead would one day lose its king, and its protection. Would he live to see the trolls come this far north? Maybe the elves would help them then, if their own forest and homes were threatened also.

Something hard bounced off of Jonathan's left shoulder. He reached up to rub his arm and shot Jason an accusing glare. It was then that he noticed Jason was at least twenty feet away, standing on the road and gesturing to Jonathan as if to ask where he was going. Jonathan looked down and realized he had left the road. He hadn't even noticed before that he was tramping through grass and freshly churned dirt.

"Lost in your daydreams again?" Jason asked.

Jonathan shrugged and hurried to catch up with his brother on the road. The two were quiet as they made their way past old Nebok's farm, with its pig sties and many chicken coops. A few minutes later they saw the Hargrove's cabin and shortly after that they were turning from the main road off toward the south. Holstead proper was still another hour away by foot toward the east, but their home was already within sight.

It was a modest house made of wood planks that had long ago turned gray and rough with age. The windows were two of the only glass windows in all of Holstead, a sign that once there had been plenty of money to support a few of the finer things life had to offer the residents of Holstead. Pa was always proud of his glass windows, quick to tell any visitor exactly when he had purchased them for his loving wife so she could watch the sun outside without letting in the bugs. Everyone in Holstead had been regaled with the tale so often that each person could recite Pa's story at the drop of a hat. Memaw was no less proud of them. On the days Jonathan didn't have to go into the fields, he had seen her wash the windows several times each day so that they always sparkled and were as clear as possible. He smiled then, as he recalled a faint memory of touching the glass when he was a little child. He could still feel the reproving slap of the wooden spoon on the back of his hand. He had only made that mistake once.

Over the windows sat the pitched roof made of wood slats and buffered with thick thatch and mud patches to fend off the rain. A front porch completed the house, extending out several feet from the front door and boasting a two-railed fence which was topped with long flower planters that Memaw tended to each day.

Jonathan peeked through the glass to the warm light inside and see if he could spy what was on the table for supper. All he could see was a covered pot with steam leaking out from one side of the lid.

"Looks like stew," Jason said. "You know what that means!" he added with a quick slap to Jonathan's back.

Jonathan nodded and his mouth watered. "Memaw's rolls and apple butter!" he said.

"Race you!" Jason challenged.

Jonathan didn't wait for Jason to start running. He sprinted for everything he was worth, hoping to be the first to get inside and smell Memaw's rolls. For the first couple of seconds, he managed to outpace his older brother. Then, as if Jonathan had stopped to take a break, Jason zipped by him. Jonathan felt a slight wave of cool, evening air and grimaced as his brother laughed and pulled away. By the time Jonathan made it to the house, Jason was already inside and seated at the table, stuffing a warm roll into his gaping mouth.

"Jason Haymaker!" Memaw rebuked. "Where are your manners?" Out came the wooden spoon and she thunked Jason's right hand. Jason quickly chewed the rest of the roll and swallowed while he held up his hands in mock surrender.

"Sorry," he offered.

Memaw sighed and shook her head of gray hair. "What am I going to do with you?" she asked as she turned back to the stone oven and pulled out another tray. Jonathan smiled wide when he saw it. Not only did they have rolls, but there were sugar cookies as well.

"I made a trip to town today," Pa said as he came out from his room near the back of the house. The old door creaked softly as he pulled it closed behind himself. "Mortimer offered me an extra sack of sugar."

"Oooo," Jonathan said as he sat next to Jason and nudged his older brother with his right elbow.

"Mortimer would like you to pay a visit to Annabel tomorrow," Pa told Jason.

"Oooo, Annabell loves Jason! Pig-face wants to marry Jason!"

18

Jason turned and scowled at Jonathan. "Better to have Pig-face than that girl who wants to marry you!" he poked.

Jonathan frowned and squinted. "No girl wants to marry me," he protested.

Jason smiled wickedly. "*Exactly.*"

"Now, boys, that's enough," Memaw scolded. "I'll give each of you one sugar cookie, but the rest are for you to take and give to Annabell tomorrow." She looked pointedly at Jason. Jason sighed.

"So I only get one cookie and the rest I have to give back to Mortimer's daughter? Doesn't sound like a fair trade."

"You may change your mind in a few years, Jason," Pa said as he sauntered to the table and pulled the sturdy, wooden chair back to sit in. He lowered himself down and rolled his sleeves up to his elbows and then rested his forearms on either side of his clay bowl. "Young girls have a way of turning into beautiful women. Give it time, and I think both of you will be recanting your words tonight."

"Assuming she will still take him," Memaw said as she turned back to the counter to grab the decanter of water. "Jason has a good look about him, but Annabell is the kind that will quickly tire of teasing. A wife shouldn't have to raise her husband into maturity."

"Ha!" Jason scoffed with a smirk. "I won't be marrying her anytime soon anyhow," he said. "I will be off to the Murkle Quags soon enough. When I return, I will have my pick of any woman I want."

Memaw lost her grip on the decanter and it slipped the last inch down to the table, sloshing a bit of water on the table. She was quick to hide the grimace on her face, but Jonathan caught it. So had Pa. The two exchanged a glance and Pa sighed.

"I'll get a cloth," Memaw said.

"No matter," Pa said. He pulled a tan handkerchief from his pant's pocket and wiped the spill quickly. "You ought not to upset her like that," Pa whispered to Jason.

Jason blushed, but he didn't back down. "I don't see the point in pretending that it isn't going to happen. The tournament is coming up, and we all know that I am going to be the top pick for the army. They'll take others too, but there is no one that can come close to my skill with a bow, and I am fair with a sword as well."

"Not as fair with a sword as those trolls are," Pa cautioned. "You know what happened to your father."

Jason closed his mouth at that and looked down at his empty bowl. After a moment he nodded and offered an apology.

Pa nodded his acceptance and then pulled the chair next to him out for Memaw to sit down.

"Let's eat, honey. I'm starved and you have been slaving over the kitchen for hours."

Memaw still had her back turned to the table. Jonathan could tell from the way she bent her head down and her hands moved up that she must have been wiping tears from her face. When she turned back to the table, she was all smiles, but it didn't hide the moistness in her slightly reddened eyes.

"He's right," she said as she sat down next to Pa. "He ought to be able to talk about it."

Pa shook his head and put a hand on Memaw's shoulder. "It's alright," he started. "We can just eat and talk about the work." He turned quickly to Jonathan to start a new conversation. "How much hay were you able to bale today?"

Memaw raised a hand and shook her head. "No, let's not pretend this isn't happening. If we do, then we'll regret it after he is gone."

Pa sat back in his chair and folded his arms. The disapproving stare he shot Jason was enough to cause even Jonathan to look down at his empty bowl.

Memaw reached out and took Pa's bowl in one hand while removing the lid from the stew pot with the other. She scooped out the thick, brown stew with the large ladle and slipped the contents into the bowl. She dished everyone at the table, ensuring to find extra pieces of meat for Jason. After she had filled her bowl she replaced the lid on the pot and then stirred her stew.

"Well, Jason, have you thought about where you would like to be assigned?" Memaw pressed.

Jonathan fidgeted with his feet, glancing between Jason and Pa.

Jason finally broke the silence and looked directly at Memaw. "I want to go to the Quags," he said. "I don't want guard duty in Fort Sym, that's for sure."

Memaw nodded and took a bite of stew, but her face drooped as surely as if she had just been told Jason had died. Pa must have noticed the hurt in her reaction as well.

"Bryce was sent to Fort Sym," Pa pointed out. "Mortimer was able to pay in order to have Bryce stationed away from the fighting." He paused and glanced at Memaw before continuing. "I don't have much, but I could make an arrangement with Sir Bingham. There is no need for you to—"

Jason shook his head and pressed the matter. "I don't want to spend my years hiding in Fort Sym. Someone has to fight the trolls and send them back into their holes."

Pa shook his head and pointed a finger at Jason. "You would do well to listen to me. Wars are not fought by the honorable, they are fought by the poor. Your commander will be a man of good upbringing, but he has no more desire to be in the swamps than I do. All of the nobles will be in Fort Sym, or perhaps as far south as Battlegrym, but none of them will serve in the Quags. Those who can afford to, pay their way into a safe station."

Jason shook his head. "Father didn't," he said pointedly. "He chose the Quags as well."

"And look what happened to him!" Pa yelled as he slammed his fist on the table. "He died, stuck by a troll's spear, and his body left to rot in the swamps without a proper burial!"

Memaw broke down and started to cry. Pa retracted his fist quickly and looked to her with soft understanding, but it was too late. The damage was done. Memaw shook off his hand when he stretched out to comfort her, and then she rose from the table and excused herself. She went into her room and closed the door behind her.

Pa dropped his spoon into his stew, angrily splashing some of it onto the table as he glowered at Jason.

"I watched your mother die of grief after we got the notice about your father."

"I remember," Jason said. "I was eight. I remember everything."

Pa leaned forward. "Then how can you be so callous? You saw what happened, you know it tore the family down. You are going to be stationed in Fort Sym, and that is the end of it!"

"How can you pay for that?" Jason asked. "The

monsoons have affected the weather here too, and some of our fields haven't yielded the same crop they used to a few years ago. You don't have the money."

Pa nodded knowingly. "Mortimer does," he said quickly. "He said if we arrange a marriage, then he would pitch in whatever I can't make up for myself. I even offered to trade the windows to him for his help."

Jonathan's eyebrows shot up. He was certain he hadn't heard Pa correctly, but when he looked at Pa's face, he saw that he had indeed heard him. Jonathan turned around and glanced at the freshly cleaned windows.

"The deal has been struck," Pa said. "Now, I don't want to talk of this anymore."

Jason stood from the table, placing a hand down on either side of his stew. "The trolls are coming," he said. "If we all stand back and watch them as the monsoons come farther north and the trolls multiply, then we will be at fault for letting our homeland slip into the expanding Quags."

Pa arched a gray eyebrow and pointed to Jason's seat. "You are not going to stand there and repeat your father's words to me as if you are some fount of wisdom, boy. Now sit."

Jason hesitated for a moment, but only a moment before he complied.

"Your father felt the same way, and I am certain he killed far more trolls than most others sent to the Quags. He was an honorable man, but he was also foolish. One man cannot stop what is coming. Fort Sym is the proper line of defense. It is a great castle with fortified walls and all sorts of weapons. Men were never meant to walk among the Murkle Quags. If we were, then the gods would have given us webbed feet and fish scales. Our place is on the dry land. If the monsoons stretch north, then we will fall back as the Quags expand."

"You say that only because you don't believe the Quags will come this far north," Jason said. His tone was even, but the defiance was more than evident in his red face and cold stare. "Just because our town might survive the monsoons, that doesn't mean we stand by and do nothing."

Pa sighed and reached down to grab the bottom hem of his shirt. He pulled it up over his chest and head and then dropped it on the floor. Jonathan stared at the myriad scars across Pa's white flesh. Slash marks ran jagged lines horizontally and diagonally. There were also circular marks of thick, purple scar tissue on his chest and left side.

"I know more of what I speak than you can comprehend," Pa said. "I fought in the Quags. I was one of a group of scouts sent to find the heart of the Quags, a place deep within The Warrens that lie in the southeastern region of the Quags. We never found it. We never came close to The Warrens. I saw them once, on one scouting expedition with two of my comrades. Our wizard was able to stop the rains and clear the skies just long enough that the three of us found the edge of The warrens, but we were separated from it by heavily flooded swamps teeming with snakes and other ungodly creatures that still haunt me in the darkness when I sleep." Pa turned his left arm over and showed a pair of small scars on his underarm. "I was hit by a serpent after taking two steps into the water.

"When my comrades pulled me out of the water, the wizard administered to my wounds, but we were attacked without mercy. A pair of crocs leapt out from the water and took Silon, each of the beasts making away with half of his body clenched in their jaws. Jaron took a third croc down with his spear, but he backed himself too close to a tree. A green viper was hiding among the vines there that he didn't even see. He slammed into the snake and it repaid the offense by biting Jaron in the neck."

Pa's eyes grew distant as he folded his arms together and ground his teeth. He took in a deep breath and frowned as he continued. "I still hear Jaron scream even today. You don't forget a sound like that."

"What did they look like?" Jason asked. "The Warrens, I mean."

Pa shook his head and slapped his hands to his thighs. "What difference does it make what they looked like?" Pa replied. "It was a vast expanse that rose above the waters and was filled with caves and shafts. It was dead, as dead as the soulless creatures that call it home. For those few moments of seeing it, two of my friends gave their lives, and I was in terrible shape. It wasn't a price worth paying. The wizard, Kragen was his name, pulled me out of there. He used magic to aid our escape after he managed to pull the venom from my arm, but it made little difference. The monsoon overpowered his spell by nightfall. We huddled together in the darkness, crouched against a large tree and shivering in the cold. We were soaked to the bone and our teeth wouldn't stop chattering. We were so cold. Even with his magic we couldn't light a fire. The howls and shrieks of the trolls sounded all around us. Their hunting parties grow strongest at night. Their eyesight isn't affected by the rain or the darkness."

Pa sighed and closed his eyes. "We never slept that night. We couldn't. We kept our weapons out, shaking and jumping at anything that sounded close. I don't know what found us, I never saw it. Could have been a croc, or maybe a troll I suppose. All I know is that one second we were huddled together, trying to listen for any sound of approaching trolls. The next moment, Kragen's staff and arm fell into my lap." Pa looked up and shook his head as he stared hard at Jason. "Only his arm and staff," he clarified. "The rest of him was gone."

Jonathan sat silently, unable to speak.

Jason dared to ask another question. "What did you do?"

Pa scoffed and slapped the table. "I made my peace with death," he said. "I said goodbye to my dear wife and apologized for failing, and then I prepared to die, but death didn't come for me then. Whatever took Kragen was satisfied with that. When the morning light broke through the clouds and swamp, I ran back to my unit. When I found them, they were all dead. Spears and arrows stuck in their bodies like…" Pa shook his head and closed his eyes. A tear slipped out from his left eye. He sniffled back the sobs trying to escape from his throat and then looked to the table. "I couldn't identify all of them," he said. "There were some bodies that didn't have heads or faces, and some that were only limbs with bits of meat and bone hanging on. There were no trolls though. The beasts had survived the battle and went on to ravage other parts of the Quags. I made my escape back to Battlegrym and told the commander all that I had seen.

"I was awarded a commendation and held up as a hero. I was the man who had found The Warrens. Commander Lisent conveniently forgot to tell the others about everything else that I had seen. For the rest of my service I was kept at Battlegrym as a personal assistant to Commander Lisent. Looking back on it now, I suppose he did that so I wouldn't scare the scores of men he sent out to retrace my steps. No one ever made it that close to The Warrens again. I was called upon to create maps and advise officers leading patrols out into the swamps, but no matter what I told them or how I warned them, none of them ever returned."

"Why haven't you told us this before?" Jason asked.

"Because I used to tell your father while he was growing up. After my return he always begged for stories from my time in the war. Your grandmother tried to stop me, and I tried not to tell them, but your father was persistent. He was so convinced that he would be a hero like his father." Pa stood up then and shook his head. "I indulged him, and his fate was no different than the countless others who tried to retrace my steps." He turned a soft, but sad eye on Jason again and shook his head. "War is not the place to earn glory and honor," he said. "The place a man proves his worth is in his own home, by how he treats his family and those around him. I failed my family once, and I won't do that again. You are going to Fort Sym, and that is final." He turned and walked to his room.

Jason stood and shot a hand out as his mouth opened to say something, but as he and Jonathan realized that there were far more scars on Pa's back than on his front, they looked to each other and were unable to utter a single word more.

Pa stopped at his door and turned back. "Before you think of snooping around for a map to The Warrens, you can forget about it. All of them were kept at Battlegrym. Your father procured the last one before he departed from Battlegrym to find The Warrens. There is no way to win this war with the trolls. The only rational thing to do is yield whatever ground that the Murkle Quags takes with its monsoons and the monsters it spawns."

CHAPTER THREE

Captain Ziegler held his fist up. The others stopped dead in their tracks behind him. The rain was falling heavily upon them, soaking them through to the bone. Raven used his magic to warm their bodies. Normally he would use his arts to halt the rain itself, but with the casualties they had already suffered, Ziegler thought it best not to draw too much attention. Using magic to halt the rain made it easier to fight, and more pleasant to trudge through the swamps, but altering the weather also brought a greater chance of discovery. The trolls had long ago discovered that if the monsoons were being stopped over a specific location, the humans were sure to be camping or marching nearby.

Once, Raven had even altered his magic so that he only created an orb around the troupe to keep them dry and warm, but somehow the trolls were able to track that as well. Still, to march a large unit of soldiers through the swamps during the monsoons was to invite disease and death. So, when the army marched out, they used wizards to alter the weather. They could at least fight against the trolls, but foot rot and dysentery were not enemies easily beaten, even with magic, and that was to say nothing of the terrible fevers that so easily beset the humans.

Despite this, Ziegler had ordered no weather shields as they fled from The Warrens back to Battlegrym. The warmth should be enough to stave off any disease, he figured. There were few enough men that Raven was easily able to keep the foot rot and fevers away, even in the deluge, so long as they made haste for Battlegrym.

Ziegler moved around a large tree layered in moss and ivy. His feet scraped through the wet ferns and his boots stuck in the thick mud that tugged at his feet with each step forward. The heavy rains masked sounds of movement. Drops as large as the end of a man's thumb pummeled the Ghosts of the Quags, as well as the ground and foliage around them. Captain Ziegler reached up with his gloved hand to steady himself on the tree. Water squished out between his fingers and the moss tore away as he put pressure on the tree. Tiny bubbles emerged from the flattened moss and the area around his hand sounded as if it was wheezing.

The little sunlight that pierced the treetops from above did little to help him. The large man peered out through the rain, straining his eyes against the silvery screen of water that shrouded his view. There was a movement some fifty yards ahead of him. A large, dark shape that walked upright and slowly stalked through the trees ahead. The rain obscured Ziegler's vision so that he could not discern whether he spied friend or foe.

He looked back to Raven and gave a quick hand signal, then he pointed to Moose and nodded to the west. The two silently turned and disappeared into the forest toward the west. They would circle around to the north, Ziegler knew. The captain then turned to Bull and pointed to the trees where the dark shape moved.

Bull stepped forward and squinted through the water coursing over his face. His eyes widened momentarily and his nostrils flared when he caught sight of the figure. Bull glanced to Ziegler and nodded confidently. Ziegler returned the nod. Bull took hold of his weapon and moved through the forest to the north.

Ziegler then motioned for Bear to follow him. The two men circled out to the east, ever watchful for sign of others in the forest nearby.

It could be that the figure they saw was a human scout, sent from Battlegrym to check the swampy forest to the south, but it was far more likely that it was a troll. Most humans would scout in pairs, or sometimes in trios. Trolls, on the other hand, were far more numerous than humans. They were also more adept at moving through the swamp without contracting any of its ill effects due to their tremendous powers of regeneration. Even the vipers and insects that could end a human life with a single bite were nothing more than small annoyances for a troll. Somehow their bodies could reject even the strongest of poisons. More than that, trolls didn't seem to care as much as the humans did about the loss of life in this war. For every troll that died, there were several more to take its place, and regardless of how many they lost in a struggle, they always fought to the last troll warrior. They never retreated

27

from battle, and they never stopped to help the wounded. This was not so with the humans.

Ziegler kept his eye on the form as it wound its way through waist high ferns and around great trees. It ducked behind a screen of thick moss stretching from a rotting bough eight feet above the ground down to the thick ferns below.

Captain Ziegler halted in his tracks and held a hand out for Bear.

"Where'd he go?" Bear whispered.

Captain Ziegler shook his head. Whatever the thing was, it was gone. Ziegler scanned the area as best he could, wiping water from his brow and squinting at the harsh rain. He couldn't see anything. He turned back to locate Bull. The large berserker must have also noticed the figure's disappearing act, for he was crouched in a crop of ferns at the base of a large, bald cypress tree.

"Something's wrong if Bull hesitates," Bear cautioned.

Ziegler drew his sword and gripped the leather-wrapped hilt. He bent to a mid-crouch, ready to sprint out as soon as he could discern where the figure was.

He waited for a few more minutes, still and focused, as his eyes scanned the area around the screen of moss. Water cascaded down the living wall as he watched.

Then, the moss bowed out toward Ziegler. The bough above the screen creaked and snapped as the moss effectively trapped something inside like a great net. A moment later Moose was trampling the ground and pummeling the lump of thrashing green with his hammer.

Ziegler rushed in, as did Bull. They arrived just as the troll managed to rip through the moss and snarl at Moose. Jagged yellow teeth flashed up at them as the troll reached out from the moss with a lean hand holding a dagger. Moose brought the hammer down quick and decisively on the troll's face, flattening everything it struck and pounding into the mud below. The sickly sound of cracking bone and squishing flesh was loud enough to be heard above the din of the torrential rain. Luckily, the moss concealed all of the gruesomeness.

The troll twitched a time or two more, and Ziegler thrust his sword down into the creature's chest for good measure.

"Always better to kill the troll twice than to let it escape,"

Ziegler commented as he withdrew his sword. He looked up to Moose with a nod of approval. "Good job."

Moose grunted.

Raven appeared from behind a crop of large trees and gestured out to Bull. "I think the troll scout caught sight of you," he said.

Bull shrugged. "That was the point. I draw his attention while the four of you close in from the sides."

Raven nodded knowingly.

"Let's move along," Ziegler said. We have another couple of miles before we reach Battlegrym. We can report this sighting when we get there."

"I could do with a dry pair of socks," Bear said.

Bull scoffed. "What's the matter Bear, toes starting to wrinkle?"

Bear picked up his right foot and turned it to the side as if he could see through the leather. "Oh, I think I am well beyond wrinkled toes."

"Are you still warm enough?" Raven asked. "Have you felt any chills or other signs of fever?"

Bear shook his head. "No, but I can feel the stinging. I know something is ripped inside the boot. The faster we get back to Battlegrym, the better I can stave off foot rot."

"Any blood?" Ziegler asked as he pointed to Bear's foot.

"Nothing seeping through yet," Bear said with a shake of his head. "Though with this rain I don't know that I would be able to see it anyway. Mud's so thick on the bottom of the boot it might be hiding it, and the rain hitting the top would wash it away before I could notice."

Captain Ziegler nodded. "Let's move."

The five of them left the troll corpse wrapped in moss and moved northward. They pressed through the large cypress trees, trudging through thickening mud that seemed to grow heavier with each step as the farther they moved north the more rocks and clumps seemed to cling to them.

Finally, after another hour of marching along, the trees broke and they saw the clearing. The muddy swamp gave way to waterlogged earth. Puddles formed all along the dead and dying patches of grass that had only a few years before been part of a vast field. That was before the monsoons moved this far north. The marching was a bit easier, if a little on the slippery side now as they crossed over the grassy field. Through the rain they could just make out the sight of a crew fixing the large boardwalk that extended out to the south. Thick posts were driven into the ground to hold up the platform of wood that stood a couple feet above the ground. It afforded Battlegrym an easier defense should the trolls ever make it this far north, Ziegler knew.

They made the platform in good time and the crew of engineers helped them up to walk on the wood. It was then that Ziegler saw they were not only repairing broken planks, but they were also preparing to build a wall. Posts were being placed at the edge of the platform every four feet. All along the platform were tall piles of boards and logs, waiting to be used for the wall. Logs were being fashioned into pikes that would presumably be aimed outward from the wall. Additionally, there were several crews of men pulling large handcarts behind them.

Ziegler stopped to watch as his men did the best they could to scrape the thick mud from their boots before traversing over the pristine platform. One of the carts held a great amount of birch bark. The men pulling this cart moved forward and started loosely nailing the rough bark to the smooth planks on the platform. No sooner had they finished then the carts behind them would come forward and shovel out quantities of sand over the bark.

"It provides better traction," one of the engineers told Ziegler as he pointed to the carts. "We have to replace the sand a lot, but the bark helps to trap the rough grains and gives our men better purchase on the platform. We'll build slanted roofs near the wall, but it would take too long to do that for the whole platform."

"The platform is bigger than I last saw it," Ziegler said.

"You have been gone for a few months," the engineer replied. "We reached our goal. This will give us a good defense if the trolls are spotted coming over the clearing. We can even build bunks out here once the walls are up. That way no one can sneak up on Battlegrym."

"Have the trolls been up here enough to make that possible?" Ziegler asked.

The engineer shrugged. "All I know is every day you are

out there looking for their home, they are sending armies north to find ours. We have had a few battles here in the clearing over the last several weeks, actually. Nothing too serious, but enough that we have redoubled our efforts to finish the platform. When it is finished it is going to create a palisade that completely surrounds Battlegrym. The castle will be in the center, with the outer walls of the palisade measuring half a mile out in every direction. The wooden platform is designed to afford our warriors better footing than the clearing would have offered now that it is constantly waterlogged." The engineer shrugged and offered a smile. "I imagine if we have the time that they'll order us to create some sort of roof over the whole deck."

Ziegler glanced back and noticed that his men were now waiting for him to finish his conversation. His eyes flicked down to Bear's foot and he noticed a thin line of red flowing out from the heel of the boot, washed along by the rainwater. He clapped the engineer on the back. "Best of luck to you. May the Gods grant you strength."

The engineer smiled and turned to leave, but stopped short, looking at the others with Captain Ziegler. "Is this all that remains? I mean, where are the others that left with you?"

Bull stepped up and placed his face directly in front of the engineer's. "Why do you think they call us the Ghosts of the Quags?"

The engineer nodded nervously and then shuffled back to work.

Ziegler turned and the men marched along the deck with him. He might have rebuked Bull for the man's harshness, but Bear was quick to do so for him, which of course started a merry argument that had all of the men along the palisade construction zone moving quickly to make way for the group. Ziegler let it go, as he found himself doing more and more lately.

When they finally saw the looming towers and walls of the stone fortress known as Battlegrym, each of the men felt a wave of relief. Their pace redoubled as their boots clapped on the boardwalk below. The gray stone of the building seemed to absorb the light of the sun that managed to filter through the thick clouds above and the sheets of rain. Spots of orange light fought the gloom from the covered lanterns and torches that were shielded from the weather. They did little to cut the gloom, but they did help the Ghosts of the Quags to find their way to the main entrance.

They passed by a large number of guards and through several mantraps, each of them blockaded and closed with a heavy portcullis of iron. The warriors would move into each one and wait for the portcullis behind them to close before the one in front of them would open.

"This is the part I hate," Bull grunted. "As if they can't see we're not trolls, we have to sit in each little holding cell and wait for them to raise the gates."

"It's a precaution," Raven said. "In case the trolls have sent an army to follow any who come into Battlegrym."

"Isn't the large boardwalk and palisade supposed to prevent surprises now?" Bull retorted. "Or are they just building it because they had nothing better to do with good wood than let it rot in the rain?" Bull looked up to the shadowy faces peering down at them from the murder holes above. "Where are the wizards?" he shouted. "Can you not at least keep the rains away from Battlegrym?"

"Close your mouth," Ziegler said curtly. He turned and narrowed an eye on Bull. "I mean it."

Bull grunted and folded his arms, but he kept his thoughts to himself.

After a matter of minutes and going through three more mantraps, the group was admitted into the castle courtyard. The floor was dirt, as this is where the horses and other animals were kept in their stables, but a roof had long ago been built over this portion of the keep. Columns of soldiers trained in the courtyard as workers hurried about with feed for the horses, or with supplies for the castle.

Ziegler led the group directly to the twenty foot tall doorway at the top of a grand staircase of gray stone. Each of the double doors stood mightily with arched tops and bands of iron bolted across the wood to reinforce them from assault. The guards stood flanking the doors, with their halberds pointed upward and their eyes focused on some point directly in front of them.

The large door on the left opened inward, revealing a man dressed in black garb with a long, hawkish nose set between a pair of narrow, ever scrutinizing eyes that glared out coldly at Captain Ziegler. The man was bald, standing with his hands clasped behind his back and his chin proudly jutting out beyond his neck.

"Where are the others?" the man asked pointedly.

Captain Ziegler sighed and inwardly cursed his luck. There were not many men he had ever met that had always seemed to rub him the wrong way, but Toles, the Master of the Keep, was one such man. It was as if Toles believed he was the steward for the king himself. It wasn't only Ziegler who felt this way either. Even Moose let out a displeasured groan when Toles opened the door.

"They're dead," Bear answered.

"Perhaps you can find us some better warriors," Bull put in sharply.

The group barreled past Toles and hardly slowed enough to allow the man to move aside.

Toles raised a hand and opened his frowning mouth. "You will have to wait your turn for an appointment," he said. "I must maintain the proper schedule, you know. It isn't easy to maintain a castle, especially one embattled as this one is."

Moose stepped toward the hawkish man and leaned down, emitting a deep growl. Toles bent backward, trying to keep a respectable distance from the giant man. Moose responded by pulling a cigar and biting it.

A moment later the cigar burned bright and the smoke swirled around Toles' face until the annoying steward had no choice but to stop talking and turn away from the group.

They walked on through the main entry chamber toward a pair of black doors on the other side.

"I thought you hated his cigars," Ziegler whispered to Raven.

Raven looked back to Moose, who nodded appreciatively and took a long drag on the thing before billowing out a cloud of smoke above them as they walked. The wizard then turned to Ziegler, unable to conceal his smug smile. He shrugged. "I said *I* don't like to smell it in *my* face."

"But it's fine for Toles?" Ziegler pressed.

Raven pressed his lips together, trying to hold back a full wave of laughter.

"Can you imagine a more pleasant way to shut the windbag up?" Bull put in harshly.

Ziegler looked back to Moose. The big man was grinning stupidly from ear to ear, holding the cigar in place with his teeth. He would never say it, but the captain had enjoyed the prank as much as the others had.

They pushed through the large, black doors and into the council hall. Unlike the entry chamber, which was essentially nothing more than a bare stone room with doors in each of its four walls, the council chamber was a long, rectangular hall with well-appointed furniture, carpets of fur, and tapestries along the walls. Sconces were bracketed into the walls and chandeliers with large candles hung from the ceiling. It was the first sign of the comfort that could be found within Battlegrym.

Ziegler pointed to a tufted red couch and looked to Bear. "Let's take a look at your foot."

Bear shook his head. "If I take my boot off, it's not going back on for a while. Better wait until after we make our report."

Captain Ziegler shook his head. "Take it off now, or I'll have Moose hold you down. I can make the report by myself. Let's take care of you now."

Bear arched a brow and lifted his right foot to the tufted couch. He bent down to loosen the buckles and latches, but a sudden pain made him wince when he tugged on the first strap. Ziegler looked to his other men. They all nodded and swooped in. Moose gently grabbed Bear by the shoulders and turned him around to sit him down on the couch. Bull knelt down and took Bear's foot between his knees and went to work freeing the latches. Raven stood near, preparing the few healing spells he knew.

The boot slid with some sticking and jerking along Bear's foot. Bear grunted and winced, but he never cried out. When Bull set the boot aside, he looked up at Bear and shook his head.

"You should have told us sooner," he said.

Captain Ziegler moved in closer to see the blood-soaked sock. "Cut it off," he said.

Bear produced a roll of wet leather and handed it to Bull. Bull unrolled the leather and found a pair of scissors. He carefully slid one edge into the back of the sock and began cutting down the back of Bear's leg. Even when the entire back of the sock was cut, it clung to Bear's flesh.

Bull huffed in disgust and handed the leather back to Bear. "Do me a favor and bite down on this," he said.

"Just pull it off," Bear insisted as he shoved the leather away.

Bull shrugged and worked his fingers along the sock, pulling only a portion of the cloth at a time. It was the worst over the back of the heel. A blister had ruptured and the wetness had prevented it from healing over. The tender skin underneath the open wound had been too wet to harden, and so it had split as well. The sock pulled at the edges, allowing a bit of blood to run out and drip over Bull's fingers. Eventually he was able to get the sock pulled away from all but the toes.

"This is where it might get tricky," Bear said. "I first felt pain in my toes."

Bull nodded. He worked the sock as gently as he could. The toes themselves were only raw or split along the pads, but there were many places between the toes that gushed with blood and had a foul stench that Bull had to turn aside more than once during the sock's removal.

"Raven, can you do anything?" Ziegler asked as the worst of the mangled flesh was revealed.

The wizard shook his head. "I can dry the wound, but some of those tears are deep enough they require sutures. It would be better to do that while the skin is still moist. If I dry the foot completely, then the skin near the rips might recede and shrink, which would make the sutures more difficult to successfully hold the skin."

Bear nodded. "He's right. Better to towel off the water and blood and then sew it up. We can use magic to dry it a bit where the skin has loosened and weakened too much, but we don't want to dry it out completely."

Ziegler nodded. "Is it bad, Bear?"

Bear scoffed. "Well, it isn't great, but I don't see any sign of infection or foot rot. I should be fine in a few days. We can manage here, Captain, if you want to go and make the report."

Ziegler looked to the others for confirming nods before leaving his men.

"We'll take care of him," Raven promised. "I'll go and

find some healers. Bull, go and fetch a surgeon. Best to use a combination of medicine and magic in this case." Raven turned to go straightway to where the healers would be.

Bull rose to his feet and looked at Moose. "You make sure that stodgy Master of the Keep doesn't harass Bear while he rests," Bull said.

Moose grinned and offered a single nod as he took a deep drag of his cigar. The end glowed brighter as the tobacco inside burned.

Captain Ziegler then turned and made his way toward the end of the council chamber. He passed the rectangular table in the center of the room without even glancing at the large map lying upon it with markings and drawings of troll camps and the proposed routes to access The Warrens. Ziegler had been in the field enough that he had the map all but memorized anyway.

He passed three doors on his left before he came to the one he wanted. He grabbed the iron ring and pulled the door toward himself. Two guards stood waiting inside a small, square room that was ten feet long by ten feet wide. A small bench sat on one wall, but otherwise the room was empty, save for the guards.

The two men took one look at Ziegler and then nodded grimly. One guard spun to the side while the other pushed the exit open. A flood of light poured into the small room. Ziegler walked through in only a few quick steps and then found himself standing in the middle of a great hall. There were several long tables in this hall, with wooden benches and chairs softened by large pillows or plush hides to sit upon. There were several officers in attendance. Some spoke amongst themselves, others played dice or cards. A few slept in the hard benches while others entertained themselves with song and drink.

Ziegler shook his head at the sight. Toles would have everyone believe that the commander was too busy to be disturbed. The reality was that nothing of importance was going on whatsoever. Ziegler removed his helmet and tucked it under his left arm as he walked between the tables toward the far side of the hall. Some of the other officers looked up at him, but no one said anything to him. Ziegler heard the whispers though, the hushed insults masked by fake smiles of greeting before he passed by. One of the officers even had the audacity to turn Ziegler's way while holding an entire turkey leg in his hand. Captain Ziegler glanced beyond the half-eaten drumstick to see a plate piled with pork ribs and more bread than any one man could conscionably eat in a day, let alone a single sitting.

They had all become accustomed to the lifestyle, Ziegler knew. While he and a few others fought in the swamps, the officers here had found enough money to buy their way into comfortable service. Most would spend a year or two at the most sitting inside Battlegrym before they would return home as war heroes. Ziegler doubted that any of them had even thought to lift a finger to help the engineers and laborers outside building the grand palisade either. No, the officers were too busy filling their gullets with wine and meat.

Ziegler passed by the glutton, resisting the urge to simply reach out and grab the drumstick out of the useless man's hand and eat it himself. He pressed on until he saw Dell, one of the few officers he actually respected.

Dell was seated with his back to the doorway that Ziegler had used. He was hunched over a small glass of wine and a heel of bread, talking to a young warrior. From the young man's wide eyes, quick glances all about, and eager attentiveness to Dell, Ziegler figured it was likely some nobleman's son that had recently arrived. The young man was the first to catch sight of Ziegler. His green eyes looked the captain over several times before glancing back to Dell.

Dell turned slowly, greeting Ziegler before he had even seen him. "Only one man that inspires that kind of look on another's face," Dell said. "How do you fare Captain Ziegler?" Dell finished turning around and rose up from his seat at the table.

Captain Ziegler reached out and grabbed Dell's forearm as Dell clasped his fingers around Ziegler's. "Dell, it's good to see you, old friend. How are you?"

Dell smiled and his blue eyes sparkled. "I am well. Here to see Commander Kilgrave?"

Ziegler nodded and looked around the room.

"He retired early for the day," Dell said. Dell motioned around the room by jutting out his jaw and looking at the others. "Babysitting the royals takes it out of him, you know how it is."

Ziegler grunted. "Heavens forbid that we actually try to

win the war."

Dell nodded. "This is Jasper, he is a good lad. He's going to join my scouts."

Jasper rose up instantly, shooting a hand over his heart. "An honor to meet you sir," Jasper said.

Ziegler nodded, but he didn't offer even so much as a smile to Jasper. "Your scouts?" he asked Dell. "I thought you were the commander of the guard here at Battlegrym."

Dell nodded. He gently turned Ziegler around to point at the officer still gnawing on the turkey drumstick. "That there is the official captain of the scouts. However, other than assign names on a roster and pretend to look at maps, all he does is eat."

"What's his name?" Ziegler asked.

Dell shrugged. "I don't remember his name, but I can think of a few things to call him."

Ziegler turned back around to face Dell. "So you are running the scouts unofficially then?"

Dell nodded. "I have good men who are willing to work hard, and I don't mind pulling double duty."

"Where is Kilgrave?" Ziegler asked. "I need more men."

Dell whistled through his teeth. "That didn't take long, did it?" Dell looked over to Jasper and motioned for him to leave. "Go and set yourself up in your quarters, son. I'll be along after the guards change shifts and assign you to a trainer." Jasper nodded and hustled out of the chamber while Dell and Ziegler watched. "He's a good one," Dell commented. "He is determined to fight the trolls, but he is smart enough that the whole mess scares the living stuffing right out of him too."

"I am sure you will mold him into a proper scout," Ziegler said.

Dell shook his head. "This isn't the same war our fathers fought," he said sadly. He cast his eyes around him. "We always had those of privilege buying their way into comfort while others fought the trolls, but it has gotten out of hand lately." Dell leaned in to whisper. "The palisade is Kilgrave's idea, he is willing to fortify Battlegrym and do what it takes to hold on to her, but there are others who would rather give up the castle and the position."

Ziegler started to respond, but Dell shook his head and motioned for the door.

"Let's get some air, away from prying ears," Dell whispered.

The two of them walked back toward the door, silent as they moved out of the hall. As they passed by the large man with the mountain of food on his plate Ziegler stopped.

"Don't," Dell whispered, but it was too late. Ziegler had already set himself to it.

Captain Ziegler reached down and snatched the drumstick out of the man's hand and took a great bite out of it himself. The officer huffed and protested, shouting and grunting.

"Who do you think you are?" the officer bellowed. "You can't do that!"

Ziegler bit into the drumstick and held it between his teeth. His right arm went to his left sleeve and he pulled the wet cloth up over his muscular arm to reveal a cover of tattoos, each in the shape of a skull. He then reached his left hand down and pulled up the left side of his tunic just enough so that the officer sitting before him could see that the tattoos also covered the left side of Ziegler's torso.

The officer blanched and turned away.

Ziegler put his clothes back in place and then reached over the glutton to take the rest of the man's food. "Meat should be for those who actually earn their living," Ziegler said softly enough so that only the glutton could hear. Nobody made a move to stop him as he took the food out from the hall.

"Was that necessary?" Dell asked as he closed the door behind them.

Ziegler shrugged, marching directly to the group gathered around Bear. He pushed his way into the throng and set the plate on the couch beside him. Bear looked down at the food and then thanked Ziegler with a nod.

Dell's eyes went down to Bear's foot and he shook his head. Then he pointed to a door on the opposite side of the hall. "Come, we can talk in my room."

The two went through a series of doors and halls until they finally approached a small room appointed with a circular table large enough for two, a short bookshelf with hardly any books upon it whatsoever, and a simple bed.

"Where are the others?" Dell asked.

Ziegler finished the drumstick before answering. "That's why I need more men," he said. He looked around for some place to put the cleaned bone.

Dell thumped a finger on the table. "Just set it down. I'll get it later."

Ziegler nodded his appreciation. "So what were you saying before?"

Dell sighed and shuffled to the bed, lowering himself down and shaking his head at the floor. "The wizards can't stop the monsoon around Battlegrym," he said.

Ziegler couldn't believe his ears. He moved to the table and sat down. "What do you mean?"

"Exactly what I said," Dell replied. "The rain is too strong. The wizards can't clear our skies for more than an hour or two a day, and that isn't nearly enough to keep Battlegrym from going under."

"Going under?" Ziegler questioned.

Dell sighed and nodded. "The castle is sinking. The rains over the past couple of years have become so intense that the ground is swallowing Battlegrym. If we don't win the war against the trolls, or maybe even if we do, Battlegrym is lost. She is going to be swallowed into the ground. She has already sunk more than half a foot since you left. Didn't you notice?"

Ziegler shook his head dumbfounded. "How can that be?"

Dell threw his hands up in the air. "The rains have doubled in ferocity. The castle is so large and heavy that as the ground softens, Battlegrym can no longer support herself. Kilgrave has turned to the palisade as a way to help us stay here and fight, but that isn't a viable solution to replace Battlegrym. Once this castle sinks, or if her weight causes her to break open, then the trolls will easily overrun this position. The best the palisade offers is a fair warning."

"What does King Roan want to do?" Ziegler asked.

"Kilgrave was ordered to abandon Battlegrym. King Roan wants us to fall back to Fort Sym. That way we can bolster the kingdom's defenses and stay out of the monsoon's reach."

"Fort Sym is hundreds of miles to the north," Ziegler countered. "Roan wants us to abandon all of that country?"

"It is lost anyway," Dell said with a flare of his hand. "The rains are changing the landscape. What was once a nice forest with rich farmland is being turned into swamp. The Murkle Quags are growing day by day. Soon they will swallow everything between here and there."

Ziegler folded his arms and grunted in disgust. "So what do we do? We just forget about all of them? We turn tail and run away now, when we are so close?"

Dell stood up and held a hand out, patting the air. "No, Kilgrave won't go for it. He has bargained with King Roan. You have one more chance."

Ziegler propped his feet up on the table and leaned back in the chair. "How did Kilgrave know I was coming back?"

Dell shook his head. "No, he didn't. But, given your past performance, he thought you might. Either way, he bargained with King Roan and convinced him that if you came back, you could have one more expedition."

"What if I didn't come back?" Ziegler pressed.

Dell smiled and he held his hands out to the side. "Then yours truly was going to lead the final expedition."

Ziegler smiled. "Was that your idea? Don't you have a wife back home to return to?"

Dell's smile faded and he shook his head. "Actually no, I don't." He moved to the bookshelf and slid a few books out of the way to reveal a metal flask. He held it up and offered a drink to Ziegler. Captain Ziegler waved it off. Dell shrugged. "I suppose that this last year was the longest she was willing to wait. When she heard that I extended for another two years of service, I received a letter saying that she would not be home when I returned."

"I'm sorry," Ziegler said.

Dell nodded and took a drink from the flask. "Me too." He sat on the table near Ziegler's feet and stared at the floor for a few moments. Then, as Ziegler watched his friend, Dell's frown broke and the beginnings of a smile pulled at the corners of his mouth.

"Why are you smiling?" Ziegler asked.

"Oh, I was just having a bit of fun at your expense. You know my Elise would never do something like that!" Dell slapped Ziegler's feet hard enough to shove them off the table and Captain

Ziegler's chair came crashing down on all fours. "Still a gullible pup, I see."

Ziegler slapped his hands on the table to steady himself and then rose to his feet. "That really isn't funny," he said.

Dell took another drink. "Go on, Kilgrave is up in his room. I am sure he is busy trying to figure out who he would assign to the final expedition. He could use your help."

"You aren't coming?" Ziegler asked.

Dell shook his head. "No, I am going to change the guard soon. The shift is almost over. I'll be along once I have a trainer assigned to that Jasper fellow I introduced you to. You should probably be informed though, that this expedition isn't going to be underway tomorrow, or anytime soon for that matter."

"Why is that?" Ziegler asked.

Dell gestured grandly with his hand, spilling a bit of amber-colored liquid from the top of his flask. "Because Kilgrave wants this to be his legacy!" Dell shouted. "The final expedition is to go down in the annals of our kingdom, to be remembered as his greatest endeavor. Kilgrave has convinced the king to double the recruits this year. All of the new ones being trained are coming here. You are going to have the largest command of your career. Why, Kilgrave himself would go with you, if not for the fact that his right leg was bitten off by a croc years ago and his wooden stump would only get stuck in the mud. Go on, go see for yourself what he has planned."

Ziegler nodded and left the room.

Dell watched him go and after the door closed the man sighed deeply. He reached into his left pocket and pulled out a folded letter. Dell's smile faded as he slid his thumb under the fold to open it up. He took another drink as he read the words on the page again. Tears formed in his eyes and he drained his flask and then set the metal container down on the table.

"Oh Elise, why'd you have to go?" he asked. He had told the truth about his joke, for Dell's wife had never been unfaithful. However, he had also told the truth about no longer having a wife to return to. The letter was from Dell's sister, who lived with Elise, informing him that she had contracted a terrible disease over the past winter and passed away.

Dell rubbed the letter with his fingers and then slid it into his pocket again. "Perhaps I will meet you soon enough," he said with a sober glance to the heavens.

CHAPTER FOUR

Jonathan sat on a grassy knoll overlooking the large canvas tents set up in the field. He rubbed the large welts forming on his left arm and watched as other young boys ferociously fought each other with wooden swords. Everyone in Holstead was gathered for the event.

Jonathan had already lost his duel.

Now he sat watching helplessly as other young men earned points and the recruiting officers took note of which would be chosen this year. Jason had already fought in several duels, and he had won each of them. Jonathan was certain his older brother would win the title of best swordsman in Holstead. He had never seen him lose to anyone before.

The tournament lasted for a couple hours while Jonathan watched from a distance. As he predicted, his older brother was handed the golden sword. It wasn't really made of gold, Jonathan knew. It was simply a wooden sword painted in gold, but Jason had done it. He was in. There were three competitions that would grant the winner automatic acceptance into the army. The rest of the boys would have to acquire a certain number of merit points from each event to buy their way in.

The crowd cheered and lauded Jason as they had done for each victor before. Lord Bingham himself gave Jason the golden sword.

After the short celebration, Jonathan rose to his feet and gathered his bow. It was time for the archery tournament. Even now he could see the targets being placed at the different distances. One would stand at twenty-five yards, another at fifty, and the final at seventy-five.

Jonathan hustled to the tent where the tournament would be tallied and scored. Others arrived in the tent before him, but he was still among the first half of Holstead's young men to sign up. After he was assigned a turn, he moved out to the line and watched as the first competitor lined up. It was Clavert Runton, another farmer's son. He was a bit older than Jonathan, but he was not as skilled at archery as Jonathan was.

Someone bumped into Jonathan from behind. He turned to see Fremon Blaire, the boy who had decisively beaten him at swords.

"I'll look forward to trouncing you again," Fremon said.

Not more than half a second after he said that, Jason walked up and shoved Fremon out of the line. "Oh sorry, didn't see you there, Fremon," Jason said sarcastically.

"You can't stand there," Fremon said as he regained his balance. "That's my place."

Jason held up the golden sword. "Nope, they said that the winner of the golden sword gets to pick his place in line. I'm bumping you back. Now if you will be so kind as to be silent, we don't need you causing a scene and distracting the archers." Jason raised a finger to his lips. Then he turned back and winked at Jonathan.

Jonathan smiled. "I don't suppose you are going to let me win the golden bow are you?"

"What, and then tell Grandmother that I am responsible for your recruitment into the army? Not a chance."

Jonathan huffed.

A stout man dressed in a brown tunic and black pants then moved out into the archery field and called for everyone's attention. "Listen up," he shouted. "This is not going to be a normal archery tournament. There won't be the usual ends of six arrows. Instead, each shooter will be allowed three arrows per target. Each shooter will have three minutes to fire all arrows. When the time is up, the bell will sound." The stout man directed everyone's attention to a man sitting in a tall chair with a bell hanging from an iron contraption over the chair. The man rang the bell three times. "When the bell sounds, the shooter is done. All arrows that have not been fired must be left in the quiver. All fired arrows will be scored. All arrows in the outer white ring will be worth one point each. An arrow that strikes the black ring inside of that is worth three points. The blue ring is worth five points, and the red ring is worth seven points. The center circle is worth nine points. For our purposes today, an arrow that completely misses a target will result in negative three points. May the best man win."

The adults gathered around the field, each clapping and

encouraging their favorite. The bell sounded once and the first archer was off in a flash. Three arrows left the bow in less than thirty seconds. They each struck the closest target in the yellow circle, but the grouping was loose. The archer managed to strike the next target only once in the yellow, and twice in the blue. He then positioned to fire at the last target, taking a bit more time and concentrating for each shot this time. The first arrow hit the red ring. The second hit the blue. The third struck the yellow, but then fell out of the target and hit the ground.

The crowd audibly groaned as the last arrow fell to the ground. Everyone could feel Clavert's disappointment, but there was no time to console him. The bell rang and the scores were tallied. The arrows were gathered and turned in. The next shooter moved up and received his nine arrows. The bell rang and the shooter began firing.

Jonathan watched each arrow fly as each of the boys before him took their turns. When it was his turn, he took in a deep breath and calmed his nerves. A man gave him the nine arrows and Jonathan placed them into his quiver. He turned and stepped up to the chalk line drawn in the grass.

The bell rang.

Jonathan burst into action. He had trained for this, he was ready. The first three arrows all struck yellow on the first target. Each arrow was grouped so closely to the other that all three touched each other and nearly made one big hole in the target rather than three separate holes. Jonathan moved to the next target and worked furiously. He drew back his string and let loose in a matter of seconds. The first arrow buried itself in the yellow of the second target. The second and third arrows did the same. Next he moved to the third target. He paused only for a moment to take in two calming breaths before he set an arrow to the string and drew it back. He tilted his bow just enough to account for the distance, and then he released. The arrow flew straight and true. It struck the center of the yellow. The other two did the same.

The crowd cheered and the stout man congratulated Jonathan on his skill.

The bell rang and his score was tallied. Eighty-one points were awarded to Jonathan.

He smiled wide and then turned to see his brother take

his position on the line, then his heart sank. A few short minutes later, Jason was also awarded eighty-one points.

"Don't look so surprised, little brother," Jason said. "You knew I was going to be tied with you no matter what you did," Jason said as he exited from the field. The two of them watched as all of the other boys took their turns. When all had finished, only Jonathan and Jason had tied. The closest archer to them was Felix Graver, who scored an impressive seventy-nine.

The stout man overseeing the tournament walked onto the field with the golden bow and held it up in the air. "We have a tie for first place," he said. "Move the targets out to ninety yards."

"You can give up now, if you like," Jason said. "You know you can't beat me."

Jonathan elbowed his brother in the gut. "You should bow out before I embarrass you," he replied. "Besides, you already have the golden sword, it's only fair that I get the bow."

Jason shrugged. "If you want it, then earn it."

The stout man approached them. "Come here boys," he said.

The two were pulled from their teasing and brought out to the cheers of the crowd. A table was placed in front of them. Each were given three arrows.

"The little one goes first," the stout man said. "Fire one arrow. Whoever has the higher score after one shot wins. Then, we will reverse it. The bigger one will fire first with one arrow. The first to win two out of three rounds will win the golden bow. The scoring system is the same, except we will add one component. If you manage to knock your opponent's arrow out of the target, you will be awarded the high score for the round."

Jason leaned over and whispered, "Your arrow is about to get split."

Jonathan pushed the words out of his mind. He took up the first arrow and set it to the string. He set his eyes on the target and drew in a deep breath as he pulled back the arrow until it touched the corner of his mouth. He let his fingers relax and the arrow soared magnificently toward the target, embedding itself in the exact center of the target.

The crowd cheered and Jonathan set his bow upon the table.

"You're up, big brother," he said confidently.

Jason wrinkled his nose and smiled as he looked to his brother and then to the target. "Great shot." Then he whipped an arrow up and set it to his string. Without hesitation he fired the arrow. The crowd held its breath for the two seconds it took for the arrow to reach its destination. Everyone erupted into loud cheers as Jonathan's arrow was split into three pieces and it fell from the target.

"Round to you," the stout man said as he pointed to Jason. "Go on, fire the next one."

Jonathan watched in dismay as Jason smugly turned his head toward the crowd and let the arrow fly. It was a trick that Jason often had done, centering his arrow on the target and then turning away while holding his arms perfectly still so as not to lose his aim. The arrow pierced the yellow circle and the crowd cheered again.

Jason set his bow down and gestured for Jonathan to take his turn.

Jonathan took up his next arrow and pulled back the string, focusing on the end of his brother's arrow. He held the bow still, arguing with himself as to when the perfect time was to fire. He became hyper-sensitive to everything around him. The noise of the crowd, the minute shaking of his body, and even the thumping of his heartbeat. Everything converged on him, threatening his focus and concentration. Somehow he managed to regain his composure. He closed his eyes and then reopened them and pinned his gaze on the back of Jason's arrow.

He fired.

The arrow sailed straight and true and the crowd gasped when Jonathan's arrow connected with the back of Jason's, but then they all let out a disappointed groan. Jonathan's arrow managed to take off a small chunk of Jason's arrow, and part of the fletching, but it was Jonathan's arrow, not Jason's, that fell to the ground.

"You are the winner," the stout man said as he turned to Jason and motioned for the golden bow to be given to him.

Jonathan stood staring in disbelief at the target. He had come so close, but it didn't matter now. His chance at joining the army with his brother was gone. He knew the next challenge. It was a four mile obstacle course run. He had trained for it as well, but he knew he would never be able to get enough points to make the threshold for joining the army. He was through. The only thing to do now was wait until next year and win the golden bow.

As the crowd dispersed and moved to the next spectating location, Jonathan remained in place, staring at the now empty target.

Jason approached from behind and placed a hand on Jonathan's shoulder. "Do you want to know the secret?" he asked.

Jonathan shrugged, staring blankly at the target.

Jason leaned down and whispered, "You have to focus on the arrowhead, not the back. You have to envision your arrow piercing the same hole. You have to pretend that the other arrow isn't even there."

Jonathan sighed and shook his head. "Little good that advice will do me now."

"Come on," Jason said. "Let's go home."

Jonathan looked up confused. "But what about the race? Aren't you going to do that as well?"

Jason shrugged. "Why should I?"

Jonathan pushed him away and shook his head. "Because you told everyone that you were going to win each category. You trained for this. It's important."

Jason shook his head and tussled Jonathan's hair. "No, it isn't. *You* are important. Right now, the only thing I want to do is get you back home and help you feel better. Besides, tonight will be our last night at home together. In the morning, I will leave with Lord Bingham. Let's go."

Despite Jonathan's sour frown, he was quite happy that his brother would rather be with him than winning glory in front of the townsfolk. It confirmed to him that the bond between brothers was what mattered most in life. Then again, that thought itself only served to make Jonathan sad again as he now fully realized that he was losing his brother in less than a day.

"I'll race you home," Jason said as he nudged Jonathan in the arm. "Last one there is a rotten egg."

Jonathan perked up at that. He knew he couldn't win, but that had never stopped him before. He took off straight away toward the house. Jason let him lead in the race until the last fifty yards or so, and then he ran at full speed, passing Jonathan by as easily as if the younger boy had been standing still.

It was no matter to Jonathan though, for tonight they played and pretended as if all was the same. Jason grabbed a long stick and the two of them beat down the tall, dry thistle plants as if they were fighting trolls side by side.

It was the last game of pretend the two brothers would share.

When the night closed in and it was too dark for them to see, they went into the house and ate a fine meal with their grandparents. Memaw had stuffed a turkey and dressed it as finely as she could. Pa had made his fabled gravy for the potatoes, prepared with the gizzard, liver, and heart of the turkey. The four of them ate and made merry as though it were summer festival feast.

When the morning came, Jason left with twelve other young men. Jonathan stood on the porch and watched his brother leave. They waved to each other maybe a hundred times, as Jason would turn every few feet and wave.

Memaw was the first to return to the house, stifling her tears only until she passed through the doorway. Pa stood with Jonathan for a long while, watching the empty road that Jason had disappeared down. After a while, Pa slapped a hand to Jonathan's back and left as well, muttering that there were no chores needing done that day.

Jonathan stood there until his legs were too tired to hold his body, and then he sat on the porch, leaning his head against the nearest rail post. Memaw brought lunch out to him, but he didn't eat it. When the sun finally dropped down below the horizon, Jonathan resigned himself to the fact that the separation was real. Jason was gone, and he didn't know if he was ever going to see him again.

CHAPTER FIVE

It wasn't easy for Jonathan to continue living at home while he knew his brother was off in faraway lands. Still, as the days slowly dragged into weeks and the weeks changed into months, the young man became used to the new dynamic. He helped Pa and Memaw as best he could, doing the majority of Jason's chores in addition to his own. Sometimes there were helpers from Holstead, a young boy named Finn and his grandfather, but they weren't of much use to Jonathan. They were millers, and not accustomed to the work in the field.

Then, every third day, a small letter would come by way of a postal rider. The rider would be dressed in brown leather trousers and a heavy leather overcoat, with two heaping saddlebags filled with letters and reports. He never had time to stop and talk with Jonathan, but he always had a letter for him. Jason made sure to write as his training allowed. Through his letters, Jonathan felt as if he were living the adventure with his brother, or at least as if their connection hadn't been entirely severed by the distance.

Jonathan cheered his brother on during the initial training in Lehemat, where Jason was able to distinguish himself from the other recruits even from the larger settlements around the kingdom. He recounted every marching maneuver, every meal, every sword lesson, and every detail of the barracks in Lehemat. Once, Jason said that he caught sight of the king, though it was from a distance. Jonathan devoured every word on the page, rereading each letter several times and nearly wearing one out before the next would come.

Pa and Memaw seemed happy too. They listened at supper time when Jonathan recounted past letters or read the newest one aloud.

They went on like this for nearly a year. They all watched Jason progress in his training through the letters. Pa would often

51

comment that Jason appeared to be more of a warrior than anyone else in the family had been. Memaw wouldn't comment, but she smiled more often than not. If she held the same worries and fears that she had expressed the night before Jason was recruited, she didn't show it, except on the few occasions when Jonathan let it slip out that he was excited to join his brother.

Jonathan spent hours training, often foregoing sleep in order to get his target practice in. He couldn't let the chores go undone, but he figured losing a couple of hours of sleep each night was well worth the sacrifice. He was going to make sure that when Lord Bingham came again, he would be chosen.

The year turned and faded away as years do whether you want them to or not. The recruiters came with Lord Bingham, ready to find the new crop of soldiers. Jonathan was certain he would win the golden bow, but this time there was no tournament.

Pa and Memaw followed Jonathan to the fields where the tournaments had been held in the past, but there were no tents set up. There was only a single, long table surrounded by ten soldiers. Lord Bingham sat in the center of the table, with another man to his left hurrying to scribble something down onto a roll of paper.

"What is this?" Jonathan asked.

Pa shook his head. "I am not sure. It doesn't look like anything I have seen Lord Bingham do before."

Memaw put a hand out on Pa's arm and shot him a concerned look. Pa only nodded and shrugged. He then put a hand on Jonathan's shoulder and the two of them walked toward the gathering crowd before the table. Whispers and rumors swirled among the townsfolk, but Jonathan wasn't listening to them. He wanted to hear what Lord Bingham was going to say.

He would have to stand there waiting for nearly an hour before Lord Bingham rose up to address the crowd.

"Thank you for coming," Lord Bingham said as the whispers died down. "I have been instructed by the king to change our recruiting methods."

Pa's fingers squeezed around Jonathan's shoulder painfully. Jonathan winced and looked up, but Pa's eyes were glued on Lord Bingham. The boy knew from the look in his grandfather's eyes that he expected something terrible.

"I am instructed to bring every male aged seventeen and

older, up to age fifty. If you fit the criteria, step forward and your name will be written on the rolls."

A wave of hesitation rolled through the crowd as heads turned and pockets of whispers rose up.

The man beside Lord Bingham blew a horn to get everyone's attention. "The king has decided that it is time to bolster our defenses. The men recruited today will all be assigned to Fort Sym. Rather than sending you off to the front lines, it is the king's order to create a wall that will separate our kingdom from the burgeoning swamps. That is also why we have expanded the age categories. We need millers, masons, builders, cooks, hunters, and woodworkers. If you don't have a skill, we will find work for you to do. Come on now, don't be modest. Everyone must do their part."

Pa's fingers released their grip on Jonathan's shoulder and Jonathan could hear his grandfather exhale a sigh of relief.

"Come on, Jonathan, there is work to be done at home."

Jonathan pulled away and pointed at the table. "This isn't fair," he said. "I have been training diligently. I deserve to go."

Pa looked down and frowned. "No one *deserves* to go to war," he said. "Come, let's return home now. You heard him yourself, they aren't looking for someone your age."

Jonathan pulled away. He couldn't bear the thought of another year without his brother. The only thing that had sustained him through this first year were the letters and the knowledge that he would win the golden bow and be able to catch up with his brother. He moved straight toward the table, sliding between others and winding his way up to Lord Bingham.

"I want to go," Jonathan said as Lord Bingham stopped in mid-sentence and turned from the man writing names on the roll.

Lord Bingham had a well-trimmed, neatly oiled mustache and beard. His brown eyes stared back at Jonathan's and the faintest of smiles crossed his lips. "You are a bit small for a seventeen year old," Lord Bingham countered. "But I admire your tenacity."

Jonathan shook his head. "I am fifteen, but I am the best archer in Holstead."

"The best?" Lord Bingham repeated as he looked to the

others around Jonathan.

A couple of people laughed behind Jonathan, but the boy didn't dignify the laughter with so much as a glance over his shoulder. "If you doubt me, I will prove it. The only person who could beat me was taken last year."

"Oh, and who was that?" Lord Bingham replied with a half-smile as he folded his arms and leaned back in his chair.

"My brother, Jason Haymaker," Jonathan said confidently. "He and I tied for first until he split my arrow. There is no other here who can beat me."

Lord Bingham's smile disappeared and he looked to the man at his left.

By that time, Pa pushed his way through the crowd and placed a hand on Jonathan's shoulder. "Forgive him, Lord Bingham, he is anxious to rejoin his brother," Pa apologized.

Lord Bingham waved it off and shook his head. "It's alright, Master Haymaker," Lord Bingham told Pa. He leaned forward then and looked into Jonathan's eyes. "I am sorry to tell you, but even if I took you today, you would not rejoin your brother."

Jonathan scrunched up his face. "Why not? I am almost as good as he is."

Lord Bingham shook his head. "It isn't that, it's the fact that you would be sent to Fort Sym."

"Where is Jason?" Pa asked as he leaned down toward the table. "I was assured *he* would be going to Fort Sym as well."

Lord Bingham sighed and motioned to his soldiers.

"Alright, that's enough. Break it up and move along," one of the soldiers said.

"We have a long line of recruits and we need to be on the road by morning," a second added.

Pa slammed a shaking fist on the table and yelled, "No!"

One of the soldiers was quick to skirt around the table. The crowd split, making way for the soldier to get to Jonathan's grandfather. Jonathan's breath caught in his throat. He had never seen Pa look so angry and determined. His loving Pa's eyes turned cold and he squared off against the approaching soldier. Pa raised a bony finger and pointed at the solider.

"I was whipping trolls in the Quags since before you were

a happy thought in your father's head, boy. You had best reconsider before tangling with the man who found The Warrens."

The soldier hesitated. The crowd took a collective step backward. Pa turned back to Lord Bingham and held his accusatory finger out at the nobleman.

"I thought we had an arrangement," Pa stated bluntly.

Lord Bingham rose to his feet and leaned in close to Pa. He kept his voice low, but Jonathan could still hear the nobleman clearly. "It isn't like that," he started. "The king ordered all of last year's recruits to the Quags. They were all transferred to Battlegrym. No one was given a different assignment. They all were trained for it, and they marched out three days ago for Battlegrym. Upon reaching it, those who are up for the task will be assigned to the Ghosts of the Quags. Others will be under Commander Kilgrave's command. The Ghosts will scout forward, trying to trail blaze for the army, and the army itself will follow behind them in a final push to The Warrens."

"And then what?" Pa pressed. "What happens after they are found by the trolls? Has anyone ever made it deep enough into The Warrens to find the trolls' nest?"

Lord Bingham shook his head. "The Ghosts of the Quags are the best we have ever had, but they have never so much as seen where the trolls live." Lord Bingham turned to Jonathan and shook his head. "I wish your brother all the strength of the gods, but he has been assigned to the Ghosts. If I were you, I would go ahead and light the funeral pyre now. No one comes back from there."

"You told me we had a deal!" Pa shouted. He launched his bony fist and punched Lord Bingham square in the nose. Pa's left fist was only a fraction of a second behind the first. It struck Bingham on the right side of the face, opening a small gash on the man's cheekbone.

Three soldiers bounded over the table and tackled Pa to the ground.

Jonathan was knocked to the ground, and someone grabbed him by the arms before he could react to what was happening. The next thing he heard was a mob of angry shouts. People closed in from both sides. Soldiers tore through the table and quickly restored order. The few villagers who had jumped in to help Jonathan and Pa were all taken to a nearby barn and seated on the floor with their hands tied behind their backs. Four armed soldiers guarded them while the rest exited the barn and the doors were closed.

None of the arrested villagers spoke. They sat on the floor half breathing and half growling as they watched the four guards. There was no way for Jonathan to know how long they sat there. His legs went numb and the sun was darkening long before the barn doors were opened again.

Lord Bingham strolled into the barn flanked by several soldiers. Jonathan felt his stomach twist into knots as the nobleman walked toward them. His shiny boots thumped across the floor heavily and the man's eyes locked onto Pa. The soldiers with him kept their hands near their weapons.

"Master Haymaker," Lord Bingham began as he stopped directly in front of Pa. "Your actions today were foolish. You nearly caused a rebellion in Holstead, what do you have to say for yourself?"

"Go stuff yourself," Pa hissed.

Jonathan's eyes went wide. He had never heard Pa speak like that before.

A soldier stormed in and raised a gauntleted hand, but Lord Bingham stopped him and roughly shoved him away. Lord Bingham then crouched on one knee in front of Pa. "My son is nineteen," Lord Bingham said. "I am a noble, a man of means, and a man of authority. Yet, my son, Felix, is marching to Battlegrym as we speak."

"I already lost a son to the war," Pa said with quiet anger. "Now you would take my oldest grandson as well."

Lord Bingham shook his head. "You must listen to me, I am telling you that even my son is being sent there. No one escaped this fate."

"Then why did you take the money that I gave you?" Pa snarled. "Something to fatten your pockets? Do you love your gold so much that you would worship it at your son's funeral?"

Lord Bingham shook his head. "The money doesn't go to me, it never did. I only passed along the bribes, but I didn't keep any portion of them."

Pa shook his head and snorted derisively.

Lord Bingham stretched out a hand and laid it softly on

Pa's shoulder. "When the king sent out his edict, I offered everything I had to the assignment officers. I sold my home and took the money to the field commander in Lehemat. Do you know what he did?"

Pa looked up at Lord Bingham.

"He thanked me for my contribution to the war fund. My wife now lives with her sister in Trieste."

"You want me to feel sorry for you?" Pa sneered.

Lord Bingham shook his head. "No. I want you to know that no one could get out of this. I passed along your bribe, as I did for tens of others with similar requests. They took the money and kept it, but all of the recruits are marching to Battlegrym." Lord Bingham rose from the floor and took two steps back. "I, myself, am going to Battlegrym as well."

Pa's anger and ferocity melted from his face then as he looked up to Lord Bingham.

"If my son is going to The Warrens, then I am going too. As soon as I take the new recruits to Lehemat for their training, I am leaving for Battlegrym. I will join a secondary group that is scheduled to follow behind the Ghosts of the Quags." Lord Bingham glanced around at the others seated on the floor. "So, hold your anger men, for the nobleman before you is already dead. I just need to catch up with the Quags, and then your justice will be delivered." He turned and addressed a nearby soldier. "Release them all. No charges, and no threats. Just, let them go home."

Jonathan was the first to be released. The others had their restraints severed and then everyone was sent home with the instruction to keep silent about what they had heard and not cause any more trouble.

Pa and Jonathan met Memaw a short ways off from the barn they had been held in. It was obvious that she, along with several other townsfolk, had been waiting there to see what would happen with those who had been arrested. She and Pa embraced. A moment later she reached out and pulled Jonathan close.

"We're alright, Memaw," Jonathan said.

Pa pushed Memaw and Jonathan away and then glanced over his shoulder at the barn. "Let's go home. I could do with a warm meal, how about you, Jonathan?"

Jonathan's brow tensed and he wondered whether he

should ask the question on his mind. Pa must have seen the consternation in Jonathan's face, for he bent low and whispered into Jonathan's ear.

"Don't believe everything you hear," Pa said. "If there was anyone who could survive The Warrens, it would be Jason. He'll come home to us, I am sure of it."

Jonathan nodded.

"Everything alright?" Memaw asked.

"Fine, right Jonathan?" Pa replied.

Jonathan nodded again. "The postman didn't leave a letter today," Jonathan said.

Memaw smiled and produced a small envelope. "Or perhaps he didn't know where he could find you," she corrected. "I haven't opened it yet."

"Let's read it at home," Pa said.

Jonathan took the letter and held it tight in his hand. The three of them returned home and ate a supper of beef stew with the previous day's rolls. The bread was a bit hard, but Jonathan liked it that way. He broke the rolls and soaked them in the stew. Jonathan wolfed everything down, hardly stopping to drink between bites as he hurried to finish.

"The letter will still be there, even if you eat normally," Pa scolded.

"Oh let him have his fun," Memaw chimed in. "After a day like today, I imagine he could use a bit of encouragement."

"I would have won the golden bow," Jonathan blurted out.

Memaw paused and took in a half breath. Then, putting on a smile to cover her concern, she nodded her agreement. "I know you would have."

Pa arched a brow at Jonathan, a subtle warning not to press the matter too far. Pa was always protective of Memaw like that. Jonathan pulled the letter up, wiping the corner of his mouth on his sleeve. He opened the letter and smiled as his eyes scanned through the words.

"You are going to read it to all of us, aren't you?" Memaw asked.

Jonathan nodded sheepishly. "Sorry Memaw." He cleared his throat. "Dear Jonathan, today I am leaving Lehemat. Orders have come down from the king that we are all going to be transferred to Battlegrym. Some of the soldiers will stay in Battlegrym, but some of us will be assigned to a veteran commander named Captain Ziegler. He leads a unit called the Ghosts of the Quags. From what I understand, he is quite the warrior. Rumor has it that he has a skull tattoo on his body for every troll he has killed. They say the tattoos cover his left arm and part of his chest. I suppose we will see when we get there. They also say that we will get new names. I am not sure who picks the names, but rumor has it that no one who fights with the Ghosts keeps their old name. I should be able to write letters until we leave Battlegrym. I have already been selected to go with the Ghosts into The Warrens. One of the captains over my training unit delivered the news personally. Too bad you aren't here, little brother. I will pretend you are with me as I slay the hideous trolls. Keep up with your chores. With any luck, you should be the winner of this year's golden bow, so it won't be long before I see you again. Give hugs to Grandfather and Grandmother."

Jonathan looked up when a spoon fell to the table. Memaw leaned over from her chair and started sobbing as Pa pulled her in tight to his chest.

"I'm sorry," Jonathan said. "I hadn't read the letter privately first, I didn't know he was going to talk about it, and then I just got so excited—"

"It's not your fault," Pa said quickly.

"You said he would be safe!" Memaw said as she pushed away. She pointed at the now boarded up holes that had once held the glass windows. "We sold our windows to keep him safe!"

Pa nodded. "Lord Bingham said his son was sent too, and he sold his entire house."

"Well, he should have to go and fight in The Warrens too then!" Memaw shouted. "Lord Bingham should be right there in front!"

Pa held Memaw's arms and nodded. "He will be," he said. "He told me in the barn, after I struck him today, that he will be joining them as well. He will look out for Jason."

Memaw shook her head and left the table. She went to her room and slammed the door.

"Don't worry," Pa told Jonathan. "Jason will come back.

Just keep writing to him, and show him we still support him. I'll go in now and talk with her." He motioned behind him with his head and then left the table.

Jonathan nodded. The scene was so much the same as it had been a year ago, only now Jonathan was left alone at the table. There was no one for him to confide in. All he could do was write a letter and hope that the postman would continue to carry Jason's letters to him.

Several weeks later, Jonathan handed the postman a letter for Jason. Jonathan also got one in return. This was the letter Jonathan had been dreading since the day Lord Bingham had told them about Battlegrym. The letter was much shorter than any of the other letters. It stated only that his new name had been assigned by Captain Ziegler himself. He was now known as Boar. It was a name fitting Jason's stubborn personality, Jonathan thought. The only other sentence was a farewell, as Jason was leaving Battlegrym early.

A week passed without any word from Jason. Jonathan went out to the road every day, anxiously waiting for the postman, but he never saw him. A month passed, and then the winter came without any word from Jason. Jonathan still diligently wrote to his brother, hiking all the way into town on the days he knew the postman would be coming. The postman smiled the first few times, commenting that such loyalty was an honorable trait. By the time the spring thaw set in upon Holstead, the postman no longer smiled at Jonathan. Instead, he looked to the young man with sad, dull eyes. Jonathan didn't miss the fact that the saddlebags were becoming more and more empty. Jonathan understood that fewer letters coming in meant more people had died.

Still, Jonathan refused to lose hope. He continued to write letters to his brother every week. Often times he saw Memaw or Pa watching him through teary eyes as he sat at the table writing, but that didn't stop him. He knew his brother was out there. Whatever hardship Jason was facing, Jonathan hoped that his letters would ease them.

Finally, Jonathan walked into town for the last time. The postman rode in, with his leather overcoat flapping behind him wildly. In addition to his saddlebags with letters in them, he held a small bundle of letters tied with twine. Jonathan jogged into town as he watched the postman dismount and talk with some of the villagers. Jonathan knew that the news must be bad if the postman was willing to get off of his horse.

Many of the villagers left with letters, but those who had sent their sons away the previous year remained behind, begging for news of their sons. The villagers were all turned away. None of them carried any letters from last year's recruits. Those young men had all been reported dead. Still, Jonathan made haste to give the postman his letter for Jason. If anyone could survive the war, Jason could. Besides, Jonathan's grandfather had survived. Surely Jason would be coming home.

When the postman saw Jonathan, the man hung his head and his shoulders rose up quickly and then fell with a burdened sigh. The postman grabbed the bundle of letters and held them out toward Jonathan.

"I never had the heart to tell you," he said apologetically. "Jason has been reported dead for some time."

Jonathan stopped in his tracks and looked at the bundle of letters. He shook his head. "No, the envelopes have been opened. He read these!" Jonathan insisted.

The postman shook his head. "I read them," he replied. "I'm sorry. I know it was wrong, but I couldn't bear to tell you."

"Why would you read the letters?" Jonathan asked. "They are for my brother."

"Your brother was lost in The Warrens, along with the rest of the Ghosts of the Quags. It's over. I only came today with the news that Battlegrym has fallen. The war is all but lost now. Only those who remain at Fort Sym still live. They will hold the line, and try to build the wall between our kingdom and the Murkle Quags, but the monsoons are growing stronger still." The postman pushed the bundle of letters out to Jonathan. "I read them because they made me smile. My job isn't easy, bringing casualty reports to so many. I needed to see some hope. Your letters helped."

Jonathan nodded slowly, letting the words sink in. Stubbornly, he pushed his new letter out to the postman. "Deliver this to Fort Sym, then," he instructed. "Tell them to hold it there until my brother returns."

The postman sighed and ran a hand through his hair as he looked up to the sky. He shook his head and then looked as though he were about to turn away.

"Take it, please," Jonathan said. "My brother needs to know that I have not forgotten him."

The postman shook his head. "Your brother no longer walks the plane of the living. You have to accept that."

Jonathan took in a breath of courage and frustration and stepped close enough to slap the letter into the man's chest. "You take my letter. That's your job. My job is to write them and support him. Your job is to take the letter to him."

The postman stood rigid. "If you wanted to support him, you shouldn't have let him go. All who fight alongside the Ghosts of the Quags die, that's the reason they are given new names, boy. The new name is to dehumanize them, to make them part of a large herd that won't feel so sorry when some of the luckless soldiers die off. Don't believe me? Ask yourself why your brother was named for an animal, and then you'll see the truth of it."

Jonathan didn't let the logic penetrate into his mind. Instead, he fired back, saying, "Captain Ziegler has a normal name. Obviously some of them live."

The postman laughed. "Ziegler is the name of *every* captain of the Ghosts of the Quags. Ziegler is an old Terrish word for 'ghost.'" The postman shook his head and sighed again as he waggled the bundle in front of Jonathan. "Ziegler is the name given to a dead captain, just as all who serve under him as soldiers are given animal names. There is no merit to me carrying your letter." The postman stepped away, dropping the bundle on the ground when he realized that Jonathan would not accept it.

Jonathan stood there, defiantly holding the letter out for the postman even long after the man had left Holstead. He didn't know what to think, or what to do. When his arm finally tired of holding the letter out, he let the envelope fall to the ground beside the bundle. It drifted back and forth until it struck the dirt, barely touching the bundle with one corner.

The boy turned and walked the empty road back to his home.

The sun had descended by the time he reached the cabin. Pa was sitting on the rocking chair out front, waiting for Jonathan. He waved when he caught sight of the boy. Jonathan wanted to wave back, but his brain was too overrun with anger and fear to send out the proper command to his arm. His feet trudged on, slowly propelling him over the dirt road to the porch one step at a time.

"I heard the news," Pa said as he rose from his chair. "I thought to come and get you, but then I figured you might need some time by yourself."

Jonathan stood at the base of the stairs to the porch, staring blankly at the ground.

"Your grandmother doesn't know yet, I haven't figured how best to tell her." Pa crossed the porch and moved to sit on the wooden steps. He patted the step next to him. "Sit," he instructed.

Jonathan turned and lowered himself down. He hung his arms over his knees and stared at a small, black rock in front of him.

"I know how you feel," Pa said. He put an arm around Jonathan's shoulders and gently pulled the young man closer. "It isn't an easy thing, and there isn't anything that will ever make it better." Pa sighed, allowing a few seconds of silence to separate his words. Then, he looked to Jonathan. "I can say that you will be able to live with it, in time. The feeling of loss never subsides, but you will get used to it."

Jonathan shirked Pa's arm off and shook his head. "Jason is alive. He isn't dead."

Pa sighed and cleared his throat. "Jonathan, you have to—"

Jonathan cut him off. "No!" Jonathan growled. "I don't have to accept it. It isn't true. Jason lives. I feel it in my bones."

"Think of how long it's been since you last got a letter," Pa said. "Jason wouldn't just let time pass without sending word."

Jonathan jumped up and pointed a stern finger at his Pa. "No. I know he is alive. Maybe he can't write letters where he is. Maybe he is so far in The Warrens that he has no way of sending letters to me, but he is alive!"

"Jonathan!" Pa shouted angrily. "He is dead! He is gone, just like your father. He is dead, like the thousands and thousands before him who ventured too deep into the Quags. Stop this foolishness. It's time you understood, time you recognized and acknowledged what has happened! If Battlegrym has been taken, it is because everyone in the Murkle Quags has been killed."

Jonathan felt a rage boil up inside him like he had never felt before. He stormed past his Pa, pulling away and pushing through when Pa tried to stop him with an outstretched hand. He ripped the door open and went straight to his bed. He grabbed his field pack and shoved a few clothes into it.

Pa was only a few paces behind him, yelling and yammering about Jonathan's stubbornness, but Jonathan didn't pay him any heed. He continued to fill his field pack and then he reached for his bow. That was when he saw Pa's hand. Pa grabbed the other end of the bow and refused to let Jonathan take it.

"Let it go!" Jonathan said. "I have to go and get Jason!"

Memaw appeared behind Pa, one arm folded across her chest and the other up to cover her mouth as tears flowed down her face. Pa shook his head and, quick as a bolt of lightning, slapped Jonathan upside the head with his other hand. Surprised, Jonathan released the bow. Pa took out his field knife and severed the bowstring in half. Had the bow been strung completely, the arms would have snapped forward, but as it was always stored properly, with the string relaxed and attached only to the top limb, the bow did little besides shake a bit as the string trembled under Pa's knife until the blade cut through.

"Pa!" Jonathan cried out. "Stop!"

Pa didn't stop. He raised the bow high over his head and brought it down on the hard floor so that a piece of the bottom limb snapped off. Then he threw the bow on the bed. "You are not leaving," he said. "I will have no more of this foolishness. I have lost enough sons."

"I am your *grandson* not your *son*!" Jonathan shouted angrily.

Pa bristled, taking a half step backward and fuming through his flared nostrils. "Whatever you are, I am not going to lose you too. Go to bed. We'll discuss this in the morning."

Pa turned and escorted Memaw back to the table area. He glanced over his shoulder at Jonathan with a disapproving scowl and a promise to thoroughly chastise the young man. But none of them would discuss the matter in the morning. Jonathan knew where Pa's bow was kept, and he slipped out into the night as quietly as an owl leaving the nest in search of a mouse. He neither said goodbye nor left a note. He just vanished into the darkness, like the Ghosts of the Quags.

CHAPTER SIX

Jonathan traveled by the road to the southwest. In his anger, he hadn't had the presence of mind to gather any coin for the journey. He filled his stomach by hunting hares alongside the road as he traveled. With the cool, early spring air, there were no berries or fruit to be had yet, but he was able to find more than enough meat to sustain himself. Hares were easy to clean and cook, and each one lasted him more than a day, even with the long trek.

By the time he arrived in Haytham, a small town roughly one hundred and fifteen miles from Holstead, he had collected four rabbit pelts. He had skinned each animal carefully, hoping that the furs might provide him with a bit of coin to make the rest of his journey somewhat easier.

He turned to the north side of the road and walked along the wagon tracks that cut through the dirt road into the center of the town. The homes here that lined the road were made with stone and wood. Most of the buildings were one story, but a few of them were as tall as two. The roofs were made with finely cut shingles and shakes. Patches of brighter shingles revealed the recent patches made in some of the roofs as the spring thaw had set in while bits of stubborn snow clung to whatever shadows they could find to avoid the sun.

As was the case in Holstead, most of the men in Haytham were gone. Women filled the streets, carrying wood, food, or other wares back and forth. There were a few older men, but not many. Jonathan had to wonder then if his furs would sell at all. Still, Haytham was a larger settlement than Holstead. It was worth trying. Perhaps he could at least barter them for some bread if he couldn't find anyone willing to part with money.

He continued along the road until he came to a main cross street. A large general store stood on the opposite corner of the intersection from him, an inn was located on his right, and a pair of houses sat on his left. The fourth corner was bare.

Jonathan shook his head and kicked the dirt for his bad

luck. The bare corner was where the market had once been. Jonathan had come to Haytham a few times over the years when they couldn't sell all of the hay from Pa's fields in Holstead. They had always been able to sell their surplus in Haytham's market.

Now there was nothing. It was as if the market had never existed.

Jonathan pushed along toward the general store.

He stepped out of the way as an older woman came out from the store with a basket filled with bread and potatoes. As she turned to nod her thanks to Jonathan, he saw she held some sort of wrapped package under her other arm. A hint of red and white flesh hung from under the package. It was pork, by the look of the color.

Jonathan moved into the store and a loud bell rang as the door struck it.

Sacks of flour were stacked half a man high directly in front of him. Off to either side of the sacks were narrow aisles of wooden shelves filled with glass jars and small wooden boxes. Jonathan moved to the left. Jars of peaches, pickles, pears, and beets filled the upper shelves while the lower shelves held crates of small, red apples, garlic, and potatoes. A nearly empty crate held a few onions, but none of them looked good enough to eat anymore. He looked down the aisle to see another set of shelves on the back wall of the store. A few loaves of bread sat in neat rows there.

Jonathan's mouth watered and he marched over to the bread.

A movement to his left caught his eye. Jonathan turned to see a red haired man walking toward him.

"What can I do for you, son?" he asked.

Jonathan pointed to a loaf of bread. "How much for a loaf?" he asked.

The red haired man eyed Jonathan and then his thin lips stretched into a smile. "Five coppers for one, or two silvers for three."

Jonathan nodded. It was a fair price, albeit more expensive than back in Holstead. A loaf there would only cost four coppers, and that was assuming Memaw didn't just make it at home as she usually did. Still, a hare's fur should easily fetch two coppers, even in Haytham. If the shopkeeper would go for it, Jonathan might be able to bargain for two loaves with his four furs. He turned and surveyed the walls around him. "Where do you keep the furs?" Jonathan asked.

"Furs?"

Jonathan nodded. "How much for a rabbit fur?"

The shopkeeper shook his head. "Afraid I don't have any," he replied. "What with all the younger men gone south, there hasn't been much hunting around these parts. Perhaps if you came back later, we might have something for you."

Jonathan smiled and pulled his field pack around and opened the flap. He pulled out the four furs and hung them over his left arm. "I have four pelts here," he said. "How about a trade?"

The shopkeeper eyed the pelts and then shook his head. "I don't need rabbit fur."

Jonathan shrugged. "Well, you just said that you have no furs. I thought we could help each other. You can have the furs, and I can take some bread."

"One loaf," the shopkeeper said.

Jonathan shook his head. "No, they are worth two coppers a piece."

"Two coppers is what I would charge for them," the shopkeeper said.

Jonathan looked at the bread and then back to the shopkeeper. "If you were willing to throw in a third loaf for free if I had eight coppers, then surely you can give me a loaf and a half. That way, I get six coppers worth of food, but you get eight coppers worth of pelts. We both win."

The shopkeeper grinned and started to chuckle so much that his belly shook. "Done." The shopkeeper moved to the bread and gathered up two loaves while Jonathan moved to set the pelts out on the wooden counter. He was careful to lay each one out so that the shopkeeper could easily see they were quality pelts.

Jonathan then opened his field pack and shoved a few things around inside to make room for the bread. He turned toward the shopkeeper but was stunned to see the man holding out two complete loaves of bread. He looked up to the smiling man curiously.

"You made me laugh, that's worth another half a loaf," the shopkeeper said with a wink.

Jonathan graciously took the food and slid it into his bag. "Thank you," he said. He then turned and left the store, eager to get back onto the road.

He journeyed for another day and a half before he came to a fork in the main road. The branch leading due south would take him to Rynder, a large city within a hundred miles of the expanding Quags. If he continued south west, then he would reach Lehemat. Either way, he would need to turn south at some point if he was to reach Fort Sym. That would be the final city where he could stock up on supplies before heading into the Murkle Quags.

As he stood thinking about which road to follow, his mind drifted to the Murkle Quags themselves. He hadn't taken much time before to think about going there. Sure, he had often daydreamed about being beside his brother, but the thought of actually going to the Quags by himself was something different. Pa's warning words tried to push their way into his mind and cast doubt over his plan, but Jonathan was resolved. His brother was alive, and he needed him. He wasn't sure how, but he knew he had to find him.

He looked back toward the northeast. He wondered whether Pa was out looking for him. Jonathan had a significant head start, but what if Pa was able to get a horse? Surely if Mortimer had been willing to lend money before, then perhaps Pa could make a new arrangement.

That settled it.

All of the recruits went to Lehemat. From there, they received their orders. Even the new recruits this last time had to go to Lehemat before going to Fort Sym. Pa would most certainly be headed toward Lehemat if he was indeed following him.

Jonathan broke out into a light jog, turning south toward Rynder.

He couldn't risk being found by Pa now. Besides, even if Pa wasn't after him, it was entirely possible he might be swept up by some officer in Lehemat and put to task. He couldn't chance that either. He had to be free enough to do what he needed to do.

Rynder was three hundred and fifty miles to the south. If the road stayed even and there were no mishaps along the way, Jonathan figured he could make the journey in about seven days.

The first two days were entirely uneventful, dull even.

Jonathan trudged over the flat dirt road as it rolled up and down over small hills and wound around larger hills. Occasionally there would be a stream along the way, providing Jonathan with fresh water. A well maintained wooden bridge stretched over each body of water he came to.

As the sun began to set upon the third day, Jonathan saw something off in the distance to the east. He couldn't quite see what it was, as his view was obscured by a large knoll, but when he came around with the bending road, he stopped suddenly when he realized there was a group of soldiers erecting large tents a couple hundred yards off the road.

Jonathan thought it best to move along. There was no need to catch their attention, and they wouldn't have any information about his brother. The young man moved to the opposite side of the road and began jogging along, hoping that he could pass them without notice.

His hopes were in vain.

Jonathan rounded a bend toward the east and nearly felt his heart leap into his throat when he saw a trio of riders approaching him on the road. Jonathan thought to hide, but there was nowhere to go. The grasslands around these parts offered little cover. There had been an elm tree just off the side of the road, but that was at least twenty yards beyond the grassy knoll behind him.

"Oi! You there, come here!" one of the soldiers shouted.

Jonathan looked at their armor, noting the black and red crest on the center soldier's shield hanging and swinging over the man's left leg.

A second soldier pulled a bow and set an arrow to the string. "Didn't you hear him? He said come over here, boy!"

Jonathan's eyebrows drew into a tight knot over his nose. He instinctively held his hands out in front of him. "I don't mean anyone any harm," Jonathan said.

"Come here!" the third soldier shouted.

The soldier in the middle dismounted and began walking toward Jonathan with a determined gait. The other two soldiers remained behind, on horseback. The archer kept his bow trained on Jonathan. The other held firm to his sword and looked all around, scanning the nearby hills.

The young man could barely breathe. What could they

possibly want with him? Wasn't it obvious that he was only a boy?

"I said come here!"

Jonathan's feet finally reacted and moved him closer to the soldier walking toward him. Fear gripped his stomach as the man drew his sword and scowled menacingly at Jonathan. Something felt very wrong about all of this.

The soldier walking toward him was about thirty yards away, but he was closing fast. The two on horseback were another ten behind that. Jonathan glanced to the archer, and then to the swordsman on foot. Their faces were so cold. Jonathan saw nothing in the men's eyes but anger. The thought occurred to him that maybe they were deserters, or possibly bandits that had killed real soldiers and now used their uniforms.

Could he outrun them to the camp of soldiers?

His eyes flicked up to the bow. The string wasn't pulled all the way back yet. The archer was just holding it, with the arrow pointing in his direction. Jonathan's feet stopped. He stood still and his muscles tensed.

"Why you stopping, boy?" The swordsman on foot growled and raised his sword threateningly. His clanking armor stifled his movement. Perhaps Jonathan could outrun them to the camp. If he could neutralize the archer... No that wasn't necessary. All Jonathan had to do was neutralize the *bow*. Jonathan jerked his shoulder around and flipped his bow over to his left hand.

"Hey!" the swordsman shouted as he began sprinting with his sword held high. Jonathan kept his eye trained on the archer as his right hand shot back and pulled an arrow from the quiver.

The archer stood in his stirrups and pulled his string back.

Jonathan nocked his arrow and drew it back with amazing speed. The two of them fired their arrows at the same time. Jonathan then tucked into a roll to his left. The archer's arrow sailed past and landed in the ground. Jonathan's arrow hit precisely where he had intended, severing the bowstring and rendering the bow useless.

Jonathan then nocked a second arrow and fired at the swordsman's sword. The arrow bounced off the steel with hardly any effect whatsoever on the weapon, but it caused the swordsman to flinch and halt in his run as he ducked for cover, giving Jonathan enough time to jump up and run away.

He sprinted for all he was worth up the grassy knoll, sliding his bow back over his shoulder so it would no longer hinder his running. The swordsman's clanking armor could be heard as he ran after him, scraping and slamming together. Then it stopped. Jonathan glanced over his shoulder with a wide grin on his face, but the smile was short lived.

The two soldiers on horseback were charging directly for him.

Jonathan redoubled his efforts, his speed fueled by fear and adrenaline. The grasses whisked over his boots as he zipped down the back of the grassy knoll. He turned slightly northward. There was no way he could make the camp, but he could make the elm tree twenty yards away.

The pounding hooves came ever closer, but Jonathan kept his eyes on the tree. Once or twice he glanced at the camp, seeing that a couple of men had come out from around one of the large tents. He waved out to them and called for help, but he didn't slow to see if they had heard him. He continued for the tree. The three men were in heavy armor. They wouldn't be able to climb after him if he could just reach the elm.

As he got closer to the elm tree, Jonathan could hear the panting breath of the horses behind him over the thundering hooves. He glanced over his shoulder just enough to see the riders gaining on him. A large hand stretched out for his back.

Jonathan reacted on impulse rather than reason, stopping suddenly and ducking low to the ground. The closing fingers tugged at his hair, but couldn't catch hold on the boy. The horsemen sped by and Jonathan was unharmed.

The riders both turned to the left, slowing their horses down enough to take another run at him.

Jonathan bolted forward, dashing in close to the riders. The closest rider, the archer with the now defunct bow, reached out with both his leg and arm, trying to stop Jonathan, but the young boy cut out to the side. The other rider had a hard time maneuvering his horse around the first, and Jonathan was able to reach the tree. He launched upward, grabbing a branch and pulling himself up. He squirreled up the tree before either rider reached the base of the trunk.

When the men got to the tree, Jonathan fired a warning

shot into the ground.

"Go away, or the next one goes into your head!" Jonathan shouted in a shaky voice. He looked over toward the camp and saw a group of several men rushing out toward him. If these were bandits, they would retreat as soon as they noticed the soldiers coming their way.

Jonathan nocked another arrow and pulled the string halfway, keeping watch on the two men below. One of them circled around the tree and grabbed at a low-hanging branch. Jonathan fired an arrow that stuck into the bough just half an inch away from the man's hand.

"I don't have to miss," Jonathan said. "Go away!"

The two men looked off in the direction of the oncoming soldiers and said something between themselves that Jonathan couldn't hear. Jonathan's confidence left him though, for the two men did not leave. They moved a few yards away from the tree and then waited patiently.

The third man was now coming over the knoll on horseback, riding at a steady trot toward them as well. Jonathan looked back to the other soldiers and he felt a terrible fear grip his heart as he realized he had just assaulted real soldiers. His mind whirled for an escape plan, but nothing coherent came to him.

Soon he heard the galloping hooves of another man on horse. Jonathan looked down. The first thing he noticed was the flowing red cape billowing out behind the rider. The new arrival talked with the other three and then turned his horse to walk it to the tree. A golden brooch secured the cloak over a set of plate mail armor. The man held a gleaming helmet in his lap and his sword hung freely from his right hip. He looked up and waved at Jonathan.

"Hello to the tree," the man called out. "I am Captain Burke, of the King's army." Jonathan froze as he looked down to Burke's face. The man smiled back from behind his thick, brown beard and placed his hands atop the saddle horn. "I don't suppose you would like to come down, would you?"

Jonathan shook his head and glanced to the first three men he had met. If they were all good soldiers, then why would they have treated him so meanly?

Captain Burke gestured to the nearby branch with the

arrow in it. "My men say you tried to attack them, is that so?"

Jonathan shook his head again. "They came after me, I was only defending myself." Jonathan looked down to the arrow shaft embedded in the elm bough. "I missed on purpose. I just wanted them to leave me alone."

"He lies!" shouted the archer on horseback. "He fired right at me, he just missed, and that's all."

"He fired at me too," the swordsman said. "I managed to block it with my sword, but he was aiming for my face."

Jonathan shouted at the men angrily. "I hit exactly what I was aiming for. I cut your bowstring with one shot." Jonathan then pointed to the swordsman. "If I wanted to hit your face, I would have."

Captain Burke and several of the others gathering around started to laugh.

"It's true," Jonathan insisted. "I can prove it too!"

Captain Burke held his hand out to silence the others. "Why did you fire at them, to defend yourself you say?"

Jonathan nodded. "That one took his sword out and was running toward me. The one with the bow nocked an arrow and was ready to shoot me. All I was doing was walking the road."

Burke nodded. "And where exactly are you headed?"

"To the Murkle Quags," Jonathan said proudly. The men erupted with laughter. Jonathan scanned their many faces and his anger burned within his heart. "I am going to the Murkle Quags!" Jonathan shouted, but his protest only drew more laughter.

After a few moments, Captain Burke wiped a tear from his eye and held his hands out to the side as he looked up at Jonathan. "And why, pray tell, is a boy like you going alone to the Murkle Quags?"

Jonathan grabbed his bow and dropped down, hopping from branch to branch until he vaulted to the ground beside Captain Burke. His eyes locked with Burke's blue orbs and he puffed his chest out as he stood upright before the captain. "Because my brother is there, and I am going to find him."

The laughter stopped. Captain Burke's smile faded and he stared at Jonathan for a short while with searching eyes. Then, he pointed to Jonathan's bow. "You say you cut my man's string with a single shot. Can you prove it?"

"Why should I?" Jonathan asked defiantly.

Captain Burke glanced over his shoulder and thumbed at the three soldiers that had started the whole mess. "Because it will show whether you were being generous or not."

Jonathan looked over to the archer and then nodded assuredly. "Put another bow at forty yards, and I will show you what I can do."

"Have him hit a man's sword too, while you're at it," the swordsman suggested as the three soldiers chuckled amongst themselves.

Jonathan pointed to the swordsman. "Hold your sword up and I will hit it as well."

The swordsman stopped laughing. His face turned hard and he clenched his jaw.

"A good idea," Burke said. "Bring me a bow." One of the soldiers from the camp brought a long bow. Captain Burke pointed to the archer on horseback. "Have him hold it." The officer then looked down to Jonathan. "Alright, kid, you have two shots. Make them count."

The swordsman stood on foot again and held his sword up, but this time he also grabbed his shield and covered his chest, neck, and head with it. The others moved aside to give the boy some space. Jonathan whipped his bow around and in less than a second he fired the weapon. The arrow ricocheted off the sword an instant later, creating a ringing sound that kept all of the soldiers in attendance quiet. Next, the archer held his bow out to the side while two others moved in with large tower shields to protect both the archer and the horse.

"The shields aren't necessary," Jonathan said. "I won't miss." He nocked another arrow and pulled it back to the corner of his mouth. He let it loose a second later and the longbow snapped straight as the string was cut in half. A low murmur rippled through the gathered soldiers.

Captain Burke laughed and slapped his leg. "Everyone back to your tents. You three, back out on the road, but do be a bit nicer if you happen to find someone wandering the road alone from now on."

The group of soldiers from the camp started laughing. The other three turned and went back out to the road, but not before each of them shot Jonathan a terribly menacing look that nearly froze his blood.

"Don't let them bother you," Burke said. "They're a bit sore that a kid bested them, but they'll get over it."

Jonathan put his bow away and nodded.

"Now what is this business about the Quags?" Burke asked.

Jonathan shrugged. "My brother was sent out with the Ghosts of the Quags before Battlegrym fell. Everyone says he is dead, but I know he is alive. I have to find him."

Burke's face grew grim and he set his hands back on the saddle horn as he bent forward and shifted his position. "I'm sure you have heard it before, but once someone is assigned to the Ghosts of the Quags, they don't come back."

Jonathan nodded soberly. "Then my brother will be the first."

Burke nodded. "Come, let me offer you a place to sleep for the night. You don't want to travel after dark out here."

"The trolls aren't this far north," Jonathan said quickly.

Burke shook his head. "Trolls no, but bandits are. That's why we are here. We patrol the roads, making a triangle from Lehemet up to Haytham, then down to Rynder and back to Lehemat. That's probably why my men were a bit over zealous when they stopped you."

"They thought I was a bandit?" Jonathan asked incredulously.

Burke grinned from the right side of his mouth. "Well, with aim like yours, I suppose you could make a mean highwayman if the Quags don't kill you first." Burke offered his hand to Jonathan. "Come on, I'll take you back to camp."

Jonathan took the proffered hand and leapt atop the chestnut horse. They rode back to camp, arriving ahead of the others walking back. There were three rows of six tents stretching out in front of one large, canvas tent. Smaller fires dotted the ground as some of the soldiers began cooking their supper. Captain Burke and Jonathan dismounted in front of the large tent, and a young man of maybe twenty came out to take the horse away.

Burke gestured to the open flap and Jonathan went inside. It was a spacious room, with a small wooden table set up in the center, and a map atop it. There was no bed, just a roll of furs with a blanket and pillow on the pile. A large leather bag sat next to the bed.

"It isn't much, but it will keep the wind off your back," Burke said. "Have you a blanket?"

Jonathan shook his head. "I have an over cloak in my field pack. That is enough."

Burke shook his head and went to his bed. He pulled a large, black fur out from the pile and shook it out. Dust and bits of fur flew off and the map on the table rustled, then Burke set the fur down a few feet away from his bed. He then went back and pulled a doeskin from the pile and set it atop the black fur.

"Thank you," Jonathan offered when he understood that Burke was making a bed for him.

"So, how will you get into the Quags?" Burke asked. "Surely you know that the king has ordered a wall be built to keep the swamps out."

Jonathan nodded and moved to the map on the table. "I was going to go to Fort Sym."

"Why?" Burke pressed.

"To see if someone there could tell me where Jason went."

"Jason?"

Jonathan nodded. "Jason Haymaker," Jonathan replied. "He's my older brother."

Burke chuckled to himself. "I should have known from the way you used your bow," he said. "I met Jason."

"You did?" Jonathan asked as his eyes shot wide and his voice rose in pitch with excitement.

"Oh yes, you don't forget a man like that!" Burke shook his head and moved over to stand on the opposite side of the map. "Never met a Haymaker anyone could forget, actually." Burke caught Jonathan's questioning look. "I know of your grandfather, and while I never met your father, I heard good things about him as well. I imagine Jason is no different." Burke paused and smiled as he reflected on it. "I tried to recruit him myself, you see. I needed a scout at the time, and he was more than the perfect candidate." Burke shrugged and leaned on the table. "I guess that's what Captain Ziegler thought as well," he added. "He was always headed straight to the Ghosts of the Quags. There was no two ways about it. Though, if he had his choice, I bet he would have gone anyway."

"He would have," Jonathan confirmed.

"Sounds like adventure runs in your blood, boy." Burke shook a finger at Jonathan and then pointed to Battlegrym on the map. "I don't know that I should tell you this, but if you can make it to Battlegrym, you just might be able to figure out where he went." Burke sighed then and shook his head as he pushed away from the table. "My conscience is going to make me remind you that he is most probably dead, though. If you go after him, you would be lucky to see so much as his body before your own death. Why not go home?"

"No, he is out there. I have to find him."

"If you are bent on fighting, stay with me. There are bandits enough on the roads that you might see some action."

Jonathan shook his head. "I'm not fighting for the king," he said flatly. "I am fighting for my brother."

Burke frowned and turned toward his bed. He walked over and set his helmet atop the pile and unclasped his red cloak. "Well, perhaps we could help each other," Burke suggested. "You could scout ahead for me, and in return I will let you accompany us to Rynder."

"I can move faster alone," Jonathan pointed out. "I can provide well enough for myself."

Burke spun on his heels and shook his head. "No, I think you misunderstand. I am not so much offering the arrangement as I am ordering it. If you reject the idea, then I will have your three friends take you home."

"You can't do that," Jonathan said. "I haven't done anything wrong."

"I could put you in the stockades in Rynder, or I could haul you to Lehemat. Assaulting the king's men is a crime."

"But I didn't, you know I didn't!"

Burke shrugged. "It would be very easy for me to claim otherwise."

"But you saw that I missed them on purpose. I showed you."

"If you want your freedom, then you must earn it. Scout

for me until we arrive in Rynder. Then, you will be free to leave."

"What is in this for you?" Jonathan asked. "Surely you already have scouts."

Burke dropped his cloak onto his bedroll and marched over to Jonathan. He bent low and poked a strong finger in Jonathan's chest. "I like you. You have a wild spirit in you, but I am afraid it will get you killed. If you scout for me, then it gives me time to talk you out of this foolish death wish of yours. No one survives the Murkle Quags."

"But you just said that if I can make it to Battlegrym, I might be able to find my brother!" Jonathan backed up, rubbing the sore spot on his chest.

Burke nodded. "And so you might, but I also said you would find your own death. Give me three days to change your mind. If we make it to Rynder and you still want to go, then I will let you go. But, if you refuse my deal, or if you try to escape early, I will hunt you down and bring you to the stockades."

Jonathan stood stunned. What could he do but say yes? Burke extended his right hand. Jonathan took it and the two shook.

"Good," Burke said as he stood back upright. "Do you have any food?"

Jonathan nodded and pointed to his field pack. "I have a couple of loaves of bread in my pack," he said. Burke moved to the field pack and rifled through it despite Jonathan trying to squirm away in protest.

"We all pool our resources together," Burke said as he took the bread. He broke off a third of one loaf and handed it to Jonathan. "You want to see what war is like, here you go." Burke then exited the tent, called out a couple of names, and gave the rest of the bread away. He reentered the tent and pointed to the furs he had given Jonathan. "Eat and then go to sleep. You will go out with the first shift of scouts. They leave before dawn."

Jonathan stared angrily at Burke, but the large man didn't seem to notice. He moved toward his bedroll and removed his armor, revealing padded leather armor underneath, which he also removed. After he was wearing only his normal clothes he left the tent, making sure to untie and close the flap behind him.

The inside of the tent went dark and Jonathan moved to sit upon the furs Burke had given him. As he ate his bread, he could hear Burke ordering others to stand guard around the tent and ensure that Jonathan didn't leave. Heavy footsteps stomped into place. Jonathan counted five men. Two in the back of the tent, one on either side, and one near the flap.

Now he was cursing himself for traveling south. Being found by Pa would have been much easier to deal with than this. Now he was a prisoner, jailed by the very soldiers he had wanted so badly to enlist with. His mind went back to that day when he and Pa were tied up and put into the barn. It seemed it was becoming a common theme with soldiers. Jonathan would have to keep that in mind before he dealt with any more of them after this was over.

He finished his bread and then laid down, thinking of how he could possibly escape. No plan he thought of seemed like it would realistically work. Unless he were to steal a horse, they could always outrun him. Even if he had a horse, he wasn't really that good with them. They had a plough horse back home, but Jonathan had never actually ridden a horse more than two or three times. Using one to escape from veteran patrolmen would be foolish. His best bet was to finish the scouting duty that Burke wanted.

Even if it slowed him down, it wouldn't dissuade him from finding Jason. If Burke decided to break their deal when they arrived in Rynder, then Jonathan could escape there, where there would be more places to hide and a thicker forest he could disappear in.

CHAPTER SEVEN

A heavy, broad-toed boot kicked Jonathan in the back long before he was ready to wake up. His eyes slowly peeled open, but he couldn't see for the darkness all around him. Another kick of the boot and Jonathan squirmed out of his bedroll.

"Get up," a voice growled in the darkness.

It wasn't Burke, Jonathan knew that much. Burke's voice was much lower, and nowhere near as nasal as the man kicking and ordering him around now. Jonathan jumped up to his feet. The man in the tent pulled on his arm and yanked him outside.

Jonathan's heart sank. He saw the three men from the day before, huddled over a fire. The smell of coffee and meat wafted on the smoke over to Jonathan's nose. The boy's stomach growled.

"Go on then, we have to eat quickly and then be off," the man holding Jonathan's arm said. Jonathan turned to look at the bald-headed man and then stumbled toward the fire.

Jonathan saw a small tin cup filled with black coffee sitting next to a plate of freshly roasted meat. "Is this for me?" Jonathan asked.

The archer nodded.

Jonathan bent down and took the food. The coffee was far too hot to drink, so he set it back on the ground and went for the meat. There were no seasonings on the food, but he was used to that already. He had been eating rabbit plain for days now. As he chewed the meat, the juices ran over his tongue and down his throat, fully wakening his stomach. He devoured the rest of the meat and then went down for the coffee. Before he could reach the cup, the swordsman grabbed it and drank it.

Jonathan stopped and stared at the man.

"That's for embarrassing me yesterday," the swordsman said as he tossed the empty cup away.

Jonathan knew the liquid was scalding hot, and so he took comfort in the fact that it must have hurt the man to tease him by stealing it, even if the swordsman didn't show it.

The archer reached over and slapped Jonathan on the shoulder as he got up to walk toward the horses. "Let's go," he said gruffly.

The third man from the previous day just looked down at Jonathan, curling his upper lip into a snarl and emitting a growling noise as he walked away.

The new man nudged Jonathan to follow them. "Go on, now. You have a long patrol ahead of you."

Jonathan turned around and looked at the bald man. "You aren't coming?" he asked.

The soldier shook his head and frowned. "Me? No, I am the cook." The bald man pointed to the fire emphatically. "I make food, and the soldiers kill things. Now go on, they have a horse ready for you."

A horse? Jonathan turned to see a fourth horse standing near the archer, who was already mounted on his horse. The three men glared at Jonathan expectantly. Jonathan reluctantly ran toward the horse. He mounted the steed and then realized that he didn't have his bow or his pack.

"Wait, I need to get my bow," Jonathan said. He hopped down, ignoring the curses and snarls the men shot his direction. He sprinted for the tent, only to see Captain Burke emerge holding Jonathan's bow and quiver. Jonathan stopped two feet from colliding into Burke and took the weapons with a nod of thanks.

"They're waiting," Burke said tersely. "Go on."

Jonathan ran back to the horse, holding his bow in his left hand and his quiver in his right hand. He stopped and stared at the horse for just a second before realizing he would need his hands free to mount the horse again. He slung his things over his shoulders, careful to situate them just the way he liked, and then he jumped onto the horse.

"Ready yet, or did you want to go back and fix your hair?" the archer asked.

Jonathan looked down, averting his eyes from the angry man's and said, "I'm ready."

"We are going to have a fun day with you," the swordsman whispered as he nudged his horse into a trot.

Jonathan looked back to the camp, hoping that perhaps this was all some sort of a ruse, a mean prank to make him want to go back home. He saw Captain Burke standing with his arms folded across his chest and his cold eyes staring directly at Jonathan. In a quick flash of his arm, he pointed for Jonathan to follow the others.

A sinking feeling pulled Jonathan's heart into his stomach and his insides twisted into a knot of dread. His horse began moving. He turned back around to see that the archer was pulling on the reins to Jonathan's horse.

"Ever ride a horse before?" the archer asked.

Jonathan nodded, not wanting to tell him that the last time had been more than five years before, and he only did it during a summer festival celebration. The archer tossed the reins to Jonathan.

"Try to keep up," he commanded. The three men kicked their horses into a gallop. Jonathan watched them speed away. He looked down and kicked his horse. The animal didn't respond. He kicked a bit harder, but the horse still didn't speed up. It trotted along after the others, but refused to obey Jonathan's command.

"Come on, let's go," Jonathan told the horse.

Suddenly one of the men let out a sharp whistle. Jonathan's horse broke into a raging gallop that nearly threw him from the saddle. He tightened his grip and hunkered low into the saddle as the horse ran over the hills and caught up with the group.

They galloped for a couple of miles before slowing the horses down to a quick trot. Jonathan would have thought that slowing down would be easier to handle, but now he found himself posting up and down as the horse *clip-clopped* along the ground. Luckily, the group slowed down even from this to a medium speed walk, which was much easier for Jonathan to control.

"Our job is to watch out for bandits, right?" Jonathan asked.

No one answered him. They just wound their way eastward, scouting the hilly area far beyond the road. Jonathan learned quickly that he was only there because Burke had ordered it. None of them were happy about the situation, least of all Jonathan. He glanced to the south several times, calculating whether he could make a break for it.

Would these three even care if he left?

He knew they would. Oh, they might not care about *him*,

but if he tried to escape, it would give them the opportunity and the excuse to hunt him down and drag him back to Burke. Jonathan looked to the swordsman and his stomach churned. There was no way Jonathan wanted to give that man a reason to beat on him.

The first day passed agonizingly slowly. As the sun began to set, the four of them dismounted and made a fire. The archer brought out a pack and pulled some dried meat out. The other two did the same.

Jonathan didn't have a pack. His was back at the camp. He watched with hungry eyes as the others ate without offering him anything. Finally, when they had finished and they moved back to their horses, Jonathan rose up and went to his horse.

"Are we headed back to camp?" Jonathan asked.

"Camp?" The archer turned around and looked at Jonathan with narrowed eyes. He pointed off to the west. "The camp has been taken down and Captain Burke and the others have begun their patrol of the road again. Their camp is now fifty or sixty miles farther away than it was when we woke today."

The swordsman cut in. "We don't join with them until two days from now. We are the far scouts, it's our job to look for dangers that the short range scouts wouldn't normally see along their patrol of the road."

"Three days?" Jonathan repeated breathlessly. "But, I don't even have any food. No one gave me a pack or anything. What am I supposed to do for three days?"

The archer shrugged. "You have a bow and a knife. I suggest you use them to find food."

Jonathan shook his head. "Fine, I'll go now."

"The sun is going down, you won't likely find any game before dark. How will you bring it back to us?"

"What do you mean how will I bring it back to you?" Jonathan asked. "You all have food in your packs."

The swordsman moved in close and snarled as he leaned in. The dark stubble only helped accentuate the evil sneer widening across his mouth. "You'll do as you're told, like all recruits do. You are here to fetch food. Not my problem if Burke didn't tell you that." The swordsman grabbed Jonathan by the shirt and tossed him onto his rump a few feet away. Jonathan landed hard, barely able to soften the fall with his hands, and not enough to keep his tailbone from screaming in sharp pain. "Get on out of here, then, if you think you can hunt at dusk." The swordsman flared his arm out to the south. "Go on, fetch me a deer."

Jonathan rose to his feet, careful to avert his gaze away from the man so he wouldn't notice that his eyes were watering from the pain in his rump. He grabbed his bow and set out on foot.

"Be back before the moon rises half way, or else we'll come after you," one of the men called out.

Jonathan waved with a single flap of his left hand out above his head, but he didn't turn around or answer the men. After he walked over a pair of hills he glanced over his shoulder to see if he had dropped out of their line of sight. Then he looked to the east. The moon was two fingers' span above the horizon. He knew he would have several hours before the moon would rise to its apex.

He broke into a jog, fast enough to put a significant distance between himself and the men, but slow enough so as not to stumble in the darkening twilight. Even with the three of them looking for him, he figured there was little chance they would be able to find him as long as he made good use of his time. If Captain Burke was heading toward Rynder, then Jonathan would go south by southwest, hopefully keeping his distance away from the large patrol and the three men scouting with him now.

He knew the geography well enough to know that if he came to the borders of the Murkle Quags, he could then hook to the east and follow the border all the way until he found Fort Sym. Rynder was situated more than a hundred miles north of the Quags, so if Jonathan was careful, he would never see Captain Burke again.

His stomach growled in protest, whining and grumbling for something to eat, but the young man pushed that out of his mind. He could hunt after he was certain the three scouts couldn't find him. It would set him back in terms of time, but if he could keep them off of his trail until they returned to Burke, then he should be clear of them enough to travel freely.

At that moment, his mind thought of his field pack. He had other supplies in there that he would need if he was to complete his journey.

Jonathan slowed to a stop and looked back in the direction he came.

"Now what?" he asked himself. He kicked at the dirt in frustration and spun around, surveying the darkening expanse around him. The fiery pinks and oranges were fading into shadows now, and more and more the moon became the primary source of light.

No, Jonathan was right to escape. Perhaps he could procure supplies at Fort Sym. His right hand instinctively brushed his pocket from the outside of his pants. The cloth folded flat against his leg, reminding him that he had no money with which to buy anything. His attention was caught by a quick movement off to his left.

There, in a clover patch jumped a large hare. Jonathan smiled. He didn't need money, he remembered. He would hunt for meat and then sell the furs when he arrived at town. Surely there would be demand for pelts at a bustling fort.

That settled it. He ran off into the night. As the moon rose ever higher, he put miles between himself and the three scouts. He didn't stop to rest until he came to a large copse of oak trees nestled together and surrounded by a thick patch of briars.

Jonathan waded into the thorny vines, picking his way carefully and slowly so as not to prick or cut himself. He guessed the plant was either a blackberry or raspberry bush, but there was no way to be certain without the fruit. He moved in until he found a break in the prickly vines and was able to curl up against the base of an oak tree. He thought about climbing the tree, but knew that he would have more success hiding in the thick bushes, not to mention that it would be much safer to sleep on the ground rather than risk falling out of a tree.

He curled up and closed his eyes.

The sounds of the grassland seemed to amplify in his ears the more quiet and still he became. Crickets chirped loudly. Grasses whispered in the midnight breeze, and sounds of wings beating the sky above were occasionally loud enough for him to hear.

As his mind started to let go of the noises and slip into the nebulous void of sleep, something snapped on the ground.

Jonathan's eyes shot open and he held his breath.

Another snap sounded from somewhere beyond the trees. That sound was quickly followed by a rustling sound. Jonathan felt his heart stop as he realized something was pulling at the thick screen of thorny vines.

"Is he in there?" a familiar voice groused from Jonathan's right.

"Dunno, I can't see a bloody thing," another man answered from the left.

Jonathan knew instantly that it was the three scouts. How had they found him? He must have traveled twelve miles or so since escaping from their camp. It seemed impossible that they could have come straight to him.

"Well?" the swordsman shouted from beyond the thorns. "Are you in there kid?"

Silence ensued for several seconds.

Jonathan heard a clicking sound. *Click-click-click.* A flash of orange flickered nearby and then died out. Jonathan realized that someone was using a tinder set.

"Let's smoke him out," one of the men said. "I bet these vines will burn nice and bright. If he is in there, and he wants to pretend like he ain't, then let the fire scare the truth out of him.

Click-click-click. Another flash of orange.

Jonathan pulled his arms and legs in tight. They wouldn't burn down a bunch of trees and bushes just to find him, would they? They had to be bluffing.

Click-click-click. Another flash, but this one didn't die down. It faded and then turned bright yellow. Streaks of thin, thorny shadows played upon the tree trunk in front of Jonathan.

The men weren't bluffing.

Jonathan shot up from the ground. "I fell asleep!" he shouted. "I couldn't find my way back so I came here and tried to find shelter."

The swordsman stomped out the few flames that had sprouted up and then started laughing. "Not only does he think we're blind, but stupid as well!"

Jonathan spun to his left as the thorny bushes rustled ferociously. In the pale moonlight he saw the archer, grim faced and frowning. A large hand reached out and grabbed Jonathan by the nape of the neck. The archer shoved him out from the small clearing and into the thorns on the opposite side.

"Aaya!" Jonathan cried out as he squirmed and jumped through the sharp bushes. The archer moved in quick, grabbing Jonathan again and tossing him clear of the thorns and to the ground beyond. Jonathan thumped to the ground and his breath flew out of him. He coughed and pushed himself up to his feet.

It was then that he noticed the archer had his bow. The archer tossed the weapon to the swordsman. "He doesn't need this anymore," the archer said.

The swordsman snatched the weapon out of the air and chuckled aloud. "Pity to waste another one," he said.

"Break it," the archer said. "We can't trust him with it."

Jonathan winced as the bow creaked and snapped into pieces. The swordsman tossed them down onto the ground, laughing all the while.

"Some scout you turned out to be," the archer chided. "We followed you this whole time, and you never once caught sight of us, did you boy?"

Jonathan sighed and his shoulders slumped. Of course they had followed him. They were testing him. "Just let me go," Jonathan pleaded. "All I want is to find my brother."

"Ha, and miss the chance to put you in the stockades?" the swordsman scoffed. "Not a chance!" He stormed up to Jonathan and seized both of the boy's shoulders. "I am going to love seeing them throw tomatoes at your ugly little face."

The archer stepped in. "You embarrassed us pretty good in front of the others," he said. "It's only proper that we show you the same courtesy."

"So this is what Burke wanted all along?" Jonathan asked.

"No," a third voice called out from a few yards away.

Jonathan turned to see the shadowy forms of a man and four horses approaching. It was the third scout. How could Jonathan not have noticed them? They were on horseback and he still had never caught a hint that he was being followed.

"Burke wanted us to show you what war was like, so we could talk you out of your idiotic quest," the archer said.

"I say we let him go. He won't survive in the Quags anyway," the swordsman put in. "Just let him walk away."

"You broke my bow," Jonathan said. "At least have the decency to give me a weapon."

"Give you a weapon?" the swordsman teased. "I don't think so. You're lucky I extinguished the fire."

Jonathan didn't doubt the man's sincerity.

"He's right," the archer said. "He should have a weapon."

"He ain't getting mine," the swordsman said quickly. "Give him yours if you want, but not mine."

The swordsman let go of Jonathan, pushing him a couple inches away and snarling.

The archer held out a short sword, handle pointed toward Jonathan. "There is a bow not far from here. If you want a bow badly enough, I will tell you how to get it."

Jonathan looked at the dark figure in front of him. The silvery light of the moon only illuminated the top of the archer's head, as the face was darkened by shadow. "Why would you help me now?" Jonathan asked.

"Because you will never be able to reach it. No one can."

"You aren't talking about Kigabané are you?" the third scout cut in. "No one can—"

The swordsman backhanded the third scout in the stomach. "Shush!"

The archer placed a hand on Jonathan's left shoulder as he pushed the short sword closer to the young boy. "Take this, in case you need it. Travel due east of here. Have you ever heard of the Kigyo?"

Jonathan shook his head. "What is that?"

The swordsman sniggered in the distance, but the archer showed no sign of emotion, other than contempt for Jonathan. "It is a land filled with dangerous snakes," he said. "There is a bow there that once belonged to a very powerful warrior. He lost the bow, and no one has been able to find it since. If you can find it, not only will you get to keep the bow, but we will give you the fourth horse so you can travel to Fort Sym."

Jonathan shook his head. "You are lying. There is no such bow is there?"

"Oh no, there is a bow," the archer assured him. "It's there alright."

"Well how long has it been there?" Jonathan asked. "It's

likely warped or rotten by now if it is just lying outside."

"Ah, you don't understand," the archer continued. "This bow is a magical bow. Its spring and strength cannot be dulled by weather."

"If there is such a bow, then why don't you go for it?" Jonathan quipped.

"The bow exists," the third scout said. "It is called Kigabané. Several men have tried to find it before, but none of them ever have. Most of them died looking. Those that didn't die, tell stories of—"

The swordsman smacked the third scout again. "That's enough, you're scaring the boy!"

"Stories of what?" Jonathan pressed. "Are there trolls there?"

"Ha!" the archer laughed. "There are things in this world worse than trolls, my dear boy."

"So what protects the bow?" Jonathan asked.

"The Kigyo," the archer replied simply as he let his hand slide off of Jonathan's shoulder. "So, what will it be? You go and fetch Kigabané, or we take you back and set you in the stockades?"

Jonathan could see no alternative. Whatever the three scouts were planning, it couldn't be as bad as being locked in the stocks. He reached out and took the short sword. "I'll go," he said flatly.

"Good," the archer said. Just then he turned enough that the silvery moonlight illuminated his wicked smile as he pointed to the east. "Due east from here. We'll wait here at the base of the trees. Don't try to sneak around us, or we will not be so nice next time."

Jonathan nodded. He hooked the short sword onto his belt and started walking.

CHAPTER EIGHT

The sun broke its bright, warm, golden rays on Jonathan's face early in the morning. The boy squinted against the light, surveying the jagged shadows before him as he pushed up to a sitting position. He had walked for several miles during the night before curling up next to a large boulder to sleep.

As his eyes adjusted, he noticed that the grass had changed in color. Instead of the vibrant green of the hills he had traveled the previous several days, he was now surrounded by a sea of yellow and brown grasses that rustled and bent with the slightest wind. The dirt was a deep, rich brown with many rocks dotting the surface. Jagged spires of brown and black rock shot up from the ground like a set of forgotten fangs from some long-lost monster. A few red poppy flowers dotted the landscape around him, but otherwise it looked as though he was walking through a valley that had been dead for a very long time.

There were no trees in these parts, aside from a few long-dead oaks that now appeared as gray, heavily cracked shells of once mighty trees. A few fallen logs littered the area between the jagged rocks.

A chirping bird caught his attention then. It squawked and flapped its wings, hopping and turning its head to look at Jonathan. Jonathan figured there must be a nest nearby, for the closer he came to the bird, the more enraged the blue-breasted creature became.

From a part of the rock unseen by Jonathan, a large, yellow snake shot out and seized the bird in its mouth. A pair of feathers exploded from the bird's body and floated gently to the rock's surface as the snake worked its jaw, unhinging it and choking the twitching creature down.

Jonathan pulled the short sword out of reflex and pointed it at the snake. The creature wasn't nearly so large as to pose a threat to him, and he knew it, but there was something about it that unnerved him. It wasn't just the sudden appearance either. He had certainly been in the forest enough times to long ago acquaint himself with the order of prey and predators. He had once seen a mountain lion pounce on a young fawn, tearing the poor creature down in an instant before ravaging it. But there was something different about this snake. Unlike the mountain lion, who couldn't have cared less about Jonathan's existence, let alone the fact that he had seen the kill, this snake watched Jonathan with his evil, vertically slit eyes. It was almost as if each flex of the snake's jaw was a threat, or perhaps as if the snake wished it *was* eating Jonathan.

The boy shook his head and pushed the obscene notion out of his head. The snake was hardly more than two feet long. There was no possible way it could think Jonathan was prey. He turned to sheathe his short sword. His left hand went down to the scabbard, trying to hold it as he lined up the tip of the sword. He was not nearly as experienced with bladed weapons as he was with a bow.

Something moved in his peripheral vision. He halted, holding the short sword just above the scabbard as he snapped his head up and looked to the grass. He saw only a brown and grey log. He shrugged it off and then looked down toward his scabbard. That was when he saw the faint, fleeting flicker of a pink forked tongue in the grass a few feet to his left.

Jonathan instinctively took a step back as he looked up to trace the tongue's movement with his eyes. An angular, scaly head shot out from the tall grass. The brown and gray beast opened its hideous, fang-filed mouth and Jonathan realized that he had not seen a log at all. Somehow he flipped the blade upright as he jumped away. The pink mouth was so large that as it closed around Jonathan's outstretched limb, his entire right hand up to the elbow fit inside, sword and all.

Jonathan jerked the blade up, triggering the snake to close its jaws. Blood shot out around Jonathan's arm and he felt the moist, hot flesh on the bottom of his arm. The snake knocked into him, sending him flying backward toward the boulder where the bird had been killed. Jonathan's back ached in pain as he slammed against the hard surface. His head snapped backward over the top of the rock, but luckily didn't hit the rock itself. The yellow snake caught Jonathan's eye for half a second before the weight of the massive snake dragged Jonathan down.

Jonathan looked down to his hand, afraid to see what was left. To his relief, the sword had saved him. The hilt firmly held the bottom jaw open, keeping the row of smaller fangs at bay while the blade dug a few inches up into the snake's head, preventing the top row of jagged fangs from striking the boy. Jonathan let go and snapped his hand out from the beast's mouth. The snake jerked away, tearing four thin lines of red across the bottom of Jonathan's forearm as the sharp teeth managed to dig in slightly.

The monstrous snake's body slithered out from the grass as it writhed and spun on the ground. The thing was well over thirty feet long, and that was just what Jonathan could see. Jonathan did the only thing he could think of, he ran.

He turned to flee the area, but before he could escape, he caught sight of another monstrously large snake in the grass before him.

"Gah!" Jonathan screamed as he dove behind a large rock sticking up from the ground. The snake launched at him, but slammed into the boulder, buying Jonathan enough time to run away. Another snake rose from the grass in the distance to the west. The long, thick body swayed as it stretched up over the foliage and flicked its tongue at Jonathan.

Jonathan turned and ran, nearly tripping over the still writhing snake at his feet. Blood squirted out onto the ground as the snake whipped around toward Jonathan. The sharp blade poked through the top of the snake's head and then the creature twitched before going still. Jonathan didn't stop to watch. He darted in and around boulders.

He could hear the other two large snakes sliding through the grass, their rough scales scraping the dry plants as they rushed toward him. He leapt up onto a large boulder and then jumped over a small depression in the ground to land on another rock. This one was flat and wide, and was situated close to another rock that rose above it. He grabbed hold of the rock and climbed, seeing another large, square boulder within jumping distance. He precariously perched on the point of the black spire just as the two large snakes circled around him below. He knew that if he missed, he would be dead.

A third snake, just as long and thick as the others,

slithered out from a hole under the spire Jonathan was perched upon. It tasted the air with its tongue and then turned its evil head up to see Jonathan. If the boy didn't know better, he would have sworn that the snake smiled at him. Jonathan looked to the large boulder ahead of him. It was at least six feet away from where he was perched, but if he could reach it, he was certain that the snakes would be unable to climb it, as it was a flat, smooth cube.

He gathered his courage and then jumped across the void. One of the snakes snapped upward, but fell far short of Jonathan as the boy sailed across. He landed hard, the solid corner of the cube digging into his bottom ribs. He curled his legs up and scrambled over the rock as another snake snapped at him. He rolled over the surface and then stood up to make sure his plan was working. Carefully he inched close to the edge and then leaned over to peer at the monsters below. One snake raised its body about four feet into the air, a little less than half the cube's height. It slithered to the rock, but could not gain purchase to wind its way up.

Jonathan sighed in relief, but then realized the other two snakes were disappearing around the side. One went around to the right while the other was disappearing around the left side. Jonathan turned to rush to the far side of the cube and see whether every rock face was just as smooth as the first, but he stopped short when he noticed a pair of skeletons on the rock. They were human. Next to them was an old spear and sword. Jonathan rushed to the spear, but discarded it when he saw the shaft was destroyed and cracked from exposure. The sword was in better shape, albeit a bit rusted from the time in the weather. From the look of the bleached bones, and the fact that only scraps of clothing remained, Jonathan knew the men had died a long time ago.

He wondered if they had met a similar fate, chased to this very rock by hideous snakes, and then starved to death as the snakes circled below. He reached down for the sword and took it in hand. There wasn't much left of the wooden handle, and the few bits that still clung to the steel tang all but crumbled when Jonathan picked it up. Still, the metal was solid and would likely be his only defense if the snakes found a way up the rock. He moved to the far side, holding the sword at the ready. A green and black snake hissed at him from below, but it could no more climb the rock than the first.

Jonathan moved to the middle of the giant boulder and sat down. He could only hope that perhaps the snakes would eventually get bored enough that he could escape when they left. He knew he couldn't possibly outrun all of them. They had been so quick to catch up to him that he doubted he would get more than a yard or two before being struck down. He also knew he couldn't fight them off. It was only luck that had saved him from the first snake.

Now there were three more, and all he had was a pile of bones and an old sword.

He waited for a long time before he dared to check the ground again. He kept hoping that the snakes would slither away, but they never did. When he finally checked over the side, he saw the snakes busily circling the boulder. There was nothing he could do.

Near the middle of the day, Jonathan caught sight of the green and black snake. It had worked its way up the other boulder adjacent to the black spire of rock that Jonathan had used to reach the cube boulder. It took several minutes, but eventually the snake wound around the spire and began reaching out to cross the void between the two rocks.

Jonathan rose to his feet and held the sword up high.

"Don't do it," Jonathan said. "Come after me, and I will be forced to kill you."

The snake stopped and turned its head to the side. It opened its mouth and hissed fiercely at the boy, and then it stretched out farther. Jonathan dropped the sword and went for the cracked spear. He knew it wasn't strong, but maybe it would be enough to fend off the snake from stretching across. He grabbed the coarse shaft near the bottom and raised it over his right shoulder like a club. The snake hissed and stretched out, nearly reaching half way to the boulder. Jonathan couldn't let the snake figure out a way to him, so he swung with all of his might.

On the ground, the snake would likely have shied away quickly, but with three feet of body precariously stretched over the air, it was slow to recoil. The spear tip slammed into the side of the snake's head, slicing a deep gash into the snake's head just below the left eye. Blood oozed out as the spear snapped in several places under the weight of the blow. Jonathan turned and grabbed the sword. Now that he knew the snake wouldn't be able to dodge a swing, he was ready.

Come on then, stretch your neck out again.

Jonathan stood firm, locking eyes with the bloodied snake.

The beast retreated and slithered down the spire, then the adjoining boulder until it was once again upon the ground. Jonathan counted his blessings that each of these three were only ten or twelve feet in length. Any more than that, and they could probably reach up to the top of the rock he was hiding on.

The young boy backed away from the edge of the boulder, making to keep an eye on the spire a short distance away. If any of the snakes tried to cross again, he would use the sword. He sat for another couple of hours before he heard a strange rustling in the grass a ways off. He watched as a large, ruby red snake slithered up onto a gray boulder maybe twenty yards away from the boulder he sat upon. The red snake turned its head and licked the air twice as it looked directly at him. Then the boy saw the other three snakes slithering toward the red one. All three of them stopped below the base of the boulder and the red snake lowered its head down to each of them.

The red snake pulled back onto the gray boulder as the three below coiled into tight springs and turned their heads to face Jonathan. The red snake lifted up several feet into the air and unfolded a grand hood which expanded behind its head. Jonathan's eyes shot wide and his mouth fell open. He had never heard of such a creature before. He glanced to the west and his feet and legs nearly twitched they wanted to run so badly.

That was when the red snake spoke.

"Run, little human, and you will not make it far, I assssssure you."

Jonathan's breath caught in his throat and it was all he could do to shake his head, for no words would come out of his mouth.

"My servants have told me that you killed one of my kin. Why would you do thisss?"

Jonathan shook his head again and dropped the sword he held. "It attacked me," Jonathan said. "I didn't want to kill it."

"You ssssay 'it' as though we are not worthy of your ressspect," the red snake hissed. "My guardssss are here to keep intrudersss out. Why are you here?"

"I didn't mean any harm," Jonathan said truthfully. "I saw the little snake eat a bird, and then the big one tried to eat me."

"Liesss! We do not eat humansss, it isss bad for our sssstomachs."

Jonathan shook his head. "Honest, he attacked me first."

The red snake hissed loudly and flicked its tongue out into the air. "Why have you come? A young boy cannot think to kill the Kigyo alone."

"Kill the what?" Jonathan stammered. "I thought the Kigyo was a place."

"No," the red snake corrected. "We are a race of intelligent creaturesssss."

Jonathan felt his heart sink. Now he knew why the other scouts had sent him here. "I was told that there is a special bow here," Jonathan explained. "I came looking for the bow, but I didn't mean to hurt anyone."

The red snake rose higher into the air, swaying and dancing as it rose high enough to show Jonathan that it could easily reach the top of the boulder he was on if it wanted. "Why come for Kigabané?"

Jonathan's shoulders slumped and he sighed as his hands slapped his thighs and he shook his head. "Some men broke my bow. I need a bow so I can find my brother. So, the men told me to come here and find the bow. They said it was magical, that the weather wouldn't damage it. If that was true, then it would help me a lot, because my brother went deep into the Murkle Quags to fight the trolls."

"TROLLSSSSS! We hate trollsssss!" the red snake hissed. "Trollssss are vile creaturesssss."

Jonathan nodded. "At least we agree on that," he whispered.

"Come with usss," the red snake said. "I will take you to our king. He will dessssside what to do with you."

Jonathan drew his brows in, glancing to each of the three snakes coiled up below the red snake. "How do I know you aren't trying to trick me?"

The red snake folded its hood and rested back on the gray boulder. "If I wanted to kill you, I could easily reach you." The red snake turned its head and spat a long stream of silvery liquid onto the ground a few feet away from the boulder Jonathan was on. The grasses hissed in protest as the acid ate them away and the dirt turned black as bits of smoke rose up from the mark. "I don't have to bite you to kill you," the snake said.

Jonathan looked to the sword and then set it next to the skeleton. His mind was terribly conflicted, with half of his thoughts being images of snakes tearing him apart and the other half reassuring words inspired by the show of spitting acid. Jonathan knew the red snake wasn't bluffing, but that didn't stop his fears from playing on his mind. He slowly moved to the edge of the boulder and took in a deep breath. He looked down to the ground and noticed the shards from the broken spear, and then he glanced back to the green and black snake. The blood oozed around the left eye still, and the snake looked none too happy to Jonathan.

The red snake must have noticed Jonathan's apprehension, for it stretched back to the green and black snake. The red hood opened, covering whatever was happening from Jonathan's sight. When the red snake recoiled back to its spot, the blood was gone and the gash was healed.

A thought came to Jonathan's mind then. "If you can heal them, then I can take you to the first snake. I don't even need my sword back. Just let me go and—"

"No," the red snake hissed. "I cannot raissse the dead."

Jonathan sighed and then decided there was no point in stalling anymore. *If you are going to kill me, then please make it fast.* He bent down to the edge and clambered down. When his legs dangled above the ground and his arms were at full length, he let go and dropped the last couple of feet to the dirt. His eyes reflexively closed when he heard slithering sounds, fully expecting to be attacked and killed.

Nothing happened. The sounds moved away from him.

Jonathan peeked out of the corner of his left eye and his shoulders and arms relaxed. The other three snakes were gone, leaving only the big red one.

"Come," it said.

Jonathan walked with the red snake, still jumping

nervously whenever he caught sight of a new snake hiding in the grass. Despite the red snake's assurances that none would harm him so long as he was under his protection, Jonathan couldn't help but look over his shoulder every few steps.

There were scores of snakes. Some small, the length of his hand, while others were like the first four he had met ranging from ten to thirty feet long. They came in all sorts of colors and patterns, but only the hooded snake was red. They walked for an hour before the red snake stopped at the edge of a large pit. Jonathan looked down and saw only darkness inside the jagged mouth of rough rock.

"Climb on my back," the red snake said.

Jonathan hesitated, glancing from the hole to the snake and then back down the hole.

He's taking me to a nest full of hungry babies.

"There isss no nessssst," the red snake said. "I take you to the king."

Jonathan startled and looked up at the snake. "You can read my mind?"

The snake flicked its tongue out and hissed. "That isss the reasssson you are ssstill alive."

Jonathan nodded as if he understood. "Do I sit on you then?" Jonathan asked, trying to sound natural despite fear cracking through in his voice.

"Ssstand behind my head. Hold onto my hood." The snake lifted its massive head and flared its hood. Jonathan moved slowly onto the snake, taking a test step onto the strong scales. "You won't hurt me," the snake said. "Grab tight."

Jonathan took a breath of courage and held the sides of the hood. The scales were rough and thick in his hand, as if he gripped something made of smoothed wood, or a thin stone perhaps. The snake lurched forward and Jonathan nearly lost his balance, but he pulled close to the hood and held firm as the snake plunged downward. Jonathan pressed his head to the back of the snake's hood, not wanting to watch their descent.

Although the drop was indeed long, Jonathan needn't have worried. The snake was able to reach the bottom before much more than half of its body had left the upper surface, so it landed softly and then sped through the tunnel.

Jonathan closed his eyes as a wave of hisses sounded all around him from the dark corners of the cavern. He hoped that they would all leave him alone, but there was still the same fear as before. Whether the red snake could sense Jonathan's fears or not, it made no more reassurances to him. It silently wound its way through and around the tunnel's various curves until they stopped in a large den that must have spanned several hundred feet in all directions.

"We are here," the red snake said.

Jonathan opened his eyes and looked around. To his surprise, bioluminescent mushrooms covered the walls, bathing the den in enough light that he could see as clearly as if he stood upon the surface with the sun shining brightly. Some of them shined blue while others were white or yellow. They clung to the walls and ceiling, appearing as oblong stars perched upon a dome of stone. The ground below them consisted of a gray slab of stone, with some cracks and depressions marring the surface. A calm, but expansive pool of water glistened beyond the stone bank, reflecting the glowing mushrooms' light and rippling softly. The water was so dark, it almost looked black. It lapped up onto the smooth, stone bank, wetting the stone and making it shine magnificently. The bank itself was weathered into a smooth angle that dipped into the pool, almost inviting Jonathan to take a swim. Had it not been for the many snakes he had just seen, he might have thought to do just that.

"Get off," the snake commanded.

"Oh!" Jonathan leapt off the red snake and held his hands out apologetically. "Sorry, I was just looking at the mushrooms. I haven't seen anything like that before."

"Sssssilenssssse," the red snake said. "Kneel before the king!"

Jonathan looked around, and then realized that the red snake was the king. That was why none of the others had attacked. Jonathan bent down to a knee and bowed his head low.

The snake folded its hood and bent low to Jonathan's face. "I am not the king, boy," he hissed quietly, then he slithered away to the entrance.

Jonathan tilted his face up slightly to look around. The surface of the water shifted and rolled as something below stirred.

A bubble rose up, and then the surface broke as a great, orange head lifted out from the water. If Jonathan had thought the other snakes were big, he was now awestruck, for they were nothing compared to the behemoth rising before him. The head was nearly as large as the cube boulder Jonathan had taken refuge upon. The neck and body were thicker than maybe ten snakes put together of the hooded snake's size.

A white and black band wrapped around the snake's neck like a collar under the skull.

"So you have come for Kigabané?" a voice said within Jonathan's mind. The boy noted that the voice was definitely not his own. It was much deeper, and reverberated within his mind. Yet, it was also different from the hooded snake as the pronunciation did not draw out the 'S' sounds in the words it spoke.

Jonathan spoke aloud, not knowing whether it was more proper to think his response or speak it normally. "Yes, to help me find my brother."

"Your brother Jason left a long time ago to fight in the Murkle Quags, is that so?"

Jonathan screwed up his face and looked at the snake king. "How did you know that?"

"The Kigyo have the ability to read minds. It is called telepathy. The gift varies according to an individual's station. The guards you met in the fields have no ability to read minds. However, my son, whom you have met before he brought you to me, can read thoughts. I can do that, as well as delve into a creature's memory. That is one of the reasons we keep to ourselves. Most other creatures do not have pleasant thoughts about our kind."

Jonathan nodded. "If you don't mind me asking, where did you come from?"

"We were born in the Murkle Quags, like so many other creatures, but our history is not why you have come. I sense you have an urgent need to return with Kigabané. The three men that sent you here, do you trust them?"

Jonathan shook his head. "No," he said honestly. "I came because I didn't see any other way to satisfy their demands. If they lock me in the stocks, then I will never find my brother."

The king snake emitted a low, growl-like sound as it swayed its head above the water. The pool rippled violently as it shifted its head and then spat at a small area on the floor where a large rock jutted up from the ground. Jonathan turned to see a covering of rock melt away to reveal a beautiful bow made of black wood hiding inside.

"Take it," the hooded snake commanded.

Jonathan turned around and looked curiously at the king. "That's it?" he asked.

The king snake offered a short nod. *"I can see that your actions, though they resulted in the death of one of my guards, were motived only by self-preservation. That is enough for me."*

Jonathan couldn't believe it had been so easy. He rose to his feet and walked the forty yards to the freshly uncovered bow. He bent down to pick it up and wrapped his hands around the smooth, cool weapon. Beside it lay a brown quiver with several arrows. He took those as well and slung the quiver over his back.

No sooner had he done so, than he felt a strange sensation course through him. A tingling ran through his hands and up his arms. His mind became warm, as if his head had been surrounded by hot steam. Terribly loud thumping sounds assaulted his ears, nearly causing him to flinch in pain. His eyes squinted against the sensations until he was able to regain his senses. Then, he noticed something strange. The hooded snake was standing before him, with his hood flared and his mouth open.

The urge to strike the red snake down came into Jonathan's mind.

Along with the compelling thought, Jonathan noticed that the terrible thumping sound was that of the hooded snake's heartbeat. As Jonathan looked at the giant snake, the heart seemed to glow purple within its body, as if calling out to Jonathan to slay the snake.

Jonathan's left hand slowly moved up to retrieve an arrow, as if an unseen power moved him.

His fingertips grazed the first arrow before he was able to snap out of it. Jonathan let go with his right hand and the bow dropped to the ground. The minute he released it, the sensations and urges vanished. Jonathan looked up to the king snake quizzically and then hurried to remove the quiver and throw it down as well.

"What was that?" Jonathan shouted.

The king snake bent low and brought its massive head

close to Jonathan's. *"That, is Kigabané. It is a bow that the trolls made to slay us all. Its arrows seek our hearts, and the bow's magic allows the archer to access unnatural speed and accuracy. It is a weapon that nearly annihilated all of my kin."*

"You fight the trolls too?" Jonathan asked. "Then why not fight with us and rid the swamps of the trolls?"

The king snake shook his head. *"It is not so easy. The trolls hunt us, and have power over us. That is why we left the swamps."*

"What kind of power?" Jonathan asked.

"Our telepathy is a product of our creation. The troll shamans use our telepathy to control us. Those who are strong enough to resist, the trolls kill. That is why we fled the swamps. You think we like the rocks and the fields? Our bodies crave the swamps and the water. That is our home, but we were driven out."

"What do you mean a product of your creation?" Jonathan pressed.

The king snake paused for a long while before he finally answered. *"It was the trolls who created us. They used dark magic to morph the naturally occurring snakes in the Quags until we became what you see before you now. For decades the trolls used us to hunt for them, to patrol their swamp for them, and to kill for them. Then, one fateful day more than two centuries ago, the first human made contact with the swamps. The trolls sent us out to find and kill all humans. The humans in the settlements far to the south called the event the Night of Fangs, but we, the Kigyo called it the Disgrace. We could sense the fear and terror in the humans. It was a dishonorable thing to force us to do. So, I led my kin to rebellion. Those Kigyo strong enough to resist the shamans' magic fought with me.*

"That is when the trolls forged Kigabané. It was a weapon to put us down and tame us once more. After losing many hundred kinfolk, we were able to overpower the troll archer who wielded it."

"I was told it was a human warrior who used it," Jonathan said.

The king snake nodded. *"That part came later. A mighty adventurer stole the bow from us as we fled the swamps. He hunted us down for what we had done during the Disgrace. We tried to flee before him, hoping that he would tire of his pursuit, but he did not. When we reached this cavern, he continued to harass any Kigyo that showed themselves upon the surface. We hid for many years. The adventurer left, likely thinking he had killed us all.*

"I don't know where he went afterward, but a few years after that,

humans tried to settle in these parts. They discovered our den, and of course my guards protected themselves. This led to the adventurer coming back to try and kill us again. I baited him into the cave and then I sat, coiled at the bottom of the pool. I knew the bow showed him our hearts, but I also knew that I could protect myself with the depths of the pool. The magic does indeed send the arrow to the heart, but it can't travel through rock or water any better than a natural arrow. The magic has its limitations. When he came close, I struck out from the water, and we have been guarding the bow ever since."

"Then why would you give it to me?" Jonathan asked. "If the bow is so powerful that it almost destroyed you, why would you trust a human with it?"

"Because when the trolls forged Kigabané, they made a simple flaw. They enchanted it to find the hearts of every Kigyo, but they forgot that the shamans who created us used snake bodies infused with enchanted troll hearts. That is what give us our ability to heal and grow so large. If the trolls had remembered that fact, they never would have made Kigabané."

"So it will help me find the trolls!" Jonathan exclaimed as he looked down to the bow.

"It will indeed, for their hearts are the same as ours. Kill the trolls, and then we will take their place in the swamps. Only then can we be free and live without fear of being hunted and killed. With the trolls gone, the humans might forgive us for the Disgrace as well. Your kin can live in peace outside of the swamp. Our two kinds can coexist, but not as long as the trolls live."

Jonathan nodded, but then he recalled the two skeletons on the rock. Before he asked the question, the king sensed his thoughts and answered his curiosity.

"The other humans that have come here all wanted the bow either to serve their greed, or to kill us. You are the first human to come who sought the bow as a way to save life. That is why we brought you down to see it. When you fought the bow's charms and refused to try to harm myself, or my son, we knew we had made the right choice."

"How do I take the bow without the magic making me try to hurt you?"

"Leave that to me," the hooded snake said. "You will ride upon my back and I will carry the bow with my tail. Itssss magic does not affect our mindssss. After I carry you out of our landsss, I will leave the bow for you and return here. Once I am far enough away, you will be able to hold it. The thoughtsssss will only come when a being with a trollsss heart isss clossse enough to you."

Jonathan nodded. "Then let's go."

"One more thing, noble warrior," the king snake began. "When the trolls are dead, I want you to leave Kigabané in their den, so no human can find it again."

Jonathan didn't have to think about that one. It was a fair deal. He nodded. "I promise I will."

CHAPTER NINE

The red snake spent several days carrying Jonathan along the border of the Murkle Quags. Jonathan told him about his plan to go to Fort Sym and inquire about his brother's last known whereabouts. He also told the snake about the patrol along the road, so the pair made sure to stick as close to the swamps as possible.

The snake was blindingly fast, and seemed hardly ever to tire. Jonathan often got the feeling that if he himself hadn't needed to stop and rest, the snake would have been happy to make the journey without stopping at all. They covered a lot of ground while keeping close to the northern border of the swamp. The red snake was surprised that the Quags had expanded so far, and was certain it was the work of the shamans.

The trees along the border of the swamp seemed sick with disease. A strange ivy covered them with black leaves and vines that sucked the vibrancy from them. What had once been a lovely, coniferous forest was now little more than a fence of dead trees overrun with ivy climbing up and moss hanging down. The damp ground squished beneath the red snake as they traveled. Small, white bubbles flared up from the soaked grasses and earth, confirming just how wet the area was.

Other than birds, the two of them saw little wildlife whatsoever. The occasional frog or toad braved the wide puddles gathered along the grass, but there was little else.

As the two of them traveled on for days, Jonathan ate frogs and rabbits, hunting them with the large snake's help. The hooded snake, on the other hand, claimed to have eaten a cow only a few days before Jonathan arrived, and therefore wouldn't be hungry again for at least another week. As they swiftly moved along the wet grasses, the hooded snake told Jonathan of the nearly mythical shamans the trolls had. More than that, though, he told him of the Kigyo and their wish to return to the swamps and live in peace. After nine days, their journey together ended.

The red snake slithered dangerously close to the swamps,

lying low and next to the tree line. He pulled his hood in and looked back to Jonathan. "Thissss is where we part wayssss, Jonathan Haymaker."

Jonathan stepped off the snake and put a hand up to his brow as he squinted in the late afternoon sun. Off in the distance, he spied what looked to be men digging and working. They were building the wall that Lord Bingham had talked about. The young man knew the snake could not risk being seen. Still, Jonathan was more than close enough to finish the journey on his own now.

"Thank you," Jonathan said. "For both the ride and for helping me find food along the way."

The snake tilted its head and then turned to slither into the tree line. Jonathan watched as the long, thick body slid effortlessly over the wet ground and into the dark trees. As the tail slithered by, it unfolded and deposited the bow on the ground as promised.

Jonathan waited for the space of about fifteen minutes, wanting to make sure that his ally had ample time to escape the reach of the bow's enchantment. Then, he picked up the bow and walked toward the workers. It took him quite some time to reach them on foot. The ground was not as friendly to his feet as it had been to the snake. He slipped more than a few times, but never fell completely to the ground. Still, it made for slow going.

When he finally reached the first group of workers, he could see that they were busy digging a trench and heaping dirt up on the side of the trench closest to the swamp. The men saw him, but none of them paid him any heed. They just keep stabbing their shovels into the wet ground and slinging the thick mud over their shoulders to build up the wall.

Jonathan walked beyond them, knowing that if he followed the wall he would eventually reach Fort Sym. He was certain that he could get information there. As he walked along the trench line, he came upon another set of workers. There were twelve tall, burly men setting pikes and poles into the heaped dirt jutting out toward the swamps. Another three hundred yards beyond them was the edge of the wall.

Seeing the end of the wall as it was being built gave Jonathan a great look at the barrier. It sat a few feet on the inside of the seven-foot wide trench. There was an outer layer of stone and brick that was roughly six feet thick. Spikes and arrow slits were being set into the outer layer that faced the swamps. Inside of that was a reinforced hallway, with sconces every few feet. Then there was another layer that faced north which was roughly another three feet in thickness. Above the hallway along the outer edge of the wall ran a battlement which would allow archers to hide behind merlons and fire upon any who dared approach. The walkway behind the crenellation was almost as wide as the entire wall, allowing for maximum maneuverability.

Jonathan passed by more carts than he could count as he wound his way through the area. Some carts held mud-cement, while others bore stone or timber. Teams of oxen pulled some of the carts while teams of horses pulled others. There were even handcarts that needed four men to move them. It was a full-out effort to finish the wall before the monsoons would start up again in the late spring and early summer.

Jonathan knew they wouldn't likely finish this year. It had taken days for him to travel from the Kigyo den, but it would take months upon months to build a wall of this stature the length of the border. After all, it had already been nearly nine months since he last saw Lord Bingham in Holstead. If this was all the more the army had been able to build in that time, it would more likely be years before the construct was completed.

All the more reason to find Jason, Jonathan knew.

He quickened his pace, hoping to reach Fort Sym soon, but when the sun began to drop in the west and workers started to build fires instead of work on the wall, Jonathan knew that was not likely to happen.

Some of the workers slipped into dirt-stained canvas tents, while others took shelter inside the wall they were building. Clouds rolled into the sky above, darkening the last of the sun's light and forcing Jonathan to find shelter as rain started to fall upon the land.

He moved into an open doorway in the wall and followed the torch light until he came to a small area that had a few stones set up in a circle on the floor. He promptly sat upon one and listened to the rain drum upon the stone above and the ground outside. It wasn't long before the ground was entirely saturated, changing the pitch of the falling drops to something lighter as the water gathered.

Rivulets of cold water filtered into the hallway as well. Jonathan looked around himself in dismay, wondering where he would sleep if the water covered the hall floor.

A stout man with a dirt covered shirt and a pair of black trousers approached.

"Mind if I join you?" the man asked.

Jonathan shook his head. It was refreshing to see some civility after his last encounter with Burke and his men. "How far is it to Fort Sym?" Jonathan asked the man.

The man sat down, and what had once looked like a solid torso now burgeoned out at the belly as the man relaxed and leaned forward. He slapped his filthy hands together and then rubbed them as he blew on his fingers. "Fort Sym?" he asked as if he hadn't heard Jonathan correctly. "You mean you aren't part of the crews?"

Jonathan shook his head. "I am too young," he explained. "I wanted to volunteer, but they wouldn't take me."

The man smiled and wiped his hands on his pants. "Ah, so you thought you could earn some coin going to Fort Sym, is that it?" The man gestured to Jonathan's bow. "That's a mighty fine weapon you have there."

Jonathan shifted in his seat uneasily, trying to guess what the man's intentions might be. "It's an heirloom," Jonathan lied.

The man took in a deep breath and shrugged his shoulders as he leaned back to rest against the stone wall. "If it is valuable, you might want to cover it before you go to Fort Sym," the man suggested. "They have a habit of appropriating things in the name of the war out here. Money goes missing. Weapons and nice clothes too. A bow like that might draw the wrong kind of attention."

"How far is it?" Jonathan repeated.

The man shrugged again. "Maybe seventy miles or so." The man closed his eyes and folded his hands across his belly. "If you don't mind, I am going to catch a wink or two before they bring me my soggy supper."

Jonathan smiled and nodded. The man sighed and sank into the wall behind him. Jonathan brought Kigabané around to set upon his lap. He looked down at the bow. He hadn't looked at it much since the first time he held it. Out of respect for the hooded snake, he had left it alone entirely for the duration for the trip thus far. But now, he was free to examine it.

Each limb curled up perfectly, with a flourish at the tip that called to mind the skill of the elves in their craftsmanship. The bow itself was black with silver inlay running over both limbs that almost looked as though it depicted swirling ivy around the bow. The grip was perfectly smooth, yet formed perfectly for Jonathan's hand. He ran his fingers over it and tightened his grip. It was as if the bow had been made for him all along. He held it up and drew the string back. It was stiff at first, but it bent to Jonathan's will easily enough. The young boy gently moved the string back into place, careful not to let the weapon dry-fire. He set it back over his lap and then moved to retrieve one of the arrows.

Like the bow, the arrow was exquisitely made. The shaft was perfectly smooth along the entire length. The fletching was made of white goose feather, something easily obtainable in the swamps as geese and swans were no strangers to the entire peninsula. A faint glint caught Jonathan's eye as he ran a finger over one of the feathers. He turned the arrow under the torchlight and found that each feather was set into the shaft and then held in place with a solder of what appeared to be silver. That was something odd that he would not have expected. He turned the arrow over and examined the tip. He found that while the core of the double-bladed tip was made of iron, the edges were also crafted with silver.

"How is that possible?" Jonathan wondered aloud.

"How is what possible?" the man across from him asked.

Jonathan slammed his eyes shut and wished he could take back his words. When he heard the large man gasp, he knew it was too late for that now.

"Son, that is no heirloom!" the man squeaked breathlessly. "That is Kigabané!"

Jonathan put the arrow away and then moved to hide the bow behind his back. "No, you're mistaken," Jonathan said.

The man leaned forward and reached out to set a hand on Jonathan's shoulder. His brown eyes grew serious as he looked at the boy. "Why are you going to Fort Sym?" he asked.

"My brother fought with the Ghosts of the Quags,"

Jonathan said simply. "I am going to find him."

"Come with me," the man instructed.

Jonathan hesitated at first, but the man stood and smiled as he waved emphatically. "Come on, I think you will like this."

"What?" Jonathan asked.

"A couple of days ago this captain rode into the camp. He said he was looking for a young boy, of course now I am guessing that was you…"

Jonathan shook his head and jumped up. "You can't make me go back to him!" Jonathan shouted.

The man drew his brow into a knot and then held his hands up innocently. "No, you don't understand, let me explain." The man looked both ways up and down the hall before continuing. "The captain had some men with him. He said that three of his scouts had lost a kid out on patrol. He told the foreman that these three scouts had told the kid to go into the lands of the Kigyo after Kigabané. He asked the foreman if he had seen a young boy with a bow. Of course we see a lot of young men with bows around here, and the foreman told the captain so, but then the captain detailed what the bow would look like." The large man pointed to the bow now on Jonathan's back. "He said it would be black with silver markings on it. I didn't notice at first because you were in the shadows a bit when I sat down, but I saw it now and I know what it is. You're him, ain't you?"

Jonathan couldn't believe his poor luck. All this way along the border of the swamp only to be caught anyway. He turned to run, but the large man seized his shoulder and held him fast in place as easily as if Jonathan was a small child. The large man leaned in close with a big toothy grin.

"Come on, you are going to like this," the man said.

"Like what?" Jonathan asked.

The man frowned. "Well, after the foreman said no one matching your description had come through, the captain became enraged. He shouted and dressed those scouts down real nice. Then, after he berated them for a few minutes, he had a few of us go and build a set of stocks for them. Come on, they're locked up in the stocks right now."

"They're locked in stocks?" Jonathan repeated.

The man nodded enthusiastically. "Yes sir, they are locked

out in the rain right now as we speak. They only get let out once a day for eating and other business, then they go back in. The captain said they were to stay there until he returned for them on his next patrol. Something about wanting them to understand who they were fighting for and making sure they wouldn't mistreat anyone again."

"Captain Burke is gone?" Jonathan pressed.

The big man nodded again and gestured down the hall. "Left the same day they came in. Said he would be back on his next round. Well, come on then, let's go see if they remember you."

"What's in it for you?" Jonathan asked.

"For me?" the big man responded. "What do you mean?"

"Why does it matter if I see them or not?" Jonathan asked.

The big man grinned. "For satisfaction!" He folded his arms over his chest and smiled wide enough that almost all Jonathan could see was the man's teeth. "I don't much care for bullies. I'll get a kick out of seeing their jaws hit the ground when you walk up with the bow. They thought they were so clever, and now you will show them that not only are you alive, but you have retrieved the legendary bow! Come on, I want to see them squirm."

Jonathan shook his head. "No, I'd rather just pass through quietly."

The big man huffed and pouted out his lower lip as his brow furrowed. Then, a moment later he smiled and nodded understandingly. "You think someone else will poach the bow from you, I understand. I know what I said earlier, and that is true, but ol' Sami will protect you."

"Who's that?" Jonathan asked.

The man frowned again and arched a single brow. "Why, it's me of course. I'm Sami Graystone. I'll let you poke back at those louts in the stocks, and then I will take you to Fort Sym myself."

"You can do that?" Jonathan asked. "I mean, what about the wall?"

Sami laughed and shrugged. "I'm the foreman's cousin. He'll let me do it." Sami then turned and motioned for Jonathan to follow him. The young boy sighed and went with the large man, hoping he wasn't making a mistake.

Sami grabbed a pair of torches from the wall and took them out into the steady rain. The torches popped and hissed against the assaulting water as the flames danced around, trying to stay alive. One of the torches died, but the second was able to remain lit despite the water.

A few men looked up from large fire pits that smelled of beans and coffee, but no one said anything to the pair. Sami and Jonathan walked up to the three stocks. The men were bent over awkwardly at the waist. Their heads and hands protruded out from the small holes and the stocks were fastened with large, iron locks.

"Don't worry, they pull the stocks off of the poles after supper to let them sleep on the ground," Sami said.

Jonathan shook his head. It wasn't that the men didn't deserve punishment for what they tried to do, but it sounded awful, and he remembered that they had threatened the very same thing to him.

One of them looked up as Sami and Jonathan approached. Water and dirt streaked the man's face so that Jonathan didn't recognize which one it was, but the man recognized Jonathan. His mouth curled into a snarl and his face grew red as he tried to crane his head up more to yell.

"You!" the man shouted. Jonathan recognized the voice as that of the swordsman.

The other two tilted their heads around to look up. When they saw Jonathan, one of the men grew very angry and shouted a curse, while the third shook his head and looked down to the ground again.

Sami, true to his word about disliking bullies, walked up to the archer and slapped him upside the head. "No one to blame for your current situation besides yourself, now watch your tongue!"

The archer didn't respond. The swordsman glowered at Jonathan, but he kept his mouth closed.

Jonathan almost felt pity for them as much as he felt satisfaction. "How long until Burke returns for you?" Jonathan asked.

"However long it takes," the swordsman growled.

Jonathan looked to the silent scout and moved over toward him. "Why did Burke send me with you?" he asked.

The man slowly moved his head up and wrinkled his nose as he thought of a response. "He wanted us to scare you away from your quest."

"By sending me to the Kigyo?" Jonathan pressed.

The scout shook his head. "No. He thought if you rode with us for three days, and then he showed you Rynder, that you would decide it was too rough of a lifestyle."

"Why would he care?"

"He had a brother who went to the Quags also. Burke tried to go after him, but he only made it as far as Battlegrym. He fought there when the fortress was overrun. He wanted to save you from that."

"So then why send me with you instead of just telling me?"

The scout sighed. "I suppose he thought you wouldn't listen to words. I don't know. Maybe he thought it would help us make amends for treating you the way we did on the road. You would have to ask him."

Jonathan turned and looked at Sami. The large man's smile was gone. He stood watching Jonathan and holding the torch in the middle of the rain. He was like a silent sentinel. Upon seeing the large man's face, Jonathan shifted from a mix of emotions to feeling mostly pity. He turned back to the third scout and held the bow under the man's face.

"Tell Burke that I found Kigabané, and that I will find my brother as well."

The scout cleared his throat. "Take me with you," he said.

Sami stepped in. "What, and let you escape the stocks so you can desert the army? Not a chance!"

The scout shook his head. "No, so I can make amends," the scout replied emphatically.

"Shut yer mouth Rourke, no one likes a softy," the swordsman spat.

Rourke shook his head. "I should have stopped them from sending you in against the Kigyo like that. Seeing the bow means you obviously have more skill than we estimated, so you might have a shot at finding your brother. If you are bent on going in, then let me go with you. If I can save your life by offering my own, then it is only proper for what I did."

114

"Oh shut up!" the swordsman snarled. "His brother was a Ghost. He's dead!"

Sami hauled off and backhanded the swordsman so hard that his head slammed against the side of the stock and jarred his neck as well. The swordsman's knees went slack and the man hung limp from the stocks.

"Sami!" a man shouted from a nearby tent. "What in Hammenfein's name are you doing?"

Jonathan looked to Sami but the big man just grinned and pointed to Jonathan. "Liam, this is the boy that captain was looking for. He actually has that bow they were talking about."

"Kigabané?" Liam inquired breathlessly. He looked to Jonathan and stared at him for a moment before shaking his head and then rushing to the swordsman. "Help me, you big oaf!"

Sami moved in and with one hand picked up the stocks holding the swordsman so that the posts could be removed. Then, he set the man down on the ground while Liam bent down to listen for breathing.

"Well, you didn't kill him, so I guess we are fine."

Jonathan pointed to Rourke. "I want this man to go with me," he said.

The archer glanced between Jonathan and Sami quickly before shouting out, "I want to go too."

Jonathan shook his head. "No, I don't trust you."

The archer started to shout something, but then Sami grinned down at the archer and raised his hand. The archer shut his mouth and looked down at the ground.

Liam rose to his feet and fumbled with a set of keys. "The captain said I wasn't to release them until he returned."

"He is going to accompany me to the Quags," Jonathan said.

Liam stopped going through the keys and looked up at Jonathan. Then he looked to Sami. "He can't be serious," he said.

Sami nodded. "I am going too," Sami said.

Liam balked, letting his hands fall to his waist. "Sami, we talked about this. You can't go down there. There is no more fighting. We are building a wall now. Battlegrym is gone, and The Warrens are too far away."

"They have my brother," Jonathan told Liam. Liam

turned and looked back at Jonathan, the droplets of water running over his face reflecting the orange light of the withering torch. "I am going to find him, no matter where he is." Jonathan then turned to Sami. "I appreciate the offer, but once I get to Fort Sym, you should come back here with your cousin."

Sami shook his head. "I served two tours in Battlegrym," he said. "I tried to sign on with the Ghosts of the Quags, but they never took me on. I know I can make it to The Warrens. If you are getting a party together, I am in."

Liam fumed as he fumbled with his keys. "Dumb as an ox, that's what I say," Liam said.

"And I am built like one too," Sami put in with a grin.

"You smell like the back end of one too!" Liam shouted as he unlocked Rourke's stock. He looked to the scout and nodded once. "I will tell Captain Burke that you did an honorable thing after the boy showed up."

"We should get moving," Sami said. "If we go through the wall, we can travel safer and out of the cold rain."

Liam shook his head and then wagged a hand at Jonathan. "Come with me, boy. I have some things you can take. I have a backpack and some supplies in my tent." He then pointed to Sami. "Make the ox carry them."

CHAPTER TEN

As Jonathan and the others emerged from the long hall in the wall, the sun broke upon their faces through a torrential downpour that soaked them within seconds. Light illuminated the clear drops that were easily as large as the top portion of Jonathan's thumb. They *thumped* down on Jonathan's body with enough force that he made sure to keep his eyes and face pointed slightly toward the ground to avoid injury.

Sami walked as if nothing could be more pleasant than an early spring rain. Rourke, on the other hand, drew his cloak tighter about himself to fend off the deluge.

Fort Sym was a marvelous sight to see. In front of the outer wall that surrounded the fortress were several wooden cottages and houses. The thick thatch on the roofs was turned a muddy brown color in the heavy rains. There were several people out patching roofs, or moving along the muddy streets with animals.

A wooden horse-drawn cart squeaked by, sloshing a bit of mud up onto Jonathan's right leg as it dropped down into a puddle in the road. A bunch of miserable looking chickens huddled together in wooden cages for warmth. Jonathan and the others walked alongside the cart for some time, passing a blacksmith who was busily pounding out something on his anvil.

A few people stopped and stared at Jonathan, or more accurately they stared at the bow on his back. Even if they didn't know what it was, it was easy to see that it was as dry as a bone. Due to its enchantment, not a drop of water was able to remain upon its surface. If anyone had ideas of trying to take it from him though, Sami was quick to put down such thought with an ever watchful glare.

The giant black haired man stood nearly six and a half feet tall, and must have weighed more than three hundred pounds. There weren't many men in all the realm who would likely tangle with a man like that. For that, Jonathan was happy to have him around.

Truth be told, he was happy to have Rourke along as well. It had been awkward at first, with Sami always eyeing the scout sideways or looking as though he were two seconds away from slapping the man upside the head, but they got through the first day alright and things felt as normal as they could all things considered.

If the buildings were interesting to see on the outside of the wall, the shops and buildings inside were much more so. There were no thatched roofs here. Each pitched roof was expertly made with shingles and boards, completed with gutters and drain pipes made of copper. The road was better as well. Though some of the mud from wagon wheels and feet was certainly brought in and smeared around the entrance, the well-built cobblestone road easily shirked off the water much better than the road of dirt and mud outside the wall.

Thirsty drains alongside the cobblestone wall gulped streams of rainwater down below the surface as well. Jonathan had heard of such things, but had never seen them in life. None of the other towns he had visited had them. He stopped and moved close to the iron grate that strained some of the twigs out of the water that disappeared into the ground below. He couldn't exactly see how far down the opening went, but the rushing sound of water was pleasant, and he smiled as he thought about who might have invented such a thing. He wondered then where the water might go. He turned back to his waiting companions and shrugged simply as he thought of several uses for a large quantity of water stored underground.

Then he looked up at the keep and all of his wonder at the simple sewer drain faded away into nothingness. Before him stood a gargantuan building of gray stone that reached at least forty feet into the sky. Each corner was built into a round tower topped with conical roofs that pointed up to the clouds. Jonathan eyed the building for several moments, noting the many windows it had, and pausing when he saw the large, rectangular stained glass pane over the entryway.

"If Pa could see this," he said aloud. He knew his Pa would be as awestruck as he was by the sight of such a grand window. The glass depicted a scene much more pleasant than the reality of the large wall just behind them would hint at. A pair of

118

horses galloped through a field of flowers with a golden sun pouring its light over them. It was simply stunning.

"I'm sure he has," Sami said as he clapped a hand on Jonathan's shoulder.

Jonathan looked up at Sami with a furrowed brow. "Who has what?" he asked.

"Your Pa, I bet he has seen this window before. After all, it would have been here during your grandfather's time in the army. It was commissioned well over eighty years ago, by the king's father."

"How do you know my Pa?" Jonathan asked.

"I don't," Sami said with a shrug. "But I know of him. He was the one that found The Warrens."

"Everyone has heard of him," Rourke put in. "And anyone who hadn't sure got an earful of it after we came back to camp without you."

"What do you mean?" Jonathan asked.

Rourke sighed and shook his head as he tugged on his cloak. "Captain Burke told us then that you were a Haymaker. We had no idea before that point."

"He didn't tell you before we set out together?" Jonathan asked.

Rourke shook his head. "If he had, I am willing to bet things would have turned out differently." Rourke motioned to the bow with his chin and offered a half smile.

"Let's get inside," Sami said.

The three of them moved to the grand double doors and pushed them open.

Jonathan expected they might be met by a guard, or perhaps a steward of some sort, but no one was in the entry way. In fact, they walked into the sweeping antechamber without seeing a single person. Sami directed them down a long, wide corridor flanked by suits of armor set up on stands with small names engraved into stone pedestals beneath them. Jonathan glanced at one to see what was written. It was the name of someone who had fallen in battle more than a century ago.

The three pushed on down the hall until they came to the door at the end. Sami pushed it open and they walked through. This room was a grand chamber, carpeted with a large, square rug of red and gold. A black dragon was embroidered into the middle of the rug, though the fibers were beginning to show wear over the center image and made it a little less enchanting than it might otherwise have been. There were no tables in the room, only a row of chairs lining each of the four walls. Tapestries depicting battle scenes with men and trolls hung over the chairs, and great iron chandeliers clung to the ceiling with long, thick chains.

"Sorry, I think this is the wrong room," Sami said with a shrug. "We needed to take the hall on the right back at the antechamber." Sami shrugged and closed the door as he ushered them back out and down the corridor. As they walked down the hallway, some men entered from the other side and began walking toward them.

The first man was tall, only an inch or two shorter than Sami. He had brown hair and was extremely muscular. A sword hung at his belt and a bow was slung over his back. He wore a set of freshly oiled chainmail and a pair of plate mail boots. He did walk with a slight limp, but otherwise he was as imposing as any soldier Jonathan could have thought of. Beside him walked an older man, maybe in his late fifties by the look of the lines on his face. In spite of the wrinkles, or perhaps because of them, the man's face caused Jonathan to stop in his tracks. There was something about the way the man carried himself that commanded respect. The white beard lining his jaw melded into his black and gray hair, nearly covering the scar on the left side of his face. He wore a full set of armor, the helmet tucked under his right arm, and a flowing, red cape billowing out behind him as he walked.

"Well don't just stand there, step aside!" the man with the limp ordered as they approached.

Sami and Rourke ducked to the right side of the hall, and Jonathan moved to the left. From his vantage point, Jonathan could see there were many men following behind the first two. He flattened himself against the wall and waited as the first couple of rows passed by. Then, someone reached out and grabbed Jonathan's arm and the whole procession came to a crashing halt as the others grumbled and mumbled.

Jonathan looked up to see Lord Bingham.

"Jonathan! Jonathan Haymaker! What are you doing here?" Lord Bingham asked.

Jonathan smiled and he took in a breath of excitement. If Lord Bingham was here, then perhaps he knew where Jason was. After all, Bingham said that he was going to fight in the Quags with the Ghosts, so perhaps he had already found Jason. "I am looking for my brother, have you seen him?"

Jonathan's heart sank as the sparkle in Lord Bingham's eyes died out. The smile faded into an open mouthed gawk that stared blankly back at the young man.

Bingham shook his head. "No, son, I haven't seen him."

"But you said you were joining the Ghosts of the Quags," Jonathan said. "You said you would be there with him. Where is he?"

Bingham mouthed something, but no words came out.

The brown haired man with the limp pushed through, ordering the others to back away. "What's all this then?" he shouted. "Who are you, and what do you want?"

Jonathan winced away from the man for a second, but then he regained his composure, emboldened by the idea that perhaps Bingham had lied that day last summer when he said he would join the Ghosts. "My name is Jonathan Haymaker, and I am looking for my brother, Jason Haymaker."

A murmur rumbled through the others nearby and Bingham backed away. The man with the limp stepped in and narrowed his eyes on Jonathan. "You're a Haymaker eh? How old are you?"

"Old enough," Jonathan answered.

"Actually, he isn't yet seventeen," Bingham cut in. "So, he isn't old enough for anything."

Jonathan stood firm, puffing out his chest and trying to look bigger than he was. "I'm old enough for the Quags," he said.

The others laughed derisively. The man with the brown hair stood silent. He looked at Jonathan for a while and then he glanced to the man with the white beard. The older man stepped in close and pointed to Jonathan's bow.

"What is that?" he asked.

Jonathan turned to him. "It's Kigabané, sir," he said.

"And it's his," Sami called out from behind the group of soldiers. "He went into the Kigyo alone and he came out with the bow. No one else has claim on it."

121

The man with the limp and the older officer turned to see who addressed them. The other soldiers moved out of the way.

"I am Sami, and this is Rourke," Sami said in answer to the unspoken question. "We're with the young man."

"You're with him?" the older officer repeated. "In what capacity?"

"We're his," Sami replied.

"I'm his scout," Rourke said. Then he thumbed to Sami. "This is the boy's muscle, though with his archery skills the boy hardly needs either of us."

The older officer balked and said, "Is that so?"

The officer with the limp turned around and eyed Jonathan from head to toe. "You want to find Jason?" he asked.

"Do you know where he is?" Jonathan asked.

The officer shook his head. "I know where he went, but I don't know where he is, or even if he is more than a pile of bones, kid. I don't mean to upset you, but you have to know that the Ghosts are called that for a reason."

"Because they're the best," Jonathan put in quickly.

The officer with the limp arched a brow and looked to the older officer.

Jonathan continued. "People tell me they are called the Ghosts because none of them ever survive, but that isn't it. They are called Ghosts because they slip in and out without being defeated. Sure, they may have had casualties, but they are also the best warriors in the kingdom. That's what Jason always told me. That's why he wanted to be a part of them."

The officer with the limp shook his head. "No, son. That is not why they are called Ghosts of the Quags. They are called Ghosts because all who are assigned to the unit are considered to be dead men. I'm sorry to disappoint you, but no one can walk into the deepest parts of the swamps and come out again."

"I will," Jonathan said quickly. "So will my brother."

The officer folded his arms and took in a deep breath as he shook his head again. "How will you find him?"

"Pa told me there is a map in Battlegrym. If I can get inside, I can find it. It's the map that Pa helped make when he found The Warrens. My brother will be working his way to the trolls' central lair. That's where I'll find my brother."

The others started to laugh again, but the older officer with the white beard held up a hand and silenced them. "My name is Commander Kilgrave. I was the commanding officer at Battlegrym. I managed to retreat with some of my men, but Battlegrym is now teeming with trolls. To go there would be a foolish plan."

Jonathan shook his head. "After surviving a den filled with giant snakes, I think I'll take my chances. Besides, one or two people can sneak in without drawing attention. It isn't the same as if I was trying to knock down the front door with an army."

The officer nodded his head and smiled. "Spoken like a true Haymaker if I ever met one," he said. He pointed to the officer with the limp and introduced him. "This is Dell, he and I were about to discuss a rescue mission. You see, there is a town that lies between here and Battlegrym. The trolls haven't made it that far north yet because the winter stopped them. So, we are trying to get the residents out before the monsoons come in full force and the trolls ravage the town."

"I am going to lead the mission," Dell said. "I can't promise you any support, but perhaps you could travel with us at least as far as Wendyn."

Jonathan couldn't believe his ears. "You aren't going to try to talk me out of it?" he asked.

Commander Kilgrave laughed and shook his head. "Wouldn't do any good if I tried," he replied. "I saw the same fire in your brother's eyes when he begged to be assigned to the Ghosts of the Quags. I saw it before that when your father did the same thing." The smile vanished and the large officer placed a heavy hand on Jonathan's shoulder. "If I let you go with Dell, then promise me that you will come back. So far the Haymaker family have shown their spirit and proven their valor, but only one out of three have returned."

"Two out of four," Jonathan corrected. "And my brother just needs a bit of help, but he's alive."

Commander Kilgrave pointed to the far end of the hall. "Come, sit in the council room with us. Bring your... men too."

CHAPTER ELEVEN

Jonathan pulled his cloak tighter around himself and secured the iron brooch as tight as it would allow him to do. He pulled the hood up over his head and took his bow in hand. He tested the string one more time and then slowly set it back into place. Then he slung the bow over his shoulder. A long, curved knife hung from his belt, a gift from Dell.

Sami stood nearby, spinning a massive hammer in his hands by holding the shaft near the head and using his other hand to twirl it. Sami had not smiled at all that morning as he stood and waited. He looked off, focusing on something beyond the stone wall and the wooden doors that separated them all from the Quags. Jonathan was still not entirely sure why Sami had come along, but he was happy to have the large man with him.

Rourke was also quiet, sitting off in a corner and burying his face in his hands as he muttered some prayer over and over. The scout had equipped himself with two additional daggers and a long spear. He had also traded out his normal boots for a pair of thick, leather boots that had iron cleats on the bottom.

Jonathan and Sami had gotten similar boots. Dell had told them that the cleats were absolutely necessary.

A cadence of heavy thumps sounded over the stone behind them. Jonathan turned to see twenty men, led by Dell, walking toward them from the open double doors at the opposite end of the large chamber.

"Are you sure you want to go through with this?" Dell asked Jonathan as he approached.

Jonathan glanced to the hardened faces standing behind Dell and then nodded. "My brother is alive out there, I know it."

Dell leaned down and whispered into Jonathan's ear. "No one would think less of a young boy for changing his mind, you know that don't you?"

Jonathan shrugged. "I am not here because I want to please others," he said simply. "I am here because I know my brother is out there, and he needs me."

"Tell me one thing," Dell pressed. "Did you really get Kigabané by yourself?"

Jonathan nodded. "I did."

Dell pressed his lips together and sighed as he nodded. "Then, let's not waste any more time." He turned to the men behind him and addressed them briefly. "Men, we march for Wendyn. We don't stop until we reach the town. As you know, it is a little less than eighty miles away. If we hasten our pace, and eat as we walk, then we should make it within a couple of days, depending on the weather and the trolls of course. As you may already be aware, the last letter we received from Wendyn stated that many of their people could not venture out from the safety of the walls, for the trolls were prowling the forest. We need to act swiftly." Dell ceased speaking and turned to Sami. The large man nodded his head and then moved to the large doors.

Jonathan watched as the iron-banded wooden door was pulled open. The morning rain had already started, though it was only a misty drizzle that clouded the green grass beyond the iron portcullis. Chains and gears popped and clanked as the portcullis was raised up to allow the troop access to the Quags. Jonathan walked in lock-step with Dell out into the open air.

Pillows of thick fog rolled across the drenched grass between them and the tall trees that marked the beginning of the forest some two hundred yards away. As with the other trees to the east, these oaks, elms, and pines had all but been destroyed by the relentless torrent of rain. Moss and ivy ate away the trees' strength while the waterlogged ground drowned them from below.

What once had been a wide, well-packed dirt road was now little more than a tan path of mud that swirled in the puddles that formed along the ground. Patches of pointy mushrooms and large-headed toadstools popped up from the water. Jonathan could feel his cleats digging into the softened ground with each step. The squishy mud squirted out either side of his boots as he walked, some splatter falling onto Dell's ankle.

They marched as quickly as Dell's slight limp would allow the group to move, making the tree line and entering the forest within only a couple of minutes of exiting from the protection of Fort Sym. Jonathan noticed how much darker everything seemed inside the forest. He looked up to see a thick, wet covering of moss stretching from tree to tree, using the outstretched branches to create a network of soggy greenery that all but blocked out the light from above. It didn't help that the rain clouds were thickening either.

The group wound their way through the darkness for miles. The rain never let up. Luckily, despite the lack of sunshine breaking through the trees and moss above, the air was actually quite warm, allowing for some amount of comfort despite the wetness.

None of the men talked. There were no songs either. Only the relentless pounding of cleated boots into the mud accompanied by the slapping raindrops that burst upon the branches above or the heavier drops that slammed into the watery ground below. Dell kept his eyes moving, sweeping all of the area around them. Jonathan tried to do the same, but then a thought came to him.

Why not hold the bow? If it would alert him to a troll's heart, then he may very well be able to see the threat before any pair of eyes might. He reached around and took the bow in hand. He felt nothing other than the cool, dry wood of the weapon in his hand.

"Did you see something?" Dell asked in hushed words.

Jonathan shook his head. "The bow is magic. It will alert me if trolls are close."

Dell looked to the boy with surprise. "I thought the bow was enchanted to kill snakes."

Jonathan shrugged, not wanting to explain the conversation that he had had with the king snake. "It does both," Jonathan said.

Dell let the topic go at that, apparently valuing silence over a history lesson.

After several hours of walking, the forest turned from a dead, soaked bunch of conifers and pines to a black and green swamp with vines now stretching through as much of the forest as the moss had been. The trees looked different too. Thick trunks that almost appeared to have many trunks fused into one rose up from the wet ground. The gray, smooth, vertical ridges and columns bent and fused with others to create unique trees that stood high above them. Dense ferns and lilies grew around the base of each tree. Thick, snake-like vines dropped low, swooping down from branches and boughs.

"Eyes open," Dell said. "No one touch or cut a vine until you are sure it isn't a snake."

The soldiers in the group all unsheathed their swords in unison, creating a ringing sound of scraping metal that echoed off the strong trees.

Off to the right, a few frogs croaked loudly. The croaks grew quieter the closer the troop marched to them. Often the sudden silence of a frog was followed by a sharp splashing sound. Jonathan tried to locate the frogs, but never saw more than a wiggling fern or ripples in the water after the creature had disappeared.

A tingling sensation rippled through Jonathan's hand and up his left arm. He stopped and pulled an arrow as he scanned the nearby ferns and trees for any sign of what was there. Dell noticed Jonathan's actions and halted the group with a hand signal. The soldiers responded by turning their backs inward toward each other and preparing for battle.

A thick, angular head dropped down from a low-hanging bough twenty yards away. Jonathan pointed to the snake and called Dell's attention to it.

"That's a pretty big beast," Dell commented. "Why not test the bow?"

Jonathan nodded. The snake flicked its tongue out, tasting the air. It turned its thick body to look at the group and then hissed, revealing a mouth filled with several rows of sharp fangs. The body was easily as thick as any of the guardian Kigyo Jonathan had seen before, and from that he could guess that the snake was probably as long as any of the guardian snakes as well, which would mean that the rest of his twenty-foot long body was coiled up in the trees.

Jonathan felt the bow call out to him. The heart began to glow within the monstrous snake. The young man nocked an arrow and let it fly. The enchanted arrow flew straight for the beast's heart, driving through the body and out the other side, causing a mess of blood to explode out the back as the snake went limp. The massive head drooped and the snake swung slowly back and forth like a scaled pendulum. With each swing, more of the body slid down from the branch above, until the whole creature slid down to the ground, crashing through a bunch of ferns and splashing onto the watery trail. Twenty feet of limp body followed the head, piling atop in a loose heap on the ground.

"Well done," Dell said.

Jonathan smiled. The tingling sensation left and the bow was quiet again. Then, to Jonathan's surprise, he heard a sliding sound in his quiver. He reached up with his hand and realized that the arrow he had fired had been magically returned to the quiver, ready for another use.

"That could come in handy," Dell whispered. He then placed a hand on Jonathan's shoulder. "Anymore danger?"

Jonathan shook his head.

"I'm starting to like that bow of yours," Dell said. He made another hand signal and the soldiers returned to their marching position. The group began jogging through the muddy swamp at a moderate pace. They kept it up for more than an hour, judging by how far they had run. Jonathan's legs ached a bit, but he was able to keep himself going by thinking of Dell's limp. If a man with an injured leg could run, then he should be able to push the aches and pains out of his mind.

Rourke was able to keep up easily enough, but it was Sami who eventually caused the group to stop. He doubled over, heaving for breath and stopping on the side of the road. Dell was quick to catch it, and halted the entire group only a few paces beyond Sami.

"Come on, you can still walk. Put your arms up over your head and keep moving!" Dell ordered.

Sami nodded through his gasps for air and slowly raised himself upright, placing both hands on top of his head and stomping forward through the mud.

They walked for the remainder of the day.

When night fell, Dell halted the group only long enough to call up four mages.

"Do we use magical light, or do we use magic to keep our torches dry?" Dell asked them.

The four glanced to each other and then one spoke. "It would require less magic to keep torches dry," he said. "However, if the boy's bow can alert us to approaching trolls, then we can gain more light by using magical light."

Dell nodded. "With more light, we can move faster," he explained to Jonathan. "What do you say, will your bow alert us in time if trolls approach?"

Jonathan nodded. "It alerted me to the snake," he said.

Dell nodded. "Yes, but this will be different. If we use magic, it might draw the trolls to us. If that happens, you will have to tell us as soon as you are aware of something. If you wait, like you did with the snake, then it might be too late to defend against them. Trolls are not snakes, they will come with magic and bows of their own, and so we need to be extremely aware of our surroundings."

Jonathan nodded. "I will do my best."

Dell nodded to the mages. "Make the light," he said. Dell then turned to Sami. "Can you run some more?" he asked pointedly.

Sami nodded. "I will do what I can."

The four mages turned inward, facing each other. They spoke an incantation in a language Jonathan had never heard before. Then a flash of light exploded between them, lighting their faces and illuminating the shadows around them. A great orb of white floated out and toward the back of the group. The thick shadows of the swamp retreated at the orb's presence as if the orb were able to cut a thick fog of darkness. A second orb appeared, and then a third, and then a fourth. Each orb took up a position around the group so that one could make a rectangle if they were able to connect the orbs with a rope. The amount of light the group now had to work with was brighter than even the noon-day sun, and Jonathan had to look away from the orbs as they hurt his eyes terribly to focus upon.

"Now work your bow," Dell commanded. "Tell me the instant you are aware of anything."

Jonathan nodded.

The group marched quickly through the swamps. They alternated their pace by running for five to ten minutes at a time, and then walking at a quick pace over the muddy road for ten to twenty minutes. They kept this pace up for the rest of the night. Dell would often look to Jonathan, but Jonathan assured him that he was not aware of any dangers.

It was still completely dark when the group finally spotted

the twelve-foot tall stone walls that encircled Wendyn. The bald cypress trees in the area thinned away, with just stumps sticking out above the dense ferns in a wide swath before the gate and wall. Great torches burned along the outside of the walls, set in massive iron sconces that were sheltered from the rain by iron slates. There were four guards protecting the gate, all of them standing on the battlements and scanning the swamp. They called out to Dell's group, easily identifying them with the magical light and hurrying to open the gates.

"Double time, men," Dell shouted. The group broke into a run. Jonathan then noticed that Sami dropped out from the group again and stood at the side of the road, grabbing his stomach and sucking in heavy breaths. Jonathan cut away from the group and went to Sami.

"Come on, we're almost there," Jonathan said.

Sami shook his head. "My lungs are burning, and my feet won't move. I need a break."

Jonathan pointed to the gate. "It's less than a hundred yards away. Come on, you can rest inside!" At that moment, Jonathan's left hand tingled. He looked down to his hand and then turned to shout at Dell. "Danger!" he called out.

The group didn't stop. They were already too far away to hear him shout over the din of their boots slamming the ground and their armor clanking and screeching.

Sami took in a deep breath and put his hands to his mouth to propel his voice as loud and far as he could manage. "DANGER!" he bellowed.

The soldiers stopped and turned instantly to put their backs to each other. Dell came sprinting around the group and shouted out to Jonathan.

"Which way?"

Jonathan put an arrow to his bow string. His mind was invaded with many beating hearts this time, not just the one as had been the case with the large snake from the tree. A purple flash glimmered in the darkness. Jonathan raised his bow and fired. A second later something howled in the night and the purple flash disappeared.

"Look right men, look right!" Dell ordered.

Jonathan could hear the officer shouting at the guards to

close the gates, but the young boy was not focused on that now. He put another arrow to the string. His arm tingled wildly and the purple flashes appeared in the shadows in great number. He saw maybe ten or fifteen. He began sending arrows out. One after another the glowing hearts faded to be replaced by the screams and howls of death.

Sami moved to flank Jonathan, holding his hammer at the ready. A few seconds later, Rourke was on Jonathan's other side, with his spear held firm. Jonathan worked his bow, unleashing arrow after arrow. For each shot he fired, a glowing heart disappeared and an arrow magically returned to the quiver.

He must have killed forty of the things before any of them reached Dell's group. He could hear the men shouting and the swords clashing against metal, but he couldn't turn to help them yet. There were more than a dozen glowing hearts sprinting their way through the trees toward him.

"Keep firing steady," Sami said. "If any of the beasts show their faces, I'll crush them before they can reach you."

Jonathan fired at a troll off to the left. Then another broke through the brush from around a large cypress tree. The beast was hideous. From the mage's light off in the distance, Jonathan could see the angular nose and the jagged teeth. Green, muscular arms wielded a pair of axes that appeared to be made of bone and stone. Jonathan turned to fire at the troll, but Sami was there in a flash, just as he had promised. His mighty hammer swung low and then upward, catching the troll in the solar plexus and lifting it up and away from the road until it crashed into the cypress tree it had hidden behind.

Jonathan let that troll go and took aim at a different one not far beyond the road. He slew it with one shot and then reloaded to kill another troll. Three more jumped out from around the cypress tree. Jonathan killed two, and Rourke drove his spear into the third, hitting the beast directly in the heart and extinguishing the purple glow.

The troll gripped the spear shaft and ripped the weapon from Rourke's hands as it fell backward onto the ground. Rourke pulled his pair of long, curved knives out and held them at the ready. The troll that Sami had hit was now rising from the ground. Its chest was caved in nearly flat, but the purple glow from the heart was bright and strong. Before Jonathan's eyes, the troll healed and the bones snapped back into place as the chest thickened out again. It howled menacingly, but Sami was there in a second and drove his hammer down through the top of the troll's skull. So powerful was the strike that the creature's spine could be heard snapping in several places as it crumpled to the ground.

"Grow back from that," Sami taunted.

Jonathan watched as the purple glow from the heart slowly faded and winked out. As it faded, so too did the tingle in Jonathan's arm. He looked out and saw there were no more glowing hearts in the area.

"Head or heart," Rourke told Jonathan. "Either one is a killing blow, otherwise you are wasting your strength hitting anything else."

Jonathan nodded. He stared down at the broken troll and was unable to take his eyes from the mangled body. He had often imagined what it would be like fighting trolls, but it was something different altogether to see it in person. The macabre image held Jonathan's gaze until Dell was able to reach him.

A hand grabbed Jonathan's shoulder. "You alright?" Dell asked.

Jonathan, finally able to pull himself from the grotesque sight, looked up to Dell and nodded. "I am."

"The first fight is always the worst, but it gets easier," Dell said. "Come on, let's get inside." Dell looked to Sami and poked the man in the chest. "Don't dawdle again, you are going to get someone killed."

Sami's shoulders slumped and he sighed as the shame he felt was stamped onto the frown on his face.

"Let's move," Dell said sharply. The group rejoined with the soldiers as they made haste for the gate. Only when the gate was firmly secured again and the entire troop was inside Wendyn did anyone relax.

Dell sent his men to find lodging in the local inn while he went to go and speak with the town's mayor. Jonathan, Sami, and Rourke were told to go to the inn as well.

The three of them followed behind the soldiers, each lost in his own thoughts. It wasn't until they pushed in through the doorway that Sami finally broke the silence.

"I am sorry, Jonathan," he said. "I didn't mean to put us in danger."

Rourke cut in before Jonathan could answer. "It wasn't your fault. The trolls were already close. It was the magic that brought them. If you hadn't stopped, then the trolls might have attacked right as we entered the city. Think of how much worse it would have been if Jonathan couldn't use his bow because there were soldiers stuck in the gateway fighting hand to hand."

Jonathan smiled and nodded. Sami smiled as well, thankful for the objective opinion.

"I'll get some food," Rourke said.

"I'll find a table for us in the corner," Sami said.

Jonathan glanced around the room and shook his head. How were they all supposed to sleep here? The main hall was long and wide, but there were only ten rooms connected to it that he could see. There was no other floor, unless there was a basement somewhere. Suddenly Jonathan realized the answer as soldiers began removing their wet armor and clothes. Some of them disappeared into the rooms, but others took up position on the tables, or underneath tables to lie down. It was definitely not something Jonathan had expected.

At least it was warm. There was a long fire pit encased in stone that ran the length of the middle of the hall. The high, vaulted ceiling had a few vents through which the smoke was able to rise and exit the building. A set of iron racks near the fire were used to hang the wet clothes on to dry.

"It would have been nice if the mages had used their magic to keep us dry," one of the nearby soldiers grumbled.

"You saw how the trolls came when we used the light," another put in. "Using magic earlier would have brought the trolls sooner."

"Bah," a third man grumbled as he wrung his shirt out near the fire pit. "They didn't come until we got near Wendyn. We would have been fine."

The man turned and sat with the others at a table while a barmaid brought them each a mug of what he could only assume was ale from the greedy way they snatched the drinks. He watched them for a second or two, and then his eyes lifted up from them and he caught sight of a young woman in the back of the inn, leaning against the wall with her arms folded across her chest. Her hair was long and black, cascading over her shoulders and down her back. She wore a long, blue tunic that was fastened in place with a thick belt around the waist. Black leggings were visible on her thighs under the bottom of the tunic and above the boots that reached nearly half way up her thighs. White sleeves poked out from under the dress, tucked into long, leather bracers wrapped around her wrists. Even from across the room Jonathan could see her emerald green eyes as she watched the soldiers in the room. She was stunningly beautiful, far more so than any of the young women he had seen in Holstead.

A long staff stood against the wall next to her. It was a simple weapon, without ornamentation or carvings of any kind, but there was something about it that piqued Jonathan's curiosity. Then he noticed that the young woman was looking back at him and he blushed and looked away. Luckily Rourke came back just then with three bowls of soup on a wooden tray, breaking the young woman's line of sight to Jonathan.

"Everything alright?" Rourke asked.

Jonathan nodded and reached out for a bowl of soup.

"Over here," Sami called out from a table a few yards away. The two of them walked to it and ate their food in silence. Jonathan fought the urge to glance back over his shoulder at the beauty leaning on the wall. He didn't want her to think him odd. He stirred his spoon through his soup and ate the larger chunks of meat and onion before picking up the bowl to drink the broth. After they had finished, Rourke pointed off to a door.

"I was able to procure a room for us. There is only one bed, but there is enough floor space for us all to share the room," Rourke said.

Jonathan nodded and looked in the direction Rourke was pointing. It was only a few feet away from where the black haired girl stood. Jonathan looked back to his bowl reflexively.

"Everything alright?" Rourke asked for the second time.

Sami grinned wide and slapped Rourke on the shoulder. "I think he fancies the girl over there," he said.

"Ah," Rourke said with a smile of his own. "Well, I suppose you will have your pick of any girl you want after you find your brother and become the first to emerge alive from The

Warrens."

Sami's smile faded and he thunked Rourke again, this time hard enough that the scout flinched. "What would you say that for?" he whispered harshly. "You say it like it ain't gonna happen, but you saw what he did with that bow when the trolls came. They were no match for him at all."

Rourke sighed and looked away.

Sami leaned over the table and tried to put on another smile. "Don't you worry, we'll watch your back through the swamps. We'll come back alive alright, you mark my words." He then pulled up a wooden tube and pried the cap loose. "I even got this at Fort Sym before we left. We can put the map in here once we find it, and it should stay dry."

"Assuming the map is dry to begin with," Rourke put in.

Sami turned a sour eye on the man. "Enough with the pessimism," Sami said.

"You don't have to come along," Jonathan told Rourke. "I am sure Captain Burke would consider the debt paid in full that you were willing to get me this far. I bet he would be happy to have you back too."

Rourke wrinkled his nose and shook his head. "It isn't that," he said. "I don't want to leave, I just feel uneasy about going, that's all."

"Then stay, and go back with the refugees," Sami put in. "The kid's right. You don't have to come along."

Rourke sighed. "I appreciate the permission, but if it's all the same to you, I'll be sticking around. I grew up in Garrick, and we take our debts very seriously there. It stems from the Konnon traditions. At least, that's what everyone in Garrick says anyway. When we wrong a person, we settle the debt not to be even, but to pay twice what we owe. Since I nearly got Jonathan killed. I am now his man until I die. There is no debate." Rourke looked at Jonathan sternly then and nodded decisively. "If you were to march into Hammenfein itself, I would march with you."

Jonathan pursed his lips and arched his right brow. "I suppose we might be doing exactly that," he said quietly.

Sami cut the silence with one of his big, toothy grins and obnoxiously confident reassurances. "Well then, we'll just have to send all of the trolls there first. We'll be marching back here before the spring is over, mark my words."

"What about you, Sami," Rourke asked. "Why are you here? You don't owe the boy anything."

Sami's smile faded and he shrugged. "I guess I just want one more crack at those trolls," he said. Something about his uneven grin queued Jonathan in to the fact that there was definitely something else there, but he wasn't going to push it. He trusted Sami, and that was enough. Jonathan looked to the table, wishing he could believe Sami's reassurances that they would live through it all.

Jonathan nodded blankly. It wasn't really something he wanted to think about right now. Sure, they had survived the attack outside Wendyn, but that was because he was able to pick off a lot of trolls as they ran toward the larger group. It wasn't until he killed a couple dozen of the things that they started to run at him. Without the group of soldiers though, any trolls they met would all be focused on the three of them. Magic bow or not, that turned the odds considerably to the enemy's favor. Jonathan could only shoot so fast. It was a numbers game, and Jonathan knew it.

"I'm beat," Jonathan said. "I'm going to bed."

He got up and shuffled his way through the other soldiers until he found his door. The black haired girl looked at him with her green eyes, but she didn't smile or say anything. Jonathan averted his eyes and pushed through into the room. He pulled off his clothes and set them over a chair. Then he hopped into bed. It was the first time in weeks that he had felt the comfort of a real bed. The soft mattress and the warm blankets welcomed his weary body, and the pillow was quick to calm his mind and let him drift off to a deep slumber.

The remainder of the night and half the morning passed before Jonathan woke to the sound of rustling armor and grumbling men outside his door. He sat up and rubbed his eyes, almost forgetting where he was. He looked around the room and saw Sami, half dressed in just his black trousers and wrestling with his boots. Rourke was nowhere to be seen.

"Where's Rourke?" Jonathan asked.

Sami shrugged. "Getting food I suppose. Dell was in here a few minutes ago. He tried to wake you, but you were out like a rock."

"Are they leaving?" Jonathan asked.

Sami nodded. "The townsfolk are ready to make the journey back. Dell has ordered everyone to be ready within the hour."

"That was a quick march," Jonathan said.

"Such is the reality of the swamps," Sami replied as he tugged at his boot and grunted. "Cursed thing must have shrunk!" Sami shouted as he tossed the cleated boot to the floor.

"Are all of the townsfolk leaving too, then?" Jonathan asked.

"I assume they are," Sami replied. "Dell said that Wendyn had a few wagons and teams of horses to make the journey a bit easier on the elderly and the children. The town also has some guards that they can add to the patrol, though I don't remember how many Dell said there were." Sami shrugged. "Sorry, just with us going deeper into the swamp, I figured it wasn't important, so I didn't pay close attention."

Jonathan nodded. "That's alright."

A knock came at the door.

Sami jumped up and rubbed his massive hands together. "That will be Rourke with the food!" Sami said with a grin. Before the big man could move, the door opened and in came one of the soldiers holding a large, black boot.

"Pardon me, but it appears I have switched boots with someone," the soldier said. The man looked down and saw the boot Sami had discarded and smiled as he went for it. "There it is. This must be yours then," he said as he held the large boot out for Sami.

Sami took it and eyed the boot for a moment before smiling wide. "Thank the gods!" Sami said. "I'd hate to go out there with one bare foot!" Sami sat back down and tugged the boot onto his foot. It slid on nicely, lacing up snug and fitting as well as it had the day before.

The other soldier left, bumping into someone as he exited the room. "Excuse me," he said as he turned to the side and slid out the doorway.

Jonathan looked up to see the young woman with the black hair come into the room. He was happily surprised at first, but then realized that he was mostly naked, covered only from the waist down with the blanket. If the girl noticed Jonathan squirm and pull the blanket up a bit tighter around himself, she didn't show it. She turned to Sami and addressed him instead.

"Did I hear you correctly last night saying that you are going to Battlegrym?" she asked.

Sami looked to Jonathan. "He's the man in charge," Sami said. Jonathan caught a winking grin from Sami after the girl turned back to him. Jonathan blushed, glancing quickly to the chair where he had placed his clothes only to discover that they were gone. "Your clothes are on the rack, Sir Jonathan," Sami said with extra emphasis on the "sir" part of the name. "I'll go and get them."

"No that's not—" Jonathan stammered through the words, but Sami wasn't listening. He left the room and promptly pulled the door closed behind himself.

"Odd fellow," the girl said after the door was closed. She stepped in closer to Jonathan, her boot heels clicking on the wooden floor. "So it is 'Sir Jonathan' is it?" she asked.

Jonathan shook his head. "Just Jonathan," he assured her. "What was your question about Battlegrym?"

The girl folded her arms. "I am going with you," she said decisively.

Jonathan looked at her curiously. "Why would you want to do that?" he asked.

"I am looking for my father," she said. "He was with the Ghosts of the Quags. He was their wizard."

Jonathan swung his legs over the bed at the mention of the Ghosts, nearly losing the blanket from his middle before regaining his composure and pulling the blanket tighter over himself again.

"There is an entire room full of men in their underwear outside your door," the girl said as she noticed Jonathan's embarrassment. "I promise I won't stare at your ankles too much."

Jonathan smirked and replied, "I don't have any underwear. I took it off to dry out while I slept." His cheeks flushed a bit and he looked at the floor, suddenly wishing he could take the words back.

"Oh," the girl said. Jonathan looked up just in time to catch the last of the small grin across her face. Then she turned away. "Well, I will let you get dressed then. I will be waiting outside when you're ready."

"My brother," Jonathan said, suddenly not wanting her to leave. The girl turned back and looked at him curiously. "My brother was also with the Ghosts of the Quags," he explained. "I am looking for him."

The young woman nodded. "Well, you have a bow, a giant, and a scout. I will add magic to the group. My father is a great wizard. I have many of his talents."

Jonathan grinned eagerly. "Can you keep us dry?" he asked.

The black haired beauty shrugged. "My father always said that magic should be used sparingly in the swamps. We'll see how it goes."

With that, she turned and left the room. No sooner had she exited than Sami came stumbling in the door with an arm full of clothes.

"They are warm and dry," he said with a big, toothy grin as he plopped the clothes on the bed. He then thumbed at the door. "So?"

"So what?" Jonathan asked roughly as he reached out for his clothes. He slipped his underwear on under the blanket and then got out of bed to finish dressing.

"How did it go?" Sami pressed.

"She was asking to join our group to find her father, not for marriage," Jonathan shot back.

Sami's smile turned into a straight lipped expression with eyes that seemed to be telling Jonathan he had missed some sort of opportunity. "The more the merrier, I suppose."

Rourke came into the room then with a plate full of bread, boiled eggs, and sausages. "No, actually the more people in our group, the harder it will be to infiltrate the swamps without being caught," he corrected. "She can't come with us."

Jonathan pulled his pants up and buttoned them. "She said she can wield magic," Jonathan said quickly. "Sounds like a smart addition if you ask me."

Rourke pulled his mouth to the left corner and wrinkled his nose before responding with, "I suppose that might be helpful."

"She is looking for her father," Jonathan continued. "She

said he was with the Ghosts of the Quags as well. Our purpose is the same, it only makes sense to help each other."

"You sure it's her magic, and not her looks that have you jumping at the chance to take her along?" Rourke asked pointedly.

Jonathan shrugged as he shook out his shirt. "She said her father was the wizard for the Ghosts, so if she has some of his talent, I assume it will be quite useful for us." He then grinned at Sami.

Sami winked back at the young man. "Her looks won't hurt either," Sami added.

Rourke sighed and shook his head. "Make sure you are thinking with your head, Jonathan. It's one thing to throw yourself into the swamps, but it's another thing to take others with you."

Jonathan tugged his shirt over his head and shoulders before straightening it over his torso. "You don't have to come, Rourke. Go back with the others if you want."

Rourke set the plate of food on the bed and folded his arms. "It isn't that, it's just that she is young."

"So am I," Jonathan pointed out.

Rourke pointed out the doorway. "Does she have any experience fighting trolls?"

Jonathan shrugged again. "I didn't have any experience doing that until last night," he rebutted.

"But you survived the Kigyo and came back with Kigabané," Rourke countered. "What has she done?"

At that moment the black haired girl stomped back into the room. Her staff was firmly in her right hand and a red, hooded cloak now hung over her shoulders. "My name is Miranda," she said pointedly. "And I came to Wendyn all by myself through the swamps just two days before any of you showed up. I was only stocking up on supplies before I headed out to Battlegrym. I am leaving with or without you to find my father. I just thought it might be smart to team together, since the two of you blathered on for over an hour last night about going to Battlegrym and such."

Jonathan smiled wide. "See, I am not *taking* her along. We're just headed the same direction."

Rourke huffed, thoroughly defeated, but clearly not happy about it. He took a piece of bread from the plate and walked toward the door. "I'll see about buying some food for the road."

"You have four mouths to feed now," Miranda put in as he passed her.

Jonathan and Sami shared a laugh at Rourke's expense.

"I like her," Sami said.

CHAPTER TWELVE

The foursome found themselves in a thick copse of bald cypress trees, looking down from a hill onto the ruins that had once been Battlegrym. The gray and black stone structure was tilted off toward the north. Another massive section of the fortress had apparently broken off and was now lying across a shattered mess of wood and stone that surrounded what had once been the main building. Ivy and thick vines now covered every surface. Skeletons still clothed in armor littered the ground, with moss and mushrooms growing out of the remains.

Around the base of the castle structure was a large depression that had swallowed much of Battlegrym into the ground. From their vantage point, Jonathan could just see the surface of the water building in the depression.

"You sure we can find the map in there?" Rourke asked.

Jonathan shrugged. "I'm not sure it is still there, but I know that's where Pa said it was."

"I'll go in with you," Sami said quickly. "Check your bow. Are there any trolls?"

Jonathan pulled his bow around again and held the weapon. He shook his head. "I don't think so."

"Why don't we all go in?" Rourke asked. "Four sets of eyes are better than two."

Sami shook his head and pointed to the sky. "It's light out for now, and the rain has stopped. As soon as the monsoon picks up again, that building is going to be slicker and deadlier than you can imagine. I was here before. I know my way around, and Jonathan knows what he is looking for. We'll go in and slip back out."

Miranda nodded. "It's a good plan. We'll keep a lookout up here."

Jonathan and Sami slipped out from the trees and half slid, half ran down the hill until they reached the clearing below. Jonathan kept a solid grip on his bow, worried that any number of trolls might be nearby.

Encouraged by the fact that the bow was not alerting him to any danger, the two sprinted up to the closest bit of rubble. Sami pried open a half busted door and made a way for them to walk inside of a large, covered deck area.

"This is new," Sami said. "They must have built this after my last tour."

"What is it?" Jonathan asked. He ducked under a few broken beams and crawled around piles of rubble and stone.

"Some sort of expansion, I suppose," Sami said with a shrug. He pointed off toward one of the exterior walls. "There is an arrow slit there. Perhaps they thought with the monsoons spreading heavier and farther than before, they needed to create a covered perimeter."

Jonathan looked down and saw a hole through the floor, noting that it was at least two and a half feet down to the water below. "They built it up from the ground too," Jonathan said.

"To keep the water out," Sami said.

Just then a large form swam past the hole Jonathan was looking down. "Sami, there's something down there!"

"Troll?" Sami said as he whipped his hammer out.

Jonathan shook his head and glanced to his bow. There was no tingling sensation, and he couldn't hear the beating of a heart. "No. Not a troll, and not a snake either."

"Big?" Sami asked as he turned and approached the hole.

Jonathan nodded.

The two of them stared down for a few moments, and then Sami slapped Jonathan's shoulder. "Maybe just a shadow," he said.

"I don't think so," Jonathan replied.

Sami shrugged. "Whatever it is, it can't get us from down there. Come on." The two of them walked over the creaking, moss-covered floorboards. They made their way toward an opening that had been created when a portion of Battlegrym had fallen down upon it. Jagged boards and beams jutted out every which way over a pile of finely hewn rocks that created a slope downward. The hallway before them was entirely blocked off. They knew they would have to go out the opening and then climb atop the structure to get closer to the entrance.

They moved to the pile of rubble and looked down. Stone

and bits of wood were piled all around them. The slope was thick, disappearing into the blue-green pool of water that had been created when the stones had fallen and another sinkhole had been created.

Jonathan peered around the rubble and saw that if they could skirt the slope, there was a section where some larger rocks had piled atop each other in such a way that they could be used to climb to the top of the structure.

"There," Jonathan said as he pointed to it.

Sami nodded. "Watch your step," he cautioned. "I don't think we would like to take a swim around here."

Jonathan started down the slope, leaning into it so he wouldn't lose his footing. A few small rocks skittered down the slippery slope and plinked into the dark waters, causing ripples that moved a pair of lily pads nearby. Jonathan pressed on, coming within a couple feet of the water's edge as he searched for handholds.

Up from the water exploded a massive form of teeth and rough skin. Jonathan wheeled around as Sami shouted out in warning. The teeth gnashed closed just as Jonathan fell back onto the slope and tucked his feet up under him. In the commotion, he let go of his bow and the weapon slid half way into the water.

A massive crocodile roared as it crashed down onto the slope, the end of its snout just inches from Jonathan's boot. Jonathan scampered up the slope on all fours, staring into the hungry eyes of the beast as it wrestled its massive body up onto the rubble.

Sami was there in a second, his hammer coming down and smashing the beast in the head. The croc's tail thrashed out from the pool, spraying Sami and Jonathan with water as it pulled away. Surprisingly, the blow did not kill it. It snapped its great jaws at Sami now, biting and gnashing its teeth. Sami sidestepped the monster and came down again and again with his hammer. Blood splattered out after the third hit and the monstrous crocodile fell limp to the stone.

That was when Sami noticed that Kigabané had slipped into the pool.

"Your bow!" Sami shouted. Jonathan called out in protest, but the big man was already springing into action. He dropped his hammer and jumped into the water with a huge splash. Sami disappeared under the depths for half a second and then came up with a big toothy grin.

"I got it," he shouted as he held the bow up in his right hand. He reached out with his left and grabbed hold of a hunk of stone so he could pull himself out of the pool.

That was when Jonathan noticed the dark form just below the surface making its way toward Sami. It wasn't quite as large as the first, but it was most definitely a croc. The ridges of its tail and back broke the water's surface as it swam nearer.

"Sami look out!" Jonathan shouted.

Sami turned to see the croc. He tossed the bow up and turned to clamber onto the pile of stones, but the stone he held gave way under his weight and he fell back into the pool. Jonathan rushed into action. Without thinking, he drew his curved knife and leapt out toward the oncoming croc. Just as the beast opened its gaping maw to attack Sami, Jonathan came down on its head, using his bodyweight to drive the blade through its tough hide and into its brain. The croc hissed and dropped into the water. Jonathan tumbled over the rough body, unable to see through the copious amount of scarlet blood pouring out around him. He tried to remove the knife, but it was wedged in too tightly. The croc's body tangled with his, and threatened to pull him under, but he pulled free and made for the surface.

Something seized his left arm and pulled him through the water. Jonathan swung out with a fist, striking out to free his arm, but he could not escape the painful grasp. Then, all at once, he was pulled out of the water and flopped unceremoniously onto the stone rubble.

"It's me, Jonathan!" Sami shouted. "Calm down!" Jonathan looked at his arm smeared with blood and realized that it was indeed Sami's hand, and not some other monster from the pool that held him fast. "Get up, we have to move," Sami ordered. The large man hoisted Jonathan up to his feet and the two scrambled to pick up their weapons and clamber up the rubble until they were on top of the structure.

Only then did Jonathan look back and see half a dozen other crocs swarming the area.

"We were lucky," Sami said. The big man thunked

Jonathan's chest. "Thanks for saving me back there."

Jonathan nodded blankly as he watched the newly arrived crocs pull and tear at the corpse that had been left on the stone. "Do crocodiles normally eat their own kind?"

Sami shrugged. "Don't really know, but I do know that they aren't eating us, so let's just keep moving."

Jonathan nodded and the two walked along the roof of the add-on structure until they arrived at the stone keep that had once been the mighty Battlegrym. They climbed onto the structure and slowly made their way up toward a window about fifteen yards above them. The whole building was slanted enough that so long as they kept low to the surface, they could climb it reasonably well.

Jonathan had a bit of trouble finding hand holds, but his cleated boots did well enough to secure him as he propelled himself along. Sami, on the other hand, was so brawny that he could easily pull himself along an arm length at a time. He reached the window before Jonathan was even half way to it. Sami swung into the opening and situated himself while he dug into his pack. He pulled out some rope and tossed the end to Jonathan.

"Grab on," he said.

Jonathan took the rope and no sooner had he done so than Sami was pulling him up the slanted wall. Jonathan turned onto his side as he slid and was dragged along the mossy stone. When he got to the widow he peered down and saw that Sami had precariously perched himself with his legs against a wall sconce beside the window.

The floor on the inside of the structure was slanted much steeper than the outside wall had been, but Sami didn't seem to mind. He moved Jonathan's hands to hold onto the window and then he tied the other end of the rope to the iron sconce. A moment later he was sliding down the rope to walk upon the opposite wall in the room.

Jonathan did the same, careful to grip the rope tightly before letting go of the window. When he made it down, he stood and brushed the moss and dirt from his pants. Broken furniture and other things were piled against the wall, and it made for slow going as they walked around and made their way toward the door.

"How are we going to find the map in this mess?" Jonathan wondered aloud.

"Easy," Sami said. "The original map is in the shrine. That's about two floors down from here. I can find it."

"How do you know that?" Jonathan asked.

"I told you, I was here before."

"Right, but how do you know the map is in the shrine?"

Sami grinned. "Because that's where they hung it. It was there as a way for us to take hope that someday we would find the lair and root out all of the trolls. I saw it often enough."

Jonathan followed Sami over to the door. The portal was busted open, with one of the hinges completely torn free and the other only barely hanging on. Luckily, the door had broken in toward them, so they could use it to climb upward. The last hinge came off when Sami put his foot on the door, but the wall it leaned against held it firm in place. They hopped through and then walked, climbing over broken stones and wood until they found a stairway.

Luckily, the stairs made the walk much easier as they were essentially now parallel with the ground. The two of them followed the stone stairs down two floors and then Sami led them down a long hallway. They had to walk over mangled suits of armor as well as broken bits of marble tables, broken chairs, and fallen tapestries as they made their way to the shrine. Jonathan fell quite a bit behind Sami, but he was still making decent progress through the hallway.

As they climbed through the rubble, Sami went on and on about how this hall had been almost an extension of the shrine, with famed warriors' armor mounted here alongside tapestries that depicted brave heroes of the past. Jonathan only half listened though, as he was much more interested in not slipping through a pile of sharp objects and tearing his leg off, or breaking an ankle.

Jonathan still had his head down, reaching hand over hand as he climbed atop the rubble, when he bumped into Sami's back. Jonathan startled and looked up.

"What's wrong?"

Sami shook his head and pointed to a pile of heavy slabs. Then he pointed up. "The floor above must have collapsed onto the entrance," he said. "How badly do we need this map?"

Jonathan sighed and ran a hand through his hair as he looked at the massive pile of stone. "Do you know the way to The

147

Warrens?" he asked.

Sami sighed. "Nope." He turned and pointed to Jonathan's bow. "Perhaps you should check and make sure we are alone before we spend the next hour or two digging stones out of the way."

Jonathan pulled his bow around and held it in his hand. He spun around in every direction, pausing for good measure, before finally nodding his head and setting the bow down against the wall. "We're clear."

Sami nodded and pointed to one side of the pile. "You start there and I will start here. Let's hurry though, before it rains again."

The two of them pulled at the stones, slowly digging their way through the pile that covered the doorway. The rocks and bits of wood were slick to the touch, but Jonathan made a good go of it, gripping each piece as well as he could and tossing it out of the way. Once, a heavy stone slipped from his grasp and nearly squished his toe as it crashed down beside his foot.

"Careful," Sami said. "A broken foot is a death sentence out here."

Jonathan nodded and redoubled his focus as they continued tearing through the pile.

Eventually, after a little more than an hour's worth of sweaty work, the two of them uncovered the doorway. It was tilted about forty five degrees, but at least the inside of the room was visible. There was a heap of broken marble statues and busts littering the left side of the tilted chamber. Sami reached over and put his hands out for Jonathan. Jonathan stepped into them and Sami hoisted him up. He climbed into the room and then quickly moved out of the way as Sami clambered in.

The room extended roughly fifteen feet to the back wall, and was only about eight feet wide. Sami almost had to duck as they walked over the rubble and looked for the map. They shifted the broken statues and other bits of stone and wood with their feet as they walked, looking for any sign of the item they sought.

"It was framed," Sami said. "It was framed and hanging on this wall." He pointed to the wall that was now tilted so that it was essentially the ceiling. Jonathan could see nails jutting out from places in the stone where the thing had been hung, but it was hard to see the farther they went into the room. The only light they had was coming in from the open doorway, and that light filtered down from the broken space above.

Jonathan moved to a pile of rubble and began digging, setting aside the shards and hunks as he made his way to the bottom. The pieces of stone clicked and clacked as he set them aside. He took comfort that the room had been kept dry by being sealed off. That should mean the map would still be usable, so long as it wasn't torn beyond repair in the collapse.

The two of them sifted through the piles of rubble for a few minutes, and then stopped when they heard something echoing out in the hallway.

"Do you hear that?" Sami asked.

Jonathan reached for his bow, but then remembered that he had left it out in the adjoining hallway. "I don't have my bow."

Plink-plink-plink. Plink-plink-plinkity-pink.

Sami shook his head. "Rain," he said simply. "Come on, dig faster."

A second later the single drops turned to a full torrent as a storm poured out over Battlegrym. Sheets of water pummeled the stone. Small rivers of water snaked their way down into the hallway outside the shrine. A few moments after that, stones began to fall. First there were small and medium sized bricks, but as the water grew in intensity and weight, the whole of Battlegrym shifted and groaned under the pressure.

"Come on, Jonathan, we have to leave."

Jonathan shook his head. "We have to find the map. We're too close!"

Sami growled in frustration and began angrily tossing bits of marble and granite aside. "This building isn't stable, you saw the sinkhole outside. We have to hurry!"

Just then the whole room shifted and the two were thrown onto their faces. Dust popped up around them and Battlegrym quaked. Jonathan looked wide-eyed to Sami. The two of them scrambled back to all fours and kept furiously digging. Then, a massive force rocked the shrine and the wall above them let out a thunderous *crrrack!* The two were thrown down again, this time much harder.

"We have to go, now!" Sami yelled. The big man jumped

up and rushed toward the doorway. Jonathan didn't argue. He leapt to his feet and started to run as well. Another massive impact shook the room and the whole shrine tilted farther, throwing the two back to their faces yet again and shifting the entire pile of rubble.

Jonathan sputtered and wiped his face free of dust. Water dropped in from above now, pouring in through a fissure in the stone. He pushed to his feet and then he saw it, the corner of a wooden frame. He turned to pull some of the rubble away. He saw the corner of a map.

"I found it!" Jonathan shouted.

"Hurry!" Sami yelled. The giant man stretched his arms up, reinforcing the wall above them as it sagged lower and lower with each passing second. "I can't hold this forever!"

Jonathan looked up to see Sami supporting the slab of stone that comprised the majority of the wall and knew he had to act fast. As he dug out the map, a few more impacts shook the room. Battlegrym creaked and groaned all around them. Jonathan worked his hands as fast as he could, uncovering the map and wrenching it free. To his horror, the map was not whole. It was ripped, presumably during the collapse. He turned it over to examine it.

"Come on, Jonathan, let's go!" Sami shouted.

Jonathan glanced to the large man and saw his shaking arms and legs. "Just a second, I have to make sure it is the right part!" Jonathan rotated the map and looked it over. A wide smile flashed across his face as he discovered that he did indeed have enough to navigate their way to The Warrens from Battlegrym. It was the northeastern portion that had been ripped away, and that was not necessary for them. Jonathan jumped up just as another impact rocked the entire chamber. Jonathan was thrown forward this time, but Sami held firm in place, growling against the effort.

"GO!" Sami shouted.

Jonathan scrambled back to his feet and darted out the doorway, jumping through and landing on the slick stones outside, slipping and hitting his side. "I'm out!" he shouted as he grimaced against the pain in his side. He pushed up and turned to the doorway. He only just caught sight of Sami's red face as a wave of water and rock broke free from above. Jonathan screamed at Sami to get out, but the man never had a chance. The wave of rock and water crashed into the section of the wall that Sami was holding up. In the instant before the room collapsed, Sami offered one final toothy grin and tossed the wooden tube to Jonathan. Then a wave of muck and dust exploded as the entire shrine collapsed and crashed through the floor below.

Jonathan screamed, with tears filling his eyes and his body trembling in horror. Battlegrym convulsed and quaked as the shrine and pile of stone broke through the subsequent floor, and then the next, and then the next, until it crashed down into a dark pool of water. Jonathan fell against the wall, screaming and crying out. He mindlessly rolled the map and stuck it into the tube that Sami had brought. After he sealed it, he put his hands on his head and drew his knees in close as shock and grief overcame his trembling body.

He didn't move, couldn't move for a long time. He let the water pour over him and build up around his body as he sat there shivering and sobbing.

It wasn't until Rourke dropped in from above using a rope that Jonathan was able to stop crying. The scout moved in and grabbed the bow and placed it into Jonathan's hands, pushing it hard enough to force the boy to take it.

"We have to go," Rourke said.

Jonathan closed his eyes. "He's dead."

Rourke placed a reassuring hand on Jonathan's shoulder and then cupped his left hand under the boy's chin. "We saw the collapse from outside. When you didn't come out, we feared the worst. Now, I know this is hard, but trust me when I say that sitting here and doing nothing will not help. Let's honor his memory by pushing forward." Rourke stood up and offered a hand.

Jonathan took Rourke's hand and pulled himself up to his feet. He then held up the sealed tube. "We found it," he said. "It was in the room where Sami said it would be."

Rourke looked down to the broken floor, nodded and took the map from Jonathan. He tucked it into his belt, using a small chain to hook it in. "That's all the more reason to push forward." Rourke pointed to the rope. "Up you go."

Jonathan and Rourke climbed out of the building, and only once they were out could Jonathan appreciate the magnitude of the collapse. Another third portion of the building had fallen to the ground, and most of the wall he had used to climb in had caved in as well. It also appeared as though the building had sunk another twenty feet into the ground. It was a miracle that Jonathan had survived such a calamity. Had it not been for Sami, he knew he would be dead.

Rourke and Jonathan found Miranda hiding in the trees atop the grassy hill. From the look on her face, Jonathan could see that she was both happy to see him, and sad that Sami was gone. Instead of saying anything, she stepped up to Jonathan's side and laid a hand on his arm. After offering a measured, meaningful look that left him with the inexplicable feeling that she understood him, she squeezed his arm reassuringly, and offered Jonathan a small kiss on the cheek. She smiled faintly and then she turned to Rourke. The scout pointed to the wooden tube at his belt and nodded.

"We have it," Rourke said.

Jonathan offered one last glance back to Battlegrym and then followed after the other two, who had already started walking again.

They made camp in a hollow dugout, using a fallen oak for a southern wall and clambering under an overhang of dirt and moss that kept the rain off of them. They ate their food in silence. Jonathan stared at the ground while the other two glanced at him occasionally.

As the darkness of night settled in over them, Rourke broke the silence. "I think it best we talk about the strategies to stay alive in the swamp," he said.

Jonathan continued to stare blankly at the ground.

Miranda nodded her head. "I have magic," she said. "I can help us build fires and such, but we'll need to use it sparingly. My father wrote in his letters that magic attracts the trolls."

"When was the last time you received a letter from your father?" Rourke asked.

"Before they left Battlegrym," Miranda replied. "He told me they were headed to The Warrens though. He said they were cutting south from Battlegrym for about one hundred and fifty miles, and then they would hook east to enter The Warrens from the west. He said they had previously made it in the farthest that way."

"Then we should follow that route," Rourke said. "With any luck, we'll find them along the way. Or, perhaps they will have thinned out the trolls along that route and at least we will have an easier time of it."

Miranda looked to Jonathan. "What about you?" she asked. "When did you last hear from your brother?"

Jonathan sighed and folded his arms across his chest as he rubbed his shoulders. "The last letter I received from him was after he was assigned his fighting name with the Ghosts of the Quags. He told me Captain Ziegler gave him the name himself, and then he wished me farewell. I never heard from him again."

"When was that?" Rourke prodded.

"A long time ago," Jonathan admitted.

Rourke put a hand out on Jonathan's shoulder. "Don't give up hope, we'll find him." Jonathan shrugged the man's hand off and leaned back against the dirt wall. Rourke turned back to Miranda. "Let's keep magic use to a bare minimum then, but go ahead and light a fire for tonight. We'll need to dry out each night in order to keep healthy in the swamps. If we let our bodies get too wet, or too cold, we won't make it very far. I can hunt, and I can look for troll tracks along our path. Jonathan is great with his bow, so as long as we see the trolls from a distance, and there aren't too many, we should be fine."

Miranda nodded and went about creating a small fire. Then the group removed their boots and socks and set them out to dry near the fire. Afterward, Miranda went and sat next to Jonathan. "You asleep?" she asked.

Jonathan shook his head.

"Where are you from?" Miranda asked.

"Holstead," Jonathan replied.

"Holstead," Miranda repeated. "Where is that?"

Jonathan looked to her as he let the fire warm and dry his feet. "It's in the northeast part of the kingdom, near Tanglewood Forest."

Miranda's eyes gleamed as she smiled and nodded her head. "I have long wished to see the forest of the elves," she confided. "I have heard they have the most beautiful cities."

"I know what you're doing," Jonathan blurted out.

153

Miranda's smile faded and she looked at him with an expression that seemed to say she had no idea what he was talking about.

Jonathan offered a hint of a smile. "Thank you," he said.

Miranda nodded. "I know what it's like," Miranda said softly. "My mother died last winter. She got really sick, and there was nothing we could do. I have been living on my own since then." She sighed and shook her head with a thin-lipped smile. "I guess that's why I want to find my father. I have to save one of them."

Jonathan nodded understandingly. He knew how she felt. "My parents are gone," he told her. "It just my grandparents and Jason left. So, I know what you mean."

The two sat in silence, staring at the flames until sleep overtook them both.

CHAPTER THIRTEEN

After walking for days, using Miranda's magic only sparingly to light fires when they found shelter enough to hide in for the nights, the trio managed to find a cave, where they could fully dry their belongings and thaw out a bit next to a large fire.

With the help of Kigabané, the trio had avoided seven different patrols of trolls. They had never seen more than four trolls at a time, but they always opted to go around them rather than fight them. The three figured it was smarter to save fighting for their last resort. Once they had almost needed to, when the trolls had come dangerously close while Miranda cast a shielding spell to keep the rain from soaking the map while they looked at it, but after her spell was done, they seemed to lose interest and they walked away.

By Rourke's best estimate, they had managed to travel another sixty miles into the swamp from Battlegrym. The going was much tougher now than it had been before though, for now there were no human roads to use. Sure, there were trails, but most of them seemed to take the trio in circles. Instead, they had to forge their own way through the swamp, avoiding large bodies of water when possible, or using trees or logs to cross them when there seemed to be no way around.

They passed by several large crocs, and had to deal with many snakes along the way, but Kigabané was quick to point out the snakes. Jonathan discovered that he didn't need to hold the bow in order to be alerted either. Whether he was growing more attuned to Kigabané's magic, or the bow had always been able to signal to him, even with it resting on his back, he didn't know. All he knew, was that without the bow, they would have been caught by trolls within miles of Battlegrym, and even if they had been able to evade the troll patrols, the snakes surely would have gotten them.

Jonathan breathed out a long sigh and looked down to the end of the cave. It wasn't very deep, only twenty feet or so, but that was enough to both shield them from the creatures outside, and protect them from anything that might have lurked in a longer tunnel.

Rourke had offered to take first watch, knowing there were dangers yet to be warry of, as the bow couldn't detect anything that wasn't a troll or a large snake. When he had taken up his post, Miranda was quick to sit next to Jonathan and pull out a piece of dried meat.

"Want some?" she asked.

Jonathan shook his head. His stomach was hungry, but his throat wouldn't agree with the idea of eating right now. He was tired, wet, and worn out from the travel.

"No thanks," he said. "I'll eat in the morning."

"Don't let the swamp get to you," Miranda said. "That's what my father wrote in his last letter to me. He said, 'never let the swamp pull you down.' I guess he knew I would be following after him."

"Why do you say that?" Jonathan asked.

Miranda shrugged as she shoved a piece of meat toward Jonathan's face. "I don't know, but why else would he write that?"

Jonathan reluctantly took the food and turned it over as he looked at it. "Maybe because the swamp is expanding," Jonathan said. "Maybe he thought it would swallow the other cities too, and he didn't want you to worry about it."

Miranda shook her head and pulled out another piece of dried meat. "No, that isn't like my father. He was never one to surrender."

"Sounds like my brother," Jonathan said with a half laugh. "Jason is as stubborn as they come." Jonathan smiled and tore a piece of meat off with his teeth and began to chew. It had a slight peppery flavor to it, but to be honest it was a bit like chewing leather. Jonathan's throat swallowed slowly, as if protesting the horridly dry food and trying to stop it from going down. His eyes watered slightly as he stretched his neck out and forced the bite down.

"Why don't you two get some sleep?" Rourke called from the cave's mouth. "I'll wake you if anything comes."

"I'll take second shift," Jonathan offered.

Rourke nodded and then turned back around to lean against the stone.

Miranda stood up in the cave and reached for her staff. "I could dry us off with magic," she offered.

Rourke turned back around quickly. "No. We have a fire. We don't need more magic right now. Let's not give the trolls any more reason to come after us."

Miranda shrugged and laid her red cloak out near the fire and then laid down on top. She looked up to Jonathan with her emerald eyes and offered a soft smile.

Jonathan returned the smile and then laid down where he was, with the fire between them. He watched as she closed her eyes and drifted off to sleep. He thought it funny then, how amidst all of the ugliness and misery that the swamp brought, there could be beauty to be found. He promised himself then that if he made it home, he would have to ask Miranda if he could call upon her. A sudden smirk flashed across his face as he laughed at himself. He knew that even if she liked him now, once she saw Jason, all of that would change.

He turned over onto his back and closed his eyes, wondering where Jason was, and what he might be doing. Was he off, still fighting trolls? Had he found the central lair, or was he still looking for it? Did such a lair even exist? Maybe Jason was searching for something that could never be found. Maybe the trolls were like the mushrooms, just born of the swamps without rhyme or reason other than the fact that the Murkle Quags seemed to spawn death and misery.

Another thought came then. An image of Jason lying face down in the brown waters of the swamp. Rain drops piercing the surface of the water around Jason and setting ripples that collided with his lifeless body. A troll's arrow stuck out from Jason's back. His corpse bobbed up and down with the ebbing water. Then, a ridged tail appeared in the water and a large crocodile swam up and dragged Jason's body down into the dark depths.

Jonathan squished his eyes shut tight and forced the image out of his mind. His brother was alive. Even if only by the power of his own hope, he knew his brother was still alive. He thought of the games they played at home. How they attacked thistles with swords and pretended they were fighting side by side against a horde of trolls. He thought of the letters Jason had written before. He imagined himself and Jason walking up the dirt path to Pa and Memaw's house once more. They would race each other, only this time they would reach the door at the same time, and then they would sit down at the table and eat Memaw's fresh rolls with her homemade apple butter.

Yes, that is how things would be. He had to believe it would end that way, otherwise why else should he risk the swamps?

The next morning, Miranda woke Jonathan and Rourke. She had taken the final shift in the night, despite Jonathan's insistence that he could take both shifts. The fire was dying down, but their clothes were dry and their spirits were up.

"The rain has stopped," Miranda said as the others began to stir.

Rourke's eyes shot open wide and he looked at her with an accusing glare. "Did you cast a weather spell?"

Miranda shook her head. "No, the rain just stopped."

"It is still early spring," Jonathan said. "The heaviest monsoons are still another month or two away."

Rourke nodded quietly and then rummaged through his pack. He pulled out a completely molded heel of bread and cast it to the ground. Then he found some dried meat and began to eat that. "We'll need to hunt for food soon," Rourke said.

Jonathan nodded knowingly. "The next time we see a goose," he promised.

"A goose?" Rourke scoffed. "When was the last time you saw a goose?"

Jonathan shrugged. "The fletching on the arrows is made from goose. Since the bow and arrows were made out here, I assume there are geese."

"Good luck with that," Rourke said.

"Don't mind him," Miranda said. "Grown men get grumpy without a lot of food. My father certainly did, anyway."

Jonathan offered her a smile and then he moved to pack up. He checked the map again and moved to the mouth of the cave. He spun around, trying to locate the sun through the trees. When he finally found it he smiled and pointed toward the east. "We'll head straight eastward today," he said.

Miranda gathered her things and nodded. Rourke finished his food and then kicked some dirt into the fire.

The three of them moved along a thick, muddy swath of

ground that wound between the cypress trees. As they walked, the cypress began to yield its ground to thick mangroves that jutted out from the murky waters. They pressed along the ground, careful to avoid any body of water that might harbor a large croc or snake in its cloudy depths.

After a while, Rourke called out to Jonathan. Jonathan and Miranda turned to see him pointing at a long, thin, green viper slithering along a branch ten yards off to the group's right.

"I thought your bow would tell you about snakes," Rourke said.

Jonathan whipped his bow around and held it in his hand and drew an arrow. Nothing happened. There was no tingling, and no heartbeat pounding in his head. Confused, Jonathan looked up to the snake and searched for the glowing heart. Nothing.

"Don't tell me you broke your bow," Rourke chided.

Jonathan shook his head. He dipped it into a nearby puddle and watched as the bow's enchantment kept the weapon entirely dry. "No, it's working fine."

"Then why didn't you know about the snake?" Rourke asked.

Jonathan shrugged. "They said it only works on troll-kin. Perhaps the other snakes we saw before, the really big ones I mean, are part of the Kigyo family. Maybe that's why I could see them before. This little guy here is nothing like the Kigyo. He's probably just a swamp viper."

"Excellent," Rourke huffed. "So now I have to watch out for vipers because if the snake isn't as long as a tree, then your bow doesn't consider it dangerous."

"Could be worse," Miranda said. "We could be swallowed up by a giant land-dwelling monkfish."

"A what?" Rourke asked.

Miranda turned and gestured with her hands to show a large mound. "You know, a land-dwelling monkfish. You walk by them and then whoop! They open their mouth and suck you in whole. You die agonizingly slowly while they bury themselves in the mud and digest you."

"That's not real," Rourke replied. He shook a hand at her and then looked to Jonathan. "Tell her that's not funny!"

Jonathan looked to Miranda, who offered him a sly wink

as she turned to continue along their chosen path. The young man had to work to hide his desire to laugh. "You aren't afraid of a fish are you, Rourke?"

Rourke's mouth fell open and his head shot forward and tilted to the side a bit. "Well, if it can eat me whole I am, but that's not real, is it?"

Jonathan turned to follow Miranda. Neither of them answered him.

"Oh come on, tell me the truth now," Rourke said. After a few moments of silence the man looked around nervously at the ground around him, then he quick-stepped to catch up with the others.

They forged on for several hours until they came to a large hill topped with a single cypress tree. Jonathan looked for a way around, not wanting to come out into such an open space and risk being seen by any patrols. The problem was that everywhere he looked seemed to be filled with that brown, murky water. He looked up to the trees, but the branches were not a feasible alternate route either.

"Up over the hill?" Miranda asked Jonathan.

"Either that or go through the water," Rourke said.

Jonathan saw the narrow neck of land that stretched forward up to the hill. It was flanked on both sides by the muddy water. He recalled how easily the large crocodile had jumped up at him at Battlegrym.

"It's pretty close to the water too," Jonathan said as he gestured to the water flanking the land-bridge.

Rourke moved to a sapling and seized it in his hands. He bent the sapling back and forward until it finally broke free from the ground and came popping up with the roots dangling and dripping with mud. Droplets of water fell from its taller branches and sprigs, but Rourke didn't seem to mind.

"What are you doing?" Jonathan asked.

Rourke moved determinedly toward the water on the right of the land-bridge. "Checking the depth so we know if there are any crocs."

Jonathan froze. He wanted to tell Rourke not to do it, but all he could see was the flashing image of the snout filled with teeth that had leapt out at him at Battlegrym.

Miranda slapped Jonathan on the shoulder. "You alright?" she asked.

Jonathan shook his head. "No, I..." he sighed and then pulled his bow out. "Yeah, I guess I am," he said. He moved in a few yards behind Rourke. The scout began slowly extending the sapling, which was half again as tall as the man was, into the murky water. He didn't insert the sapling far before it struck ground.

"Three inches," Rourke called out. He then moved away from the land bridge and tested a spot about a yard away. The sapling went in twice as far. "Six inches," he called out. He repeated the process until he had tested the depth about ten feet away from the land-bridge. "I would say we are safe on the right side," he said. "The deepest spot is less than a foot. No big croc could hide there. If they come from that side, we'll see them."

Rourke then moved to the left side and tested the water. The sapling drove down much farther, almost a foot deep right next to the land-bridge. The sapling shook and Rourke jumped back yelling and shouting.

Jonathan startled and reached for an arrow as Rourke ran away from the sapling. Jonathan drew his arrow back and waited, but nothing happened.

Rourke bent over and slapped his hands together. "Oh you should have seen your faces!" he shouted. "That's what you get for telling stories earlier. Never mess with a scout. We've seen it all, and we know how to get you back."

Jonathan eased his bowstring back into place and shook his head. "That wasn't funny," he said.

Rourke shrugged and retrieved the sapling. "It's only about four or five inches deep here. I just pressed it into the mud to make it look deeper. Come on, we can walk across." Rourke tossed the sapling into the water on the left and then walked over the land bridge. Jonathan shook his head and started after him. Miranda mumbled something about burning Rourke's boots so he'd have to finish the journey barefoot and then moved to catch up with Jonathan.

Jonathan stopped in mid step as the cypress on top of the hill appeared to shake. "Rourke," Jonathan called out. "Wait a second."

Rourke turned back around and held his arms out. "Come

on. We should cross before we risk being seen." He turned back to the hill and set one foot onto its base, when the whole brown and green mass of land rose up. In a flash that took all of one second, a great mouth opened and a weird sucking sound filled the air. Even Jonathan and Miranda were pulled forward a bit by the force, but Rourke was gulped down into a massive mouth. The lips snapped shut after Rourke disappeared, echoing through the swamp.

"Monkfish!" Miranda cried out.

"What!?" Jonathan yelled. "I thought you were joking!"

Miranda ran forward with her staff up high. "Come on, we have to stop it before it buries itself in the mud."

Just then a pair of terrible, gargantuan eyes the size of large, round shields opened on either side of what Jonathan had thought was a moss-covered hill. Fleshy lids blinked over the slimy eyes as massive flippers rose from the murky waters on either side, and the beast began to turn away. Mud and water splashed everywhere, and a giant, flat, paddle-like tail emerged from the water as well.

Jonathan watched in horror as Miranda sprinted up the side of the monkfish. In a panic, he fired two arrows at the behemoth, but they did little more than pierce its thick, blubbery skin. Certainly they didn't do any lasting damage, for the giant monkfish didn't even react to them.

Jonathan hurried to catch up with Miranda. He slung his bow over his shoulder and used his hands and feet to climb up the slippery side as the fish hurried with its flippers and tail to submerge itself.

Miranda stood near the large thing that had looked like a cypress tree from far away. She drew her knife and stabbed it into the protrusion. The fish shuddered and thrashed, throwing Jonathan down.

"It's his antenna," Miranda called out. "Come and try to cut it while I look for the fish's blow-hole."

"His what?" Jonathan shouted back as he clambered to his feet. If not for the iron cleats, he may never have made it to the large antenna, but thankfully the spikes dug enough into the fish's skin that he was able to reach it. He grabbed the growth in his left hand as he worked the knife with his right.

Miranda chanted the words to a spell and gathered fire

around her staff. "Hold your breath!" Miranda shouted.

Jonathan gawked as a large hole opened only a few feet away from the large, tree-like growth. A cloud of green gas emerged. Miranda covered her mouth and nose with her left arm and she directed a great fireball with her staff. The fire shot down through the open blowhole and a moment later the great fish screeched and convulsed.

"Again, keep cutting!" Miranda shouted.

Jonathan looked back to his task and kept slicing the growth with the knife. Lines of blueish green blood poured out from the cuts, and the antenna shivered and trembled. As the cloud of green gas from the monkfish's blowhole reached Jonathan, he felt weak, and his stomach twisted into knots. The stench was unbelievable. His eyes stung and he started choking.

"Keep cutting it, the gas won't hurt you!"

Jonathan jabbed the knife deep into the antenna.

He heard the slimy hole suck open again. Another fireball went down and the fish twitched and thrashed so violently that both of them were thrown from its back. They tumbled down to land in the shallow water and then had to clamber out of the way as one of the fins slammed down into the muck and mud where they had just been.

A terrible shriek filled the air and the monkfish opened its mouth. Out it spewed a glob of goo and ooze. Bits of crocodile and several fish came out along with Rourke. The putrid mess splashed into the murky water and then then fish went still. A column of thick, black smoke rose up from the blow-hole, and the antenna fell flat onto the fish's back.

Jonathan and Miranda went to help Rourke, but the man was quick to escape the murky water and shake the bits of goo off. He drew a knife and pointed it at Miranda.

"I thought you said you were joking!" Rourke shouted.

Jonathan stepped between them and held his hands out. "Calm down," he said.

"I thought I was joking," Miranda said honestly. She looked to the beast and shrugged. "My dad told me about them in one of his letters, but he said they had died off before he got to the swamps."

"Your dad?" Rourke asked breathlessly. He then pointed

a knife at the monster and shook his head. "Your father was very, very wrong."

The three of them stood there for a moment, staring at each other. Then, as bits of slime and ooze dripped from Rourke's outstretched arm they began, one by one, to smile and then laugh.

Rourke put his knife away and smoothed his hair back, trying to squeeze the grime and slime out of it. "It isn't funny," he said as he turned with his nose in the air.

Jonathan and Miranda shared a glance at each other and then moved to follow Rourke.

"We can eat it," Miranda said.

"Is that what your father says?" Rourke shot back over his shoulder. "Because I am NOT eating anything that smells that badly. If he was wrong about its existence, I am going to assume he is wrong about eating it."

Miranda huffed, but she didn't refute the argument.

Rourke turned around and held his arms out. "Besides, why is it that a fish that big is still sitting here, untouched by crocs or trolls, unless its meat is bad?"

"He has a point there," Jonathan put in.

Miranda shrugged it off. "Just as well. I had to use a bit of magic to get you out, so we should probably get moving."

"Get me out?" Rourke said as he raised a brow. "I got myself out, I will have you know," he said while he pointed one of his knives at his chest."

"Oh really, how did you manage that?" Miranda inquired.

Rourke smiled and sheathed his knife. "I found the monster's uvula, and I cut it off. That's when he spit me out."

"Well he wouldn't have spat you out if we hadn't kept him from burying himself in the mud," Miranda replied.

Rourke shrugged. "Sure he would have."

"And where would you go after he spat you into a wall of mud submerged in thirty feet of water?"

Rourke smiled. "A scout always finds a way," he said as he turned around. "Now let's go. If you used magic, the trolls will know where we are."

The trio pressed on until dusk. They looked for a place to take shelter, but there were no rock formations to be found. They made do with a large mangrove tree that grew on a dry hillside.

Rourke fashioned a few thin pikes and stuck them in the ground facing away from their shelter. Miranda set another fire, and Jonathan checked the area for vipers and other dangerous creatures. Once camp was established, they ate the last of their dried meat in silence.

As night began to fall, Jonathan's left hand started to tingle. He flipped his bow around and took it in hand. His right hand shot out for an arrow.

"See something?" Rourke asked.

Jonathan rose from the mangrove tree and peered into the distance. To his dismay, a large semicircle of glowing hearts was closing in on their location. They were moving slowly, and were about eighty yards out beyond the trees and brush.

"They haven't seen us yet," Jonathan whispered. "They are far away still."

"Can we escape," Rourke asked.

"In the darkness?" Miranda shot back. "The trolls will either find us, or we will have to use magical light, in which case they will follow us. I think we have to stand and fight."

Jonathan nodded. "She's right. I'll do what I can. There aren't as many as outside of Wendyn. We should be able to win as long as I can get clear shots."

Rourke drew his knives. "Very well, then. Let's get this over with."

Jonathan drew an arrow and let it fly. A few seconds later, a purple heart winked out. A terrible cry erupted from the swamp as it came alive with more than a score of warriors. Splashing footsteps sounded in the distance as the trolls came rushing toward them.

Jonathan fired again and again. Each time his arrow struck down a troll before returning to the quiver. Jonathan stepped out to the side a bit to get a better angle on a troll. In addition to the glowing heart, he could see the beast clearly. It was sprinting toward him with an axe in each hand. It snarled and howled menacingly. Jonathan pulled the arrow back and focused on the troll's chest. He let the arrow fly, and an instant later the creature fell to the ground. As it fell, the arrow shaft struck a tree trunk and broke. That arrow did not return to Jonathan's quiver.

Jonathan continued to work furiously, firing as the trolls

moved in.

Overhead, a trio of fireballs soared out and blasted into a pair of trolls, burning holes through their chests and dropping them to the watery ground in a smoldering heap.

A troll came in from the right, but Rourke was quick to engage it. He ducked under a sword and worked his knives up into the troll's heart, then he pulled free and stabbed the troll through the back for good measure.

Two more trolls jumped out from behind a large mangrove tree, but Jonathan stopped each one with an arrow to the heart. Jonathan locked eyes on another target, and pulled out another arrow. Just as he nocked the arrow, Rourke slammed into him and tackled him to the ground. Jonathan was about to shout at Rourke, but then he saw the arrow that had sunk into the tree directly behind where he had been standing.

"Mind the troll archers first," Rourke said.

The two jumped up and Jonathan scoured the field for the troll that had fired the arrow. None of the trolls running toward them had bows. He then turned his eyes to the trees. He saw three trolls hiding among the branches, or rather he saw their glowing hearts through the screen of leaves. Jonathan fired. One, two, three, all of the trolls dropped to the ground. Unfortunately, Jonathan also saw that each of those three arrows broke during the fall. Now he was down by four arrows, leaving eight.

There was no time to mourn their loss now. Trolls were closing in, sprinting across the shallow waters and coming in fast. Miranda took on another troll with her magic, but she missed its vital areas. It ran out into the open where Rourke finished the troll before it could reach the young woman.

Jonathan fired seven more times and then the battle was over. Troll bodies littered the swamp from a few feet in front of them all the way out to nearly eighty yards away.

"They must have been tracking us," Rourke said. "Couldn't have been too hard for them, what with us using magic to start fires and all."

"Not to mention the spells I had to use on the monkfish," Miranda put in.

Rourke wiped his knives off on the dead troll and smiled garishly. "I still maintain that I had it completely under control,"

Rourke said. "Now, if you'll excuse me, I have to see a man about a horse."

"You have to what?" Miranda asked.

Jonathan sniggered and pulled Miranda away. "Better you don't know," he said. They walked only a short distance before they heard Rourke scream.

"I'm going to kill him!" Miranda snarled. "It isn't funny anymore," she shouted as she turned around. "Oh dear," she gasped.

Jonathan whipped around and saw a bright green viper latched onto Rourke's neck. The two ran toward him as fast as they could. Rourke stumbled out away from the tree, clutching and pulling at the snake.

Then he stopped and stood still. A wide smile crossed his lips and he flopped the viper onto the ground. As it rolled and its white belly pointed up, they could see the red knife wound in the viper's body, just behind the head.

"As I said," Rourke began as he polished his nails on his shirt, "Rourke is always prepared."

Miranda stamped her right foot and made a sound that was something between a growl and a scream. She wagged a finger at the man, but instead of saying anything, she turned and stormed off.

Rourke was still smiling when he walked up to Jonathan. "I saw the snake," he said. "I figured we could use the meat."

"That wasn't very nice," Jonathan commented.

"What, hunting the snake?" Rourke asked with feigned innocence. He shrugged and bent down to pick it up. "You don't have to eat it if you don't want to."

"No, I mean," Jonathan sighed. "Never mind."

"Miranda, be a good girl and start a fire if you would please," Rourke called out.

Miranda set her magic to the fire she had already been working on before the trolls had come. The flames burned high and bright, enough to clearly illuminate the quickly darkening swamp. Rourke brought the snake to the fire and went to work cleaning it. He cut the head off first and was quick to kick it away.

Jonathan watched as the jaws grotesquely continued to open and bite down. Rourke saw his gaze and he thumbed over at the head.

"It can still kill you," he said soberly. "You should treat a severed viper head exactly the same as you would treat a whole viper, with extreme caution. Without its body it is even angrier than usual, but it's still just as deadly."

"How long can it do that?" Jonathan asked.

Rourke shrugged. "Hours, maybe a whole day. Never really sat and timed it, but I know it takes a long time."

Miranda shot a fireball at the severed head, blasting it to bits. Then she folded her arms and glared at the ground.

"I guess that is one way to take care of it," Rourke said. He ripped the guts out from the snake and tossed them over his shoulder as far as he could, then he stuck the body on a stick and set it over the fire. "Sorry," he said.

Miranda glanced at him, but she didn't acknowledge his words.

"If it's any consolation, the inside of that monkfish thing was horrible. I don't think I will ever get that smell out of my nose. It was kind of worth the extra prank, if you ask me."

"No more pranks," Jonathan said when Miranda remained silent.

Rourke nodded and continued to cook the snake.

"After the snake is done, we should make torches and keep moving," Jonathan said. "If they found us once, they can find us again if we stay put. Besides, we had to use magic."

Rourke nodded and rotated the snake. "It won't be long now," he said. "We can eat it as we walk."

The trio was up within half an hour, pulling out whatever wood they could find that was dry enough to burn as a torch to light their way. They continued pushing eastward for several hours until they came to a large mound of stone. Jonathan crept up to it and looked beyond the rocks. A smile crossed his lips then and he looked back to the others.

"We found it, we found The Warrens."

CHAPTER FOURTEEN

The sun broke over the trio early the next morning. A light drizzle started with the first rays of light. It broke into a full downpour before the three had even begun walking out over the barren landscape. They saw a clearing of rocks and pits as far east and south as the eye could see. Jagged, brown and black rocks jutted up from the ground, and great depressions filled with lichen-covered boulders dug down into the valley.

Pools of murky water filled some of the depressions, but it was not the same as the swamp had been. It was as if the rocky landscape somehow drained the rains away and whisked the water off somewhere else. Still, they were careful to stay clear of the pools, just in case there were any crocs or other dangers hiding therein. They walked for two miles, climbing over mounds of stone and leaping from boulder to boulder. Had they not just emerged from the swamp, they would have sworn that this place was desolate and void of life.

There was no sign of any trolls, or anything at all really. The rain bounced off the slick stone endlessly, mocking their vain attempt to find the lair of the trolls. They stopped after the fourth mile and sat upon a large rock together.

Rourke went for the map, but Jonathan told him it was no use.

"Pa never made it this far," he said. "He saw The Warrens from the edge of the swamp, but he never set foot inside them."

"So how do we find Shadowbore, the trolls' den?" Rourke asked.

Jonathan shrugged. "I guess now we follow Kigabané. When it senses trolls, we go toward the danger instead of away."

The other two didn't respond to that notion. They all sat there, staring out over the vast expanse of mounds and depressions. They ate the remainder of the chewy, stringy snake meat and then they pushed onward.

Eventually they came to a depression that had a tunnel in the bottom. The rain made the area around the tunnel extremely slick, but Jonathan went down toward it anyway. His heart thumped inside his chest. His eyes were glued to the dark hole as he slowly stretched his foot out one after the other to work his way down. A warmth rose up from the pit, carrying with it a strong odor. It wasn't exactly foul, but it wasn't pleasant either. It was kind of like the smell a bear's den might have during a long winter's hibernation, a bit musky and somewhat dank.

Jonathan froze as his hand began to tingle. He looked up to the other two and nodded his head. He pointed down to the tunnel. "They're down there," he said.

Miranda and Rourke were quick to join him. The three of them silently crept down to the opening and then went inside. To their pleasant surprise, the tunnel shot off at a steep angle, but it did not descend down for long before leveling out to a nearly flat tunnel system.

"It's so dark," Miranda whispered. "Should I conjure light?"

"No," Rourke whispered harshly. "We don't need to announce our presence. We go in quietly, slowly, letting our eyes adjust as much as they can." Rourke reached out and nudged Jonathan. "You can see them even in the dark, right?"

Jonathan nodded, as if they could see his response in the pitch-black tunnel. Rourke nudged him again. "Yes, I can see their hearts," Jonathan replied.

They pushed on slowly. They followed the tunnel around a bend to the left and just as their eyes began to adjust, they caught the flicker of light upon the tunnel walls. Shadows danced upon the wall as well, and the tingling in Jonathan's hand grew stronger. He started to hear the heartbeats in his mind. He knew they were getting close.

"How many," Rourke asked.

Jonathan shook his head. "Don't know yet."

Rourke pushed ahead and motioned for the other two to stay put. The scout crept around the long bend and leaned over the edge, peering further down the tunnel. A few seconds later, he quick-stepped his way back to the others.

"What did you see?" Miranda whispered.

"Seven trolls," Rourke said. "There are six of them in a circle around a really big one. The six have their arms up in the air and are waving from side to side while the big one in the center is standing and has his head bowed down." Rourke turned to Jonathan. "Can you take them all quick enough that they can't call for help?"

"Does the tunnel go any further?" Jonathan asked.

Rourke nodded. "There are three tunnels branching off of the chamber the seven trolls are in. I think it's a shrine of some sort. There was a large carving made of stone behind the group. I couldn't get a great look at it, but it might be some kind of deity or something."

Jonathan then remembered the words that the king snake had spoken about the troll shamans. He steeled his nerves and nodded to Rourke. "We have to kill the shaman," he said resolutely. "I think that is their source of power. I think the shamans are expanding the monsoons."

"Shamans?" Miranda asked skeptically. "If their shamans could expand the monsoons and make the Murkle Quags grow, then why not do that decades, or even a century ago when the war was new? Why wait until now?"

Jonathan shook his head. "I don't know," he said with a shrug. "But it doesn't matter now. Stay here. I will take the seven."

"Good luck," Rourke said.

Jonathan moved silently toward the end of the bend. The light grew brighter and brighter until he peeked around and saw several large braziers made of iron pans set upon columns of stone. Orange flames danced above each brazier, flooding the chamber with light.

Jonathan saw the glowing hearts, but then he noticed a problem. Only the seated trolls had glowing hearts. The shaman did not. It didn't deter him from his mission though. The trolls were only forty yards away. It would be an easy target set for him, even without the magical help of the bow.

He reached up over his shoulder and grabbed an arrow. He decided he would start with the trolls seated behind the shaman, as they were facing his direction. The three in back first, then the shaman, and then the three closest to him with their backs turned.

He drew the bow back and released. He pulled the next arrow without watching the first land. He fired the second arrow only a moment later, and then the third. He drew the fourth and focused on the troll's chest. He fired the arrow and it sailed true, striking down the shaman as easily as the others. The remaining trolls jumped up to their feet, shouting and hollering. Three more arrows flew and then they died.

Jonathan waited as the arrows returned to his quiver. Then he counted them with his hand. Instead of the eight he started with after losing the four in the previous night's battle, he only had seven. One of them must have broken, he figured.

He cursed his luck, but then realized that the tingling in his arm was not fading. It was growing. The sound of pounding hearts flooded his mind. He looked on in horror as trolls came spilling into the chamber from two of the three tunnels.

He turned to Rourke and Miranda. "Run!" he shouted. Jonathan then stepped out and started firing arrow after arrow into the multitude of trolls. He worked the bow so fast that his first arrow hardly had time to reappear in his quiver by the time the seventh was in flight. He took down at least thirty before he had to turn and run himself.

He sprinted up the tunnel, periodically firing an arrow over his shoulder and hoping that the magic would direct the arrow to a troll and kill it. His strategy must have worked, for every arrow he shot like that reappeared in his quiver a couple seconds after he heard a scream of agony.

Miranda was standing directly in front of the entrance to the tunnel by the time Jonathan could see the exit. Rourke was nearby, with his hand stretched down for Jonathan. The young archer leapt up, grabbing Rourke's hand and scrambling out of the tunnel as fast as he could. He turned just in time to see Miranda send a series of fireballs down into the tunnel. Horrid screams and shrieks ripped through the air as fireball after fireball rolled through the tunnel.

"Can you collapse the tunnel?" Rourke asked.

"I'm trying!" Miranda replied.

Miranda worked her spell furiously. Her black hair whipped up around her face as she chanted the spell over and over, summoning numerous fireballs that rocked and shook the tunnel as they ripped through the trolls. Finally, a great blast of smoke and dirt erupted out from the hole and rocks collapsed inward, sealing it off.

Miranda turned and smiled at them as she dug her staff into the ground before her.

"Not bad, if I do say so myself," she said with a wry smile.

Jonathan exhaled and dropped onto the rocks behind him to rest. "How do we know if this is the central lair?" he asked.

He never got an answer.

Rourke leapt up and grabbed Miranda by the shoulders, swinging her around and throwing her down toward Jonathan. Rourke's body went rigid, and then he fell to his knees. He slumped forward to reveal an arrow shaft protruding out of his back.

Jonathan jumped up and fired at the troll that had appeared at the rim of the depression. The troll fell dead, and the arrow reappeared in Jonathan's quiver. Jonathan then ran out to Rourke and helped the man to his feet. Rourke looked at Jonathan and then his eyes went wide. The scout shoved Jonathan to the side just as another arrow pierced him in the front. This time Miranda was the one who slew the troll, whipping a single bolt of fire from her staff and driving it through the creature's skull. Jonathan regained his footing and began firing at trolls as they appeared at the top of the rim. Some had bows, while others had swords or spears.

Rourke let out a mighty cry to Basei, the demigod of war, and then he charged up the far side of the depression. Despite the arrows in his body, he worked his blades furiously, dropping three trolls before he reached the rim. He sidestepped a spear thrust, stabbed the troll in the heart, sheathed his knives, and ripped the spear away to use it himself. He flipped the weapon over in an instant and then skewered three trolls through the heart one after the other.

The scout then tossed the dead trolls down into the rocky depression and went back to using his knives. Jonathan killed two trolls that tried to attack Rourke from behind, buying the scout more time as he worked through the enemy. Rourke jammed one knife into a troll's temple and then whirled around to finish another with a double-thrust to the heart. Then another arrow pierced Rourke's back. He cried out in anger and arched his back.

173

Another arrow shot through his left forearm. His left hand dropped the knife, but he charged on with his single knife in his right hand.

Jonathan worked his bow with every ounce of speed he could muster while Miranda slew troll after troll with her fireballs.

Rourke charged ahead, taking a spear to the stomach while he lashed out and stabbed another troll. He released his knife and then brought his arm down to break the spear shaft. Another troll jumped in with an axe. Rourke ducked under the first swing and plucked the arrow from his chest. With a mighty yell he lunged upward with the arrow, using it as a mini-spear, and drove it up through the soft tissue under the troll's jaw, through his neck, and up into his brain.

Then, the valiant scout fell into the depression, devoid of strength and life.

Miranda and Jonathan finished off the remaining six trolls and then rushed to Rourke's side.

Jonathan listened in vain for any sign of breath from the man. With tears on his face he reached out and closed Rourke's eyes. Miranda bent down and set a hand on Jonathan's shoulder. Jonathan leaned into her and she wrapped him in an embrace as he let the tears silently fall down his face. The tingling in his left arm was gone. The heartbeats no longer assaulted his mind, but the victory was a hollow one.

Jonathan rose to his feet after a while and Miranda stood as well. Her hand slipped down to Jonathan's and the two climbed out from the pit together.

They continued on, neither of them sure which way to go. They walked eastward, following the same line they had been treading for days now. They passed by several more holes and pits, but they didn't find any more trolls. They were smaller dens with nothing inside.

Eventually, the sun began to set and the rain turned bitterly cold. The two of them turned southward where they saw a large rock formation that could afford them some shelter. Jonathan was careful to scan the area with Kigabané's power, but when they found nothing around, the two of them decided it was best to move into the rock structure. It shielded them from the rain and the wind.

They opted not to make a fire that night. There was no wood at all to be had, which meant that Miranda would have to magically feed the fire continuously. Neither thought that was the best idea, so they huddled together for warmth while they both watched the darkness outside the rocks.

Flashes of silver lightning streaked through the sky, followed by terrible thunder that shook the pair to their very centers. Neither of them slept for several hours. To make matters worse, both of them could feel the pangs of hunger as their stomachs growled and cramped, but they had nothing to feed themselves with.

Eventually, sometime around midnight, Miranda succumbed to sleep. Jonathan let her head fall on his shoulder and he kept watch over her. It was far too dark to see anything, except during the flashes of lightning, but he knew that Kigabané would alert him to any trolls that came near. For the night, he would be their guard.

When the morning finally came, Miranda woke to find Jonathan still awake next to her. She pushed off from his shoulder and then looked outside. "Is it still raining?" she asked, even though she could clearly see that it was.

"It is," Jonathan said.

"Were you awake all night?" Miranda asked.

Jonathan nodded slowly, his eyes still scanning what he could see outside of their shelter.

"Would the bow work if I held it?" Miranda asked.

Jonathan looked at her curiously.

"If the bow is enchanted to work no matter who uses it, then we should take shifts. You can sleep part of the night while I hold the bow, and I will sleep while you hold it. You can't stay awake forever."

Jonathan nodded and held the bow out for her. "Wake me if you feel anything strange," he said. "And if you don't, then wake me in an hour or two. We shouldn't stay here for too long."

Miranda nodded and took the bow to keep watch while Jonathan slept.

It didn't take him long before he was snoring lightly and his mouth had gone slack with his head tilted back against the stone.

Once she was certain he was asleep, the black haired girl went out from the shelter and climbed atop the rock formation to get a better look around. The rain soaked her within minutes, causing her clothing to cling to her body in ways that were anything but comfortable. She sat upon the top of the rock, drawing her cloak tighter around her to fend off the wind. All she could see in any direction were the same, bleak rocks. There were no mountains, no trees, no animals, and no sign that they were anywhere close to finding her father. There was nothing.

After a few more minutes, she descended the rocks and went back into the shelter. Instead of waking Jonathan within an hour or two, she let him sleep until mid-day when he woke on his own.

"Ready to go?" she asked with a cheerful smile.

Jonathan yawned and stretched as he rubbed the back of his neck. He stood and reached out for his bow. "Anything?"

Miranda sighed and shook her head. "Absolutely nothing," she replied. "Where should we go?"

Jonathan pulled out the map and stretched it out in his hands. "I know it doesn't show much, but I bet if we head east we will be walking through the middle of The Warrens. That has to give us the best chance of finding something." Jonathan looked to Miranda and pursed his lips. "What do you think?"

Miranda shrugged. "I suppose that is as good a plan as any," she said. "Let's go.

The two of them set out into the open. The rain had died down, leaving a hazy fog across the landscape that wafted on the cool breeze. They walked for four miles over the rough terrain before they found another tunnel. This one was not in a pit, like the first had been. It had been carved into the side of a large, rocky hill.

Jonathan looked to the green eyed girl for her approval. She nodded. That was all he needed. He brought out his bow and moved in. The two of them crept through the dark tunnel and followed its winding paths until, like in the first tunnel, they saw firelight. Jonathan signaled for Miranda to stay put while he went on with his bow.

To his surprise, his arm didn't tingle. He didn't hear any heartbeats either. However, he did see shadows moving along the wall as the tunnel curved down and to the right. He inched toward the edge. He put his back to the smooth wall of stone, wondering if his bow had finally lost its enchantment, or if maybe there was some other magic that interfered with it, like when he had been unable to see the shaman's heart in the first tunnel. He took in a couple of breaths, trying to build his courage.

Jonathan slowly moved his head to peer around the side of the wall. He saw a large stone table flanked by tall braziers like those in the first tunnel. A figure moved in the distance. Jonathan leaned over more, peering around the corner as far as he could to see what it was.

That's when something grabbed his head and pulled him around the corner with such force that his feet left the ground and he nearly flew into the chamber. He cried out in terror, trying to aim his bow, but something ripped it from him and tossed him to the ground as if he were nothing more than a rag doll.

Jonathan landed on the stone and bounced. A pain ripped through his back and he cried out as the sharpness ran up his spine and caused him to arch his back.

"What have we here?" a voice asked.

Jonathan looked up, expecting to see some hideous troll, but instead he saw a pair of men. One was roughly six feet tall, with a pair of knives similar to Rourke's in his hands. The other man was absolutely gigantic. He stood easily seven feet tall, and his arms were so thick and strong that he made Sami look small. The large man narrowed his eyes on Jonathan and bit onto the back end of a cigar. He drew in a deep breath and the end glowed red hot.

CHAPTER FIFTEEN

Miranda heard the scream and ran down the hallway. She gathered a pair of fireballs, letting them hover over her staff as she ran. Her footsteps fell lightly upon the stone, yet they propelled her with graceful ease and speed. She rounded the corner to see Jonathan Haymaker being helped to his feet by an absolute mountain of a man.

Jonathan caught sight of her and held out a hand to stop her. "It's alright," he said.

The huge man turned around, smoking a cigar as he eyed her briefly before looking at her spell of fireballs.

Another man stood nearby and was quick to speak up. "You can extinguish those, young lady. We only fight against trolls."

Miranda gawked with her mouth open. She winked the fireballs out and then rushed into the chamber, looking around excitedly.

"Young lady, what are you doing?" the smaller man asked.

Miranda wasn't listening. She recognized Bear and Moose easily from her father's letters. These were the Ghosts of the Murkle Quags. That meant she had found him. Her father was here somewhere. She jogged toward the middle of the chamber and looked around. She saw a broad shouldered man just under six feet tall, bald, and mean looking. That was Bull, she knew. She spun around and saw a large man stoking a fire. He stood up and rubbed his hands clean of soot as he turned to look at her. He wore a pair of brown trousers, but his shirt was drying near the fire.

His entire left side was marked by black tattoos of skulls.

"Captain Ziegler," she called out.

The man squinted at her and approached. "And who might you be?" he asked.

"I am looking for my father," she said. "You called him Raven."

Ziegler stopped in mid-step and looked to the others.

"You're Raven's daughter?" Bull asked as he folded his

arms.

Jonathan and the others came in close to her. It was then that she realized Jonathan's brother wasn't here either. She turned to him and tried to find the right words to say.

Jonathan shook his head. "They aren't dead," he said quickly before Miranda could say anything. "They're still alive, I know it."

"Who are you talking about, boy?" Captain Ziegler said as he came close to Jonathan.

Jonathan looked up at the man, noting his many tattoos. Ziegler had three purple scars running at an angle down his right cheek. There was a heavy scar on his left shoulder, thick and pink. He was older than Jonathan had expected, with gray hair on his head, but he looked no less capable than any of the others.

"You killed a lot of trolls," Jonathan noted as he pointed to the tattoos.

Ziegler looked down and huffed. "These aren't the trolls I killed," he said grimly.

The shorter bald man cut in, grinning wickedly as he pointed to Ziegler. "If he had a tattoo for every troll he killed, he'd be working on his third full set by now."

Jonathan frowned. "My brother said they were for each troll," he said.

Ziegler shook his head. "They're for each Ghost of the Quags that died under my command."

The words burrowed into Jonathan's ears and shot down his spine like a streak of ice. There were so many tattoos. The thought that his brother might be represented by one of them was almost more than he could bear.

Ziegler pointed to the bald man next to him. "This is Bull." He then pointed to each person in the circle around Jonathan and Miranda. "I'm Captain Ziegler, that's Bear, and you already met Moose."

Jonathan looked at each of them and then he stared back at Ziegler's tattoos. He wanted to ask the question, but the words caught in his throat.

"The two of you came alone?" Ziegler pressed.

Miranda was the first to respond. "There were two others with us," she said.

"Two?" Bull groused. "How in Hammenfein's name did you make it this far with only four people?"

Miranda pointed to Jonathan.

Jonathan pulled his bow around and held it out. "This bow lets me see trolls from a distance," he said.

Ziegler reached out and took the bow in hand. He turned it over in his palms and then tossed it to Bear. Bear held it up close to his eyes and smiled.

"It's magic," Bear said.

"How did you get a magic bow?" Ziegler asked.

Jonathan shrugged. "I got it from the Kigyo."

Bear offered the bow back to Jonathan. "Any man who could get Kigabané would be a welcome asset to our group," Bear said.

Ziegler then turned to Miranda. "And you are Raven's daughter?" he asked.

Miranda nodded. "I am."

"Have you the same talent for magic as your father?"

Miranda sighed, stealing a quick glance at Jonathan before looking to the ground. "No. I can manipulate and create fire, but I am not much good otherwise."

"I thought you could control the weather," Jonathan put in quickly.

"I never actually said I could," Miranda said sheepishly.

Jonathan shook his head. Now that his words were working again he looked up to Ziegler. "Where is my brother?" he asked.

Ziegler's eyebrows shot up. "'Fraid you'll have to be a bit more specific than that. I met a lot of brothers in my years in the swamp."

Moose reached out and turned Jonathan to him. The man's massive right hand tilted Jonathan's chin up and then turned his face right and then left. Moose reached up to his cigar and pulled it out as he exhaled a thick cloud of smoke.

"He looks like Boar," Moose said.

"Your brother is Boar?" Bear asked with an anxious nod.

Jonathan nodded and pulled away from the giant man. "My brother is Jason Haymaker, but you called him Boar."

Ziegler offered a faint hint of a smile. "Well then, in that

180

case I am happy to report that I have good news for both of you. They are alive, though I don't know how much longer they will stay that way."

"What do you mean?" Miranda cut in.

"They were taken," Bull cut in. "Our last encounter about a week ago. A pit opened up in the ground that we didn't see and they snatched them both."

"Why would they take prisoners?" Jonathan asked.

Ziegler shrugged. "Don't know the answer to that. I have never seen it before."

"How do you know they are still alive?" Raven asked.

Ziegler sighed. "Well, I don't know exactly. It's just a feeling I have." He turned and put a hand out on Jonathan's shoulder. "Your brother is a good soldier, one of the best I have ever seen. Are you anything like him?"

Jonathan nodded. "Even without the magic, I am just as good with a bow."

Ziegler nodded and smiled. "Then come, eat. We have some food that we can offer. We'll go over the plan and then we'll head out before the sun rises."

"You'll take us with you?" Miranda asked.

Ziegler nodded. "Fireballs are incredibly useful against trolls. They can't regenerate any part of their body that is burned. If I had to choose a mage who only knew one spell, it would be you."

"And Kigabané will allow us to sneak into the lair," Bear put in from behind.

Jonathan started to smile for the first time since entering the tunnel. "You know where it is?"

Ziegler smiled wide. "Your brother found Shadowbore," he said.

"Cocky little Boar," Bull spat. "He was always saying he would be the first to find it."

"And he was," Ziegler added. "Now it falls to us to get him, and Raven, out alive."

Ziegler motioned for the others to follow him back to a long, stone table. There were no plates or bowls to eat with, but neither Jonathan nor Miranda cared about that once they saw the roasted meat set before them. They tore into the savory flesh with abandon, ripping off hunks nearly too large to chew before swallowing them down.

"Easy now," Bear said as the others began to eat as well. "It would be a shame to come all this way only to die choking on croc meat."

Jonathan chewed quickly and choked down another bite. "Where have you been all this time?"

Captain Ziegler answered. "We have been hunting trolls. The Warrens are a mess of tunnels and dens. We didn't find the main lair until very recently. Up until then we were exploring and clearing every tunnel we found."

"And what of my father?" Miranda asked excitedly. "How has he been?"

Ziegler smiled softly. "Both Raven and Boar have been very well. Two of our best, actually. Up until our last encounter, they were right there with us each step of the way." Jonathan was about to jump in with another question but Ziegler raised his hand and cut them off. "Eat. There will be time for questions later. Eat now, regain your strength. We have some hard days ahead of us yet."

Jonathan and Miranda did as instructed, eating until they had to sit back for the ache in their stomachs. They hadn't seen this much food since they left Wendyn. There was only a small amount of water to be shared, but it was fresh and clean, and helped wash down the last few bites of food.

When all had finished their meal, Ziegler grabbed a large, white stone and began to draw an outline by carving it into the table. Jonathan watched intently, seeing a map of The Warrens taking shape.

Bull nudged him in the side with his elbow and asked, "How many trolls did you kill this week?" Then he raised the canteen to his mouth and started to drink.

Jonathan shrugged and looked at Miranda. "I don't know, a hundred or so each."

Bull squirted water out his nose and choked on his drink.

"Well that takes the wind out of your sails, doesn't it Bull," Bear said.

"That's not possible!" Bull said as he slammed the canteen down. He pointed at Moose while glaring at Jonathan. "That mountain over there has only killed twenty this week. I am in

182

the lead by seven. How is it that you could kill one hundred trolls?"

"Let it go Bull," Bear said. "Just accept that you'll never be in the lead for long."

Bull shook his reddening, bald head and swiveled his arm around to point at Jonathan. "Tell me the truth boy."

Jonathan stopped and tried to count the trolls. "I don't know, maybe closer to eighty I guess. She might have more. We had a whole slew of them chasing us through a tunnel, and she burned 'em all up and collapsed the entrance, but I took down at least eighty with my bow."

"Hogwash," Bull growled. "Those numbers don't count. They're using magic. The numbers should be cut in half."

Half of eighty is still thirteen more than what you took this week, Bull," Bear pointed out smugly.

"Enough," Ziegler said suddenly. The table grew quiet and turned to look at the drawing etched into the table top. "We are here. Shadowbore is a day's march to the south." Ziegler marked a large 'X' on the table, followed by a circle. Then he cut smaller dots near the circle. "These are the guard tunnels that we saw. Remember, the trolls have built trap doors here, so we have to be on our best."

"I can see the trolls from about eighty or ninety yards away," Jonathan put in. "I can help locate the trap doors, because the bow will show me where the trolls are by making their hearts glow."

"Can you see them through stone?" Ziegler asked.

"A bit," Jonathan said. "I can't see through solid rock that is more than a few feet thick, but I can see through boulders or trees."

"Kigabané is powerful magic," Bear said. "It will come in handy."

"I still call it cheating," Bull groused.

Ziegler turned to Bull. "You'll be happy that we are cheating, given how many trolls there are in Shadowbore."

Bull arched a brow and then nodded in agreement. "I will," he admitted.

Ziegler turned to Jonathan. "The first order of business is to find Boar and Raven. We will try to find the tunnel they were trapped in. We find them alive, and they will not only bolster our numbers by an additional thirty percent, but they can maybe tell us something about the tunnels, or the trolls, that will be useful."

Jonathan raised his hand.

"This isn't school, boy, if you have something to say, just say it."

"The shamans are the key," Jonathan said. "They are the ones using magic to expand the monsoons. If we kill the shamans, we can break their expansion."

Bear slapped his hand on the table and let out a whistle. "I like this one."

Ziegler smiled and offered a nod of respect. "How did you learn of this?"

Jonathan told them about the Kigyo, and what the King Snake had said about the shamans. He then explained how the rains lessened after he had slain the shaman in another tunnel.

"That fits with our experience as well," Bear commented. "Every time we wiped a smaller tunnel clean of trolls, the rains did lessen."

Ziegler stroked his chin. "Could be," he said. "Either way, it gives us a chain of command to try and disrupt. Perhaps if we find a leading shaman in Shadowbore, it would be the equivalent to slaying a king."

"That might only piss them all off," Bull said gruffly. "I know if our king was killed by a group of assassins, I'd be out for blood."

Jonathan leaned in and spoke. "But, not if the king was the one with the most powerful magic." Everyone turned to look at him. "I mean, if the lead shaman is the one responsible for expanding the swamps, the trolls won't be able to attack when the monsoons weaken and the swamplands recede to their former state. If they come at us over dry land and valleys, then we will be able to use fire, and not just magical fire, but torches and catapults to send them back. If we kill their strongest shaman, and any other shamans we find, they will have no choice but to stay here in the swamps."

"But then what?" Bull asked. "We run away and let the trolls breed like an infestation of cockroaches until they are strong enough to march out from their holes again?"

"We close the tunnels," Miranda put in quickly. "Like I

did with the other tunnel. None of the trolls were able to make it out. We set fire to the tunnels and then we collapse them."

"You can cave-in a dozen tunnels?" Bear asked.

Miranda shrugged. "I can close at least one or two. If we find my father, he can do more. As long as the shamans are dead, we can halt the trolls by trapping them in their tunnels."

Bull shook his head. "No," he said. "If you close an anthill by covering it, the ants always dig back out. It would only be a matter of time."

"The Kigyo," Jonathan said as he slapped the table. "They can finish it!"

Bull and the others all shot Jonathan a puzzled look. "The Kigyo don't like the trolls any more than we do. The king told me that peace can exist between humans and Kigyo only if the trolls are gone. If we kill the shamans, then we can send the Kigyo into the Murkle Quags to finish the rest of the trolls."

"But the trolls ran the Kigyo out the first time," Bear reminded him. "That's what you said."

Jonathan nodded. "Because they had Kigabané. Without that, the Kigyo could sneak through the swamps better than even the trolls can. Some of them even spit acid. They would be a terrible force to reckon with."

Ziegler nodded and took in a deep breath. "Do you think the Kigyo would be willing to do it?"

Jonathan nodded quickly. "If the shamans are dead, the Kigyo would prefer living in the swamps again. They could finish the fight. Then, they could have the Murkle Quags, and we can keep the dry parts of our kingdom."

Ziegler tapped a knuckle on the table and then pointed to Jonathan. "You are hereby inducted as a Ghost of the Quags. From this moment forward, your name shall be 'Snake,' and we will try this plan of yours, for the Gods know it is the best option we have been able to find."

The others wrapped their knuckles on the table and called his name enthusiastically.

Jonathan smiled for a second, but then the smile faded and he looked down at the table. The cheers died down and Miranda nudged him under the table with her foot.

"Something wrong?" she asked.

"Don't take this the wrong way, but I am not a Ghost," he said. "I mean, I always wanted to be one of you. I used to imagine fighting the trolls and conquering them, but now that I am here…" Jonathan shook his head. "Sami and Rourke died trying to bring me here, and after fighting real trolls, everything is so much different from what I imagined it would be." Jonathan paused and then took in a deep breath. "I will fight alongside you, but I am here for my brother. I am no Ghost, and I don't wish to become another tattoo in a forgotten war. My name is Jonathan Haymaker. My father died fighting the trolls. My brother, Jason Haymaker, was captured by the trolls. My Pa, Wilkin Haymaker, was the first to discover The Warrens' existence." He pointed across to Miranda. "That isn't a younger Raven, this is Miranda, a loving daughter who has come to look for her father."

Miranda smiled and cut in. "His name is Gabriel," she said.

"So, while I know this might sound rude, I want to be called by my name. Whether I die or live, I want people to know me as Jonathan Haymaker. I am not an animal, and I am not a ghost."

Silence overtook the table as the men awkwardly exchanged glances. Captain Ziegler sat at the table and no one spoke for some time. Finally, Moose stood up and extinguished his cigar on the table.

"My name is Lucas Oaks. My family lived in Falstead for generations, until the monsoons came and the trolls chased us out." Moose sat back down and offered a nod to Jonathan. "I am pleased to fight beside you, Jonathan Haymaker."

Bear spoke next. "I am Winnifred Barrister, son of Harold Barrister, one of the most reputable lawyers in the capitol city. I come from Lehemat."

"Winnifred?" Bull teased. "Oh I am not going to let that one go. From now on I am going to call you 'Winnie.'"

Bear smiled back and offered a single nod. "My name is Winnifred." He drew his knife and pointed it at Bull for emphasis. "Call me 'Winnie,' and you will not long have a tongue to speak with."

"And you?" Moose asked in his booming voice. Bull tilted his head to the side and arched a brow.

"Sure, why not?" Bull commented. He held his hands out and said, "I am Damon Meaks, son of Rutger Meaks, who like his father and grandfather before him fought and died in the swamps. I have a wife back home, and a young son I have not seen for many years. I fight for them."

The table then turned to Captain Ziegler. The man stood. He extended his tattooed arm and pointed to one of the skulls. "This is Mikel." He moved on to each tattoo nearby and began introducing them. "This is Stephen, and this is Blane. This one is Gerald, and this is Frear. This one here is Niam, and this is Jerat." He continued as the others sat there in silence. One by one he gave the names of each of his tattoos. When he finished with his arm he moved on to introduce the names of the skulls tattooed onto his chest and torso. He finished by sliding the left side of his trousers down enough to expose his hip while he named eighteen more people. By the time the last name fell from his lips, there was not a dry eye in the room.

Captain Ziegler looked up at Jonathan then and took in a deep breath. "My name, is Tray Maloy. Thirty years ago, my wife and two daughters were killed by a troll raiding party in a small village that used to stand to the northeast of Battlegrym. I survived, but only after a spear tore through my shoulder and a troll gave me this." He pointed up to the three scars on his cheek. "The soldiers came, but only after the village was burning. Some of the men had lit the blaze to chase away the trolls. It worked, but nearly everyone had been killed before the flames grew big enough to send the monsters running.

"I met a man called Captain Ziegler. He picked me out from the rubble and took me along with the other survivors back to Battlegrym. Most of the refugees left and went north. I stayed behind. When my arm was usable again, and my other wounds had healed, I trekked out into the forest and found Captain Ziegler, but he wouldn't take me into the Ghosts. I joined the army and was stationed at Battlegrym for fifteen years from the time I was twenty-two until I turned thirty-seven. I saw three men take the title of Captain Ziegler before I realized that the name meant nothing more than the animal names given to those brave souls who fought as ghosts. I joined the Ghosts of the Quags when I was forty-two, after I left Battlegrym and found the Ghosts deep in the Murkle Quags. I took over command once I was the oldest member of the Ghosts, when I was forty-three. By that time, I had seen all of the Ghosts who had been serving before me die. When I took over leadership of this unit, and Commander Kilgrave helped me choose the first men who would become my team from a roster of hand-picked veterans, I vowed to remember each man who served as one of my Ghosts.

"I kept with the tradition of naming people after animals. I also kept the group small, no more than thirty-five men at our largest numbers. We became even better at deep swamp scouting. I still lost more men then I would ever care to have done." Ziegler's hand went up to touch the tattoos on his chest. "As time went along, Bear, Moose, Bull, and Raven joined the group. We were the longest standing core the Ghosts had ever known. We have spent nearly eight years together. We have seen many comrades fall by disease or a troll's spear. When I met Jason, he seemed no different than the many others before him. I named him Boar for his stubbornness, and for his ability to fight ferociously. Now I see that I dishonored him. His name is Jason Haymaker. He is a brother, a son, and a grandson, and I will do everything in my power to bring him out of Shadowbore."

Bull raised his hand in mock reverence. "Just a thought, but are we going to call each other by our real names now, or do we still use our Ghost names? I mean, I need to know if I should shout 'Bear' or 'Winnie' in a fight."

"That's it, I'm castrating Bull," Bear said as he stood up.

Captain Ziegler shook his head and smacked his hand on the table. He shot Bull a sour glare and then motioned for Bear to be seated. "Out of deference to Jonathan, he shall go by his given name, as will Raven's daughter, Miranda. The rest of us will use our Ghost names. I don't need the two of you fighting over names when we should be focusing on trolls."

"Right," Bull said with a satisfied nod and a grin. "Besides, I bet it would be too confusing for Moose to start trying to memorize new names now anyhow, seeing as he has used our Ghost names for years."

Moose emitted a throaty growl.

"That's enough, Bull," Captain Ziegler said. Something about the tone caused Bull to look down at the table and close his mouth. Ziegler then took in a deep breath and glanced at each of the others. "Let's get out there and bring our friends home!"

The others pounded their fists on the table and shouted in agreement.

"Let's skewer those sons of Khefir!" Bull yelled.

"For our friends!" Bear called out.

"No!" Moose said as he rose from the table. "For our brothers!"

CHAPTER SIXTEEN

The group set out from the cave over the barren, cold rocks. They moved silently, taking down a pair of trolls out on patrol, moving ever closer to Shadowbore. The rains assaulted them fiercely every step of the way, limiting visibility and making the journey colder than any spring Jonathan had ever known.

They stopped halfway through the day when Jonathan noted a hidden den full of trolls. The bow alerted him by sending the now-familiar tingling sensation through his hand. As he took the bow out and readied himself, the others stopped and watched him.

He crept over a pair of rocks slick with rain and covered in orange and gray lichen. He stared down to a slab of stone, and then he saw the faint, glowing heart behind it. He looked back to Ziegler and signaled the location. Moose and Bear circled around the left, while Ziegler and Bull stalked up behind Jonathan.

"How many, can you tell?" Ziegler asked.

Jonathan shook his head. "The stone is either very thick, or perhaps the others are farther back in the tunnel. I can only see one."

Ziegler nodded and stood to signal to Moose and Bear, but Jonathan nudged the captain in the side.

"Two more just appeared," Jonathan said. "I see three now."

"They know we are here, maybe," Bull put in.

Jonathan shook his head. "They don't appear to be moving too close to the stone. They are grouping together. Maybe they are eating, or talking."

Ziegler signaled with his fingers to Moose and Bear. The two soldiers nodded and slowly made their way toward the stone. Captain Ziegler then bent back down and set a hand on Jonathan's shoulder. "They lift the door, you take out the guards."

Jonathan nodded. He slid a bit closer to the doorway and then stood, with an arrow set to the bowstring.

Moose and Bear took several minutes to traverse the last

twenty feet. They were so slow, it was almost painful for Jonathan to watch, but at least they were quiet. The two men neared the massive slab and then signaled to Jonathan that they would tip it forward toward him, affording a wide opening to shoot into. Jonathan drew the string back and waited.

Moose and Bear exploded into action, throwing the doorway open. Light burst in from the outside and the trolls shielded their eyes. Jonathan let loose three arrows in less than two seconds. Three bodies slumped to the ground.

"Go!" Ziegler commanded in a whisper as he and Bull started down toward the opening.

Moose was the first one inside, followed by Bear. Ziegler and Bull were next, followed by Jonathan and then Miranda. Jonathan looked down to the trolls and saw hunks of meat spilled along the floor of the cave.

"They were eating," Bull said with surprise written on his face. "Good job, kid," he offered.

Ziegler then pointed to Jonathan and gestured with his head down the cave. "Take point. If you see anything, we'll be two paces behind you."

Jonathan didn't have to be told twice. He quickstepped past the others and tiptoed down the darkening tunnel. He followed it around a bend to the left, and then back again toward the right. Then he stopped as he approached a set of stairs that had been carved into the stone. He moved slowly, not wanting to misstep in the darkness. The stairs descended down twenty feet before the tunnel leveled out again and then veered to the left.

The young archer kept his breathing steady, slowly putting one foot out in front of the other. Kigabané was not alerting him to any dangers, but still something felt wrong to him. The damp, musty air assaulted his nose with a putrid odor.

He heard something, like rustling leaves perhaps, or maybe something dragging across loose dirt over stone. Jonathan paused and held his breath, listening and waiting.

Nothing happened.

He moved forward as the tunnel narrowed. He looked back, but could barely make out the dark forms following him.

Something moved in the darkness again. Jonathan froze. He turned back to the others. "We need light," he said.

"No light," Ziegler whispered. "If we use magic now, they will know where we are, and not just the trolls in this tunnel, but everywhere."

Flustered, Jonathan sighed and pushed back. "I can't see anything, and the bow isn't telling me there are any more trolls, but I hear something moving in the darkness. There's something out there, and I don't want to go in blind."

"Then we leave," Ziegler said.

"What do you mean we leave?" Bull whispered in the dark. "If the boy is afraid of the dark, then let me go."

"Enough, Bull," Ziegler said harshly. "It isn't vital to our mission. We are going for Boar and Raven. We killed the guards above that could surprise us, and that is good enough. Let's double back and get moving to Shadowbore."

"What, and leave the tunnel alone?" Bull asked.

"Shut your mouth and move," Ziegler commanded.

The group made their way back up through the tunnel, up the stairs and around the many bends until they emerged into the daylight. Moose and Bear set the slab of stone back over the tunnel. Then they made their way farther across the desolate rocks.

None of them spoke much. It seemed that the veteran warriors were more than used to the silence. It was almost as if they preferred it, communicating with their hands and eyes more than with their words. Miranda walked in the middle of the pack, with Moose and Bear off to the left, Bull to the right and Ziegler in the rear. Jonathan took point, as they all thought it best, given that his bow could alert them to dangers the naked eye could miss.

He glanced back every now and again at Miranda, trying to conceal his interest by then glancing around to Moose or even farther back to Ziegler. She noticed his peeking on a couple of occasions, but didn't say anything about it. She would just avert her eyes elsewhere and continue walking. Most of the time, however, his eyes scanned the endless gray in front of him. The water had soaked him thoroughly enough that it now felt a part of him. His boots squished with each step, hemorrhaging gobs of water from the sides as his feet forced out the liquid.

The worst part was the wind. As the sun dropped down, the wind picked up, howling over the rocks and sweeping the rain into Jonathan's face with a terrible sting. Each heavy drop was shattered into tiny, sharp particles that ripped and poked at his skin. He had to half-close his eyes to shield himself from the rain. The storm grew fierce enough that Jonathan had to lean into the wind to keep from being blown off balance.

They pushed through that horrid weather for an hour before Ziegler whistled. Jonathan turned to see him pointing to Bull. Jonathan looked to Bull and saw the man waving for Jonathan to come over. Jonathan hurried toward him, pulling his cloak in tight and trying not to slip up on the rocks as the wind pushed the cloak and tangled it between his legs. Jonathan arrived to see the bald-headed man standing next to a black boulder.

"Can you see any trolls here?" Bull asked as he pointed down.

Jonathan focused on the rock and the ground beneath, but shook his head.

Bull waved the others over. He then set his arms around the stone and hoisted it up as if it were nothing more than a sack of potatoes. Bull set the rock aside and pointed down.

Jonathan moved in, happy to be out of the weather, but apprehensive about the new tunnel. He bit his lip as he dropped down into a descent of four and a half feet before he touched the bottom. The soft earth beneath his feet gave way as the water and rain from above had already found its way down and softened it for him.

"Make way then," Bull said. Miranda was the next to enter the tunnel. Jonathan stepped aside and was pushed further into the hole as all of the others dropped down one by one. The archer pulled Kigabané around from his shoulder and held it firm in his hand. It still surprised him every time he gripped the dry wood. No matter how much water assaulted them, the weapon was always protected. He found himself wishing the same enchantment had been placed on him.

"Any sign of trolls?" Ziegler asked, ripping Jonathan away from his thoughts.

Jonathan shook his head. "Nothing," he said.

"Good. Follow me. We camped in this tunnel after your brother was captured. It opens up into a chamber about fifty yards from here. There are no offshoots though, it's just a den. So, if there are no trolls, then we can camp here for the night."

Jonathan kept close to Ziegler until they made it into the chamber. Their eyes attuned themselves to the dark just enough that they could keep from bumping into each other, but they couldn't really see anything. Jonathan only knew they had reached the chamber because the left side of the wall opened up and there was nothing left to put his hand along as he walked.

"Bear, you have your tinder kit?" Ziegler asked.

Jonathan heard some shuffling in the darkness. *Click-click-click*. A spark flashed, and the tiny light nearly blinded Jonathan. His eyes contracted so sharply that they ached, but then they opened up as Bear nurtured a baby flame atop a small candle. The thing was no bigger than a man's middle finger, but the light it provided cut through most of the darkness in the chamber.

Jonathan looked around and saw a pile of green and gray bodies off in the corner.

"We'll set up camp over here," Ziegler said as he pointed to the opposite end of the chamber.

The others walked by Jonathan as the boy continued to stare at the dead trolls. Dried blood lined their bodies, and their limbs were contorted in unspeakable ways, as if they had been dumped in a hurry and then left.

Jonathan knew that was exactly what had happened. If the Ghosts had camped here before, then that meant they must have killed the previous inhabitants. Not wanting to waste the time burying the bodies, they had just piled them off to one side.

He broke his stare and turned away from the repulsive sight. He moved up to the others and they began arranging their weapons and packs around the floor.

"We don't have anything to build a larger fire with," Bear said. "Shall we ask the girl to dry our socks?"

Jonathan looked to Ziegler, the dancing candlelight played upon the man's form as he turned and shook his head. "We can make do with wet feet for a day. Pull your boots and socks off so your feet can dry out in the air. No reason to risk using magic this close. We make for Shadowbore tomorrow."

Ziegler didn't say it, but Jonathan understood the implication. Either they would win tomorrow and have all the time in the world to build a proper fire to dry themselves, or they would all be dead, and there would no longer be a need for dry socks.

Jonathan frowned and dropped onto the floor. He pulled his boots off and then peeled his socks from his feet. He couldn't see very well in the candlelight, as Bear had moved farther away from him, but his toes seemed to feel fine. He wiggled them and spread them, letting the air work around his cold, wet flesh. Then, he moved in with his hands to check the skin on his feet. His toes were a bit wrinkled, but no worse than they had been at other times along the journey.

Miranda's staff slapped to the ground next to him. Jonathan looked up to see the young woman sit nearby and pull her boots and socks off as well. She moved them off to the side and then smiled at him briefly.

"I'm nervous," she said.

He nodded. "We'll find them," Jonathan promised.

Miranda nodded again and then smiled as she pulled a few strands of wet hair off of her face. She had already removed her cloak and laid it out a few feet away on the ground. She put her hands down behind her and then bit her lip as she looked to her knees. "You never questioned me," she said after a moment.

Jonathan looked at her, but he didn't say anything. He wasn't sure where she was going with the conversation.

She turned to him and smiled. "Thank you for that," she said.

Jonathan shrugged. "What was there to question?" he asked.

Miranda's smile widened and she lowered herself down to rest upon her elbows. "Do you think we will actually return home?" she asked, changing the subject slightly.

Jonathan thought of Rourke and Sami. There was a large part of him that didn't believe they would live through the night, let alone the day ahead, but he was not about to say that to her. How could he? He took in a breath and then nodded with feigned confidence. "I know we will," he said as he put on a smile for her.

Miranda laughed once and shook her head. "You're not very good at lying are you?" she asked. Jonathan's eyebrows shot up and he started to protest, but Miranda kept laughing. "Don't look so insulted," she said. "It's actually a nice quality to have."

Jonathan shrugged. "I suppose if I had to be bad at something, there are worse options."

Miranda nodded. "So what will you do *if* we do survive," she said as she wiggled her feet just enough to kick his leg playfully. "Will you go back to your farm and cut hay for the rest of your life?"

Jonathan cocked his head to the side. "I guess I haven't thought about it much lately," he said honestly. "I suppose that would be the proper thing to do. Pa and Memaw could use the help around the fields. I certainly don't want to be a soldier anymore if I get out of here."

"Ah, so you want to settle down and start a family do you?" Miranda pressed.

Jonathan looked to her and his cheeks flushed. He turned away, though there wasn't any way she could see him blush in the dim light of Bear's candle. "I suppose someday," he said. "I can think of worse things to do with one's life than to work a field and raise a family." He cleared his throat and threw the focus on her. "What about you?"

"Would I work a field?" Miranda asked playfully.

"No, I mean what would you do?"

Miranda dropped down and put her hands behind her head. "I suppose I would go to study magic in Lehemat. That's what my father did when he was my age. Or maybe I would go and travel to Teo."

"The elven trading port?"

"Yep," Miranda replied excitedly. "I think I have seen enough swamp and rain. I want to see Tanglewood Forest and one of the elven cities. If I went to Teo, then maybe I could even find a ship and go sailing to other ports, see parts of the world that I have only read about in books."

"You know," Jonathan started, "Tirnog is only a couple hundred miles north of Holstead. I heard it's a beautiful city, and it would get you farther into Tanglewood Forest than going to Teo would." The young boy fidgeted with his thumbs, wondering how she might like the idea.

"Ah, but Teo is set upon the beautiful cliffs overlooking the sea," Miranda replied. "The port bustles below while the towers stand upon the cliffs and you can see for hundreds of miles across the ocean."

Jonathan suddenly felt dumb for suggesting Tirnog.

"Yeah, I guess Tirnog doesn't have anything like that," he said sheepishly.

A few moments of silence ensued and then Miranda leaned up onto an elbow and looked at Jonathan. "Although," she began. "I suppose if I went to Tirnog, I could stop in to see you and your fields, if that's alright I mean."

Jonathan smiled wide. "I could even show you the way to Tirnog from my house," he offered, though he had surely never been anywhere near Tirnog in all of his life.

"How about you just propose marriage and get it over with?" Bull snorted from a few yards away.

Miranda dropped down onto her back and the conversation, as well as the moment, were now finished. Jonathan sighed and began to lay down as well. He might have started thinking about what he would do if Miranda did show up at his home, but Ziegler approached and silently grabbed his shoulder, stealing all chances Jonathan might have had to imagine such things.

"Come with me," Ziegler said in a low whisper.

Jonathan grabbed his bow and the two of them slowly made their way to the tunnel. The candlelight barely did more than outline Ziegler's face by the time they reached the tunnel, but Jonathan could still tell that something was weighing upon Ziegler's mind.

"What is it?" Jonathan asked.

Ziegler was silent for a moment, glancing back to the group and then to Jonathan. "There is something you need to know," he said. "I will do everything I can to get Jason and Miranda back home." Captain Ziegler stopped talking and Jonathan scrunched up his brow as he wondered what the point of saying that was. Ziegler reached out and grabbed Jonathan's shoulder and squeezed. "I tell you this, because I need something from you."

"What?" Jonathan asked.

"Before your brother was captured, he scouted out part of Shadowbore. He found a waterway inside that led deeper into the lair. It seemed to run parallel with the tunnel itself, leading down into the trolls' home. The actual tunnel itself is blocked and guarded by many trolls, as well as different kinds of traps. Jason thought that if we could go down the waterway, we could surprise the trolls."

"Did you try it?" Jonathan asked.

Ziegler shook his head. "Raven decided that it was best to use magic to scout the way. If the waterway ended underground, then it would be suicide. So, after a bit of debate we used Raven's magic. We broke the head off of an arrow and then created three pieces of wood from the shaft. Raven cast a spell over each one and then sent them through the waterway. I'm not sure exactly what he did, but somehow the magic on the pieces of the arrow formed an image that appeared in front of the three of us. It was nearly the same as if we were looking through a window, except there was no glass. It was just an image brought about by Raven's magic."

"That's how you got caught," Jonathan surmised. "You used magic and the trolls could sense it."

Ziegler nodded. "But we also found the way into the central lair. The waterway is the key. It leads directly into the central lair. We got a good look around before the spell was detected and we had to escape. The waterway opens into a pool inside of a large chamber. Unlike the others we have ever found, this chamber was extremely ornate. There is a throne made of bones and gold. It sits behind a large alter of obsidian. There is a troll king there. He was much larger than any troll we had ever seen before. He was wearing strange robes too, with a blue amulet around his neck. I can't be sure, but it seems to me that if there were a troll in charge of making the monsoons larger, then it would be him."

An uneasy feeling hooked itself around Jonathan's stomach, and goosebumps rippled across his forearms. "And you want me to go through the waterway?" he asked.

Ziegler nodded slowly. "I don't ask this lightly," he said. "Raven's magic also revealed that the hole opening up into the pool is too small for any of us to get through. It would be suicide for me, or even someone as large as Jason."

"Suicide for me too," Jonathan noted.

"You could make it through the opening. I saw it, and I know you could swim through," Ziegler said.

"But after the king is dead, I will not be able to swim back up the waterway, will I?"

Ziegler sighed heavily. "No. The angle is too steep and the current is far too strong." His hand squeezed Jonathan's shoulder tighter again. "You don't have to agree to it now. Take the night and think on it. I know you only came to save your brother, but I think you might be the best chance we have to end this war. Look at you, a boy by all accounts, and yet you are the only one who could retrieve a magical bow that enables you to kill trolls. Despite all odds, you have not only braved the Murkle Quags, but survived all the way to The Warrens. You are within striking distance of Shadowbore. The gods have placed you here for a reason."

"I'll do it," Jonathan said. Ziegler stopped with his mouth open and stared at the young man. "Just be sure that Jason gets home."

Ziegler nodded solemnly. "I will."

Jonathan glanced over at Miranda and his shoulders fell slack. There would be no future day when she visited him in Holstead, he knew. He looked back to Ziegler and thought about the plan for a moment before asking, "How will you know if I have succeeded?"

Ziegler smiled wide. After what I have seen of your archery skills, I have no doubt that you will succeed. Besides, if we are right, and it is the shamans that have amplified the monsoons, then the rains should stop upon the king's death. Raven was certain that the king has much greater magical abilities than the other shamans. Beyond that, there is always the hope that killing the leader will cause the others to break up, or possibly retreat altogether."

"What if they don't, or what if the king isn't there when I swim out from the pool?" Jonathan asked.

Ziegler leaned in. "Don't let fear and doubt cloud your judgment. It is a solid plan, and at this point it is the smartest one. The only other option is a frontal assault with everyone fighting their way down to that throne room."

Jonathan sighed and nodded. "No, I can do it. Just get Jason back home."

CHAPTER SEVENTEEN

The group was back out in the rain before the morning's first light. Ziegler led them, with Jonathan at his side scanning with his enchanted bow for trolls. The wind was even worse than it had been before, chilling them all to the bone and quashing their spirits. The rain was lighter, but in the harshness of the winds it felt colder and more bitter than the previous day's large drops.

The silvery moon broke through the clouds for quick intermissions only to be covered up again as the wind above carried the clouds eastward. Ziegler used the additional light to speed the group along their journey, slowing when the darkness was full and nearly running when the moonlight streamed down upon them.

Soon they came to a large mound of rocks. Jonathan signaled that he saw two trolls. At first he thought they were in the mound, but he quickly realized as the glowing hearts split and walked in opposite directions that they were patrolling around the outside.

Ziegler signaled for everyone to lay low to the ground.

Jonathan drew an arrow back and waited for the first troll to move out into the open. He fired and the troll fell without a sound. He drew another arrow and dropped the second just as easily. The two arrows returned to his quiver and he signaled that all of the enemies were gone.

Captain Ziegler moved in close to Jonathan and put a hand on his shoulder. "This is it," he said. "Behind those rocks is the cave where they took your brother and Raven. We'll go on ahead, and the others will go after your brother."

"Can't I at least see him?" Jonathan asked.

Ziegler shook his head. "Better that we split up now. Don't worry. Moose will lead the others to make sure your brother gets out alive, but we can't risk all of us going in there and getting caught. You and I need to go to Shadowbore."

Jonathan glanced over to Miranda. He could only faintly see her in the dim light filtering through the clouds above. Then he turned to Ziegler and nodded. "Let's go."

*****

"Where are they going?" Miranda asked as she saw Jonathan and Ziegler run off toward the south.

"They have something they need to do," Bear said cryptically.

"What?" Miranda pressed. "Jonathan's brother is in this cave right?"

"As is Raven," Bear answered.

Bull came up and put his massive hand on her shoulder. "We focus on getting your father and Jason." It was the sympathy in his eyes that gave it away for her. In her short time with him, she had only seen the brash braggart that her father had talked about and so eloquently described in his letters. To see him show any amount of empathy was beyond alarming to her.

"They're going to Shadowbore, aren't they?" Miranda guessed.

Moose walked up and pointed to the mound of rocks.

"Come on, then," Bear said. "We have some trolls to kill and people to rescue."

Miranda stared off at Jonathan, watching his cloak wave in the wind as he disappeared into the darkness. "He didn't even say goodbye," she whispered to herself.

"Let's go, love," Bull said as he gently pushed her toward the mound of rocks.

Miranda turned to follow Moose, but the large man had disappeared into the shadows. "Where did he go?"

Bear cracked a grin and shrugged. "No one's sure how he does it, but he puts the literal meaning into the word Ghost, if you know what I mean."

She glanced all around, but saw no sign of the giant.

"Come on, he's going to get a head start again," Bull complained. The three of them broke into a light jog. They rounded the mound of rocks, passing by one of the slain trolls and stopping at the open entrance.

"Remember, no magic unless I say so," Bear told Miranda.

The young girl nodded and held her staff out in a guard

201

position. Bear and Bull went in first and she followed after them. Unlike the other tunnels, there were lights in this one. Torches set into the stone hung every twenty feet or so, illuminating everything.

Off in the distance the trio could hear the sound of a sharp crack, followed by a distinct *thud*.

"Snake-eggs," Bull cursed. "Moose has already got one."

An instant later there were some muffled thumping sounds. A slight groan could be heard and then another *crraaack!* Bull pushed by Bear and quickened his pace while trying to remain as silent as possible.

They came to a small chamber where a troll guard lay dead on the floor. His head hung limp off to one side and his tongue was flopped out of his mouth. The small chamber then broke off into three more tunnels. Two were dark, one was illuminated by torches.

Bear moved up to the tunnel with the torches and put his ear out, listening for any sign of Moose. He shook his head and frowned as he turned back to the others.

"We can cover all three tunnels," Miranda offered.

Bear shook his head. "We can cover two," he said. "Moose likely took one of the two dark tunnels. He does best in the shadows. So we can either all go down the lit tunnel, or we can split up."

"How do we know which tunnel Moose took?" Miranda asked.

Bull approached the tunnel on the left and listened closely as he put a finger to his lips.

Miranda heard faint thumping sounds coming from the right tunnel. She pointed to it and Bull and Bear nodded.

"Right then, Bull, you take Miranda down the dark tunnel. I'll take this one."

"You'll be alright alone?" Miranda asked.

Bear winked as he drew his pair of knives. "Don't worry about me, worry about the trolls."

"Let's go!" Bull whispered harshly. "Moose has already got at least three or four kills by now."

"Race you to twenty," Bear teased.

Bull growled and turned down the tunnel.

Miranda ran quickly to follow the bald headed warrior.

They silently rushed through the tunnel as it broke away to the left and descended into the ground. The air grew warmer, despite the cold air above, and even though it was dark, it was not pitch black. There were small gems in the ceiling of the cave that gave off a strange, red glow. The light was enough that they could see where they were going, as well as make out the texture of the walls around them.

After following the tunnel for two minutes, it spiraled down at an alarming pitch. Miranda and Bull had to step sideways in order to keep from slipping and tumbling down the red hallway. Round and round they walked until they came to a long hallway that appeared to have several offshoots to either side. At the end of the hall sat a troll. It rested upon a large stone, with its back leaning against the wall and its head and neck crimped so that its chin rested on its chest. Its hands sat upon its bulbous belly, rising and dropping with each ear-splitting snore.

Bull motioned for Miranda to stay put. She moved close to the wall, trying to make herself as hard to see as possible in case the troll opened its eyes. Bull moved through the hall. He paused at each branch off the tunnel and peered around the wall before hopping across the opening and then waiting to see if the troll had been disturbed by his sudden movement. The bald-headed warrior leveled his sword as he neared the sleeping troll, and then he lashed out as quickly as a viper and drove his blade up through the large belly and into the chest. He pulled his sword out and then brought it up to stab directly down into the chest.

Miranda put a hand to her mouth as a copious amount of blood spilled to the floor, splattering loudly as the troll flopped over to land on its side. Bull then turned and motioned for Miranda to join him. He turned immediately to the opening on his left and disappeared.

The young woman paused at the first opening, but was quickly relieved when she saw nothing more than a den maybe twelve feet deep and eight feet wide. She inspected each opening and found them to be similar. Then, when she arrived at the last offshoot, her heart leapt into her throat.

Bull was helping a man to his feet. He was weak, barely able to stand on his own and reaching out for Bull's support. He had a messy beard and a mat of unkempt dark hair on his head.

Miranda rushed in to him and nearly knocked him over as she hugged him tight.

"Father!" she cried.

"M-Miranda!" Raven said in a cracking voice as he slowly put his arms around her. "My girl, what are you doing here?"

Miranda squeezed him tight and buried the side of her face into his chest. His body felt cool and thin, but he was alive. She cried tears of joy and then pushed away so she could wipe her face. "It's good to see you again," she said.

"Daughter, why have you come?" Raven asked. "You should never have come."

Miranda looked to see that Bull was cutting another man loose. A thick rope extending from an iron ring in the wall was tied to the man's neck. His arms were bound around a pole laid horizontally across his back so that he couldn't use his arms, and his feet were bound together at the ankles. Even in the dim light of the red stones, Miranda could see the likeness to Jonathan.

"You're Jason Haymaker," she said.

The young man lifted his head and looked at her with puzzled eyes. "How do you know my name?"

Bull finished cutting him loose and then pulled Jason to his feet. "Boar," he said as he pointed to Miranda. "This is Raven's daughter, Miranda. She is a friend of your brother's."

"My brother?" Jason asked. "What do you mean?"

Miranda shot her father a quick glance and then went to Jason and took one of his hands in hers. "Jonathan helped me find my father, and he was here too. He went with Ziegler to Shadowbore."

"Shadowbore?" Jason asked. "Jonathan was here?"

Bull nodded. "A fine warrior he is too," he said. "He was dead set on finding you, no matter the cost."

"Why is he going to Shadowbore?" Jason pressed.

"The waterway," Raven said. The other three turned to him. "I am guessing that Jonathan is a younger brother?"

"No, he can't!" Jason said loudly. Bull slapped a hand to the man's mouth and held it firmly.

"Quiet down, Moose and Bear are up in the other tunnels. We don't need to attract any more attention." Bull stared at Jason's eyes for a moment and then slowly removed his hand. "Now,

204

Jonathon wanted us to get you home."

Jason shook his head. "Most of the other trolls left last night."

"Why?" Bull asked.

Raven answered. "Couldn't say for certain. I can't understand their language. All I know, is we were originally held in the upper chambers. They examined us for a while, and then they took my staff. A group of them left the tunnel, with my staff, and the others brought us down to this level."

"Then last night they came in shouting and hollering. They had broken Raven's staff and they seemed pretty angry," Jason put in.

Raven smirked. "I was hoping that perhaps they had tried to use it and it backfired on them, but there is no way to be sure."

"They were after your magic?" Bull asked.

Raven shrugged. "All I know is most of them left after that. We could tell because the tunnels became almost deathly quiet from that time up until you arrived. I'm guessing if they thought you would come for us, they would have stayed here to fight."

"We need to find Bear and Moose," Bull said. "Ziegler said we were to get you both home as soon as we found you."

"Then you shouldn't have told me my brother was here," Jason said flatly. "I'm not leaving without him."

Bull grinned wide. "That's exactly why I told you. I ain't for leaving the kid to the monsters in Shadowbore either."

"We should help Bear and Moose," Raven said. "Let's clear this den before we move on. If we don't, then they might be able to raise an alarm."

Bull turned to Raven. "Can you walk?" he asked.

Miranda handed her father her staff and he took it in hand. "Easily enough."

Bull turned back to Jason. "What about you, can you fight?"

Jason narrowed his eyes and offered a single nod. "Give me a sword and let's finish this."

*****

Jonathan and Ziegler crept into the large opening slowly.

Jonathan had already spotted and killed four guards, and now the entrance was clear. They stepped into Shadowbore and snuck down into the first chamber. Several tunnels broke off from this chamber, but Ziegler pointed to the farthest right tunnel.

"The waterway is down this one," he said. The two of them walked along the shadows for several hundred yards. Jonathan noticed several hearts as they approached a second chamber. Firelight danced out into the entrance to the tunnel, playing upon the wall near Jonathan.

"I see three," Jonathan said.

Ziegler nodded. "The entrance to the waterway is in this chamber. It isn't large, but you should manage. Take these trolls out, and then you should be able to make it."

Jonathan took a couple of breaths to steady his nerves. Then he set his jaw and walked out to the opening of the chamber. Three arrows flew and three trolls fell. Unfortunately, one troll dropped onto the arrow and snapped the shaft, so now Jonathan only had six arrows left. He didn't let that bother him though. He only needed one for the king.

Ziegler ran into the room and pulled Jonathan along by the arm after the trolls were dead. He took him to a place in the wall where there was a moveable stone slab. He gripped it, and with a grunting effort, pulled it free.

"This is it," Ziegler said. "This is what your brother found."

Jonathan looked at it and his heart sank into his stomach. The waterway was little more than a granite chute. From the looks of it, he would have to hold his breath the entire way down. The water ran so fast that he knew there was zero chance of swimming back up.

"Hold your bow across your chest," Ziegler said. "You don't want it breaking before you reach the throne room."

Jonathan nodded. He handed the bow and the quiver to Ziegler while he climbed up to sit on the rock at the edge of the opening. Ziegler then gave him the weapons back and Jonathan held them close to his chest. He closed his eyes and then looked to Ziegler.

Captain Ziegler put a hand on Jonathan's forearm and squeezed. "Jonathan Haymaker, it has been a deep honor."

Jonathan faked a smile and shook his head. "Tell my brother…" the words caught in his throat.

"I will," Ziegler promised. "Now, get that troll king."

Jonathan cleared his lungs and then took in a deep breath. He slid into the rushing water and the current swept him away in a flash.

The rushing water sounded like thunder as he coursed down the chute. The smooth rock had him slipping and sliding up the sides as he zipped down at incredible speeds. Sometimes he nearly fell vertically while at other times the water pushed him along a level plane. He kept his eyes squished shut and his lungs tight as he raced through the waterway. There was no way of knowing how far he had travelled, but the journey came to an awkward end as he spun out of the chute and into a larger, orb-like structure. The water rolled him over and over until he finally saw the opening that would allow him to exit to the deeper pool above. He caught a glimpse of sparkling orange flames dancing beyond the surface above and knew that was where he needed to be.

Jonathan struggled to right himself, wasting precious seconds fighting against the swirling current as he tried to angle himself toward the opening. He nearly panicked as his lungs began to burn and ache. They almost involuntarily expelled his breath to prepare to suck in a breath, but the young man held onto his air and closed off his windpipe with the sheer power of will. Then he cleared his mind, and allowed the current to work for him. He stopped fighting it and used it, gaining momentum until he finally was able to break out and grab the rim of the opening, but he wasn't clear yet. The opening was tight, even for him.

Jonathan slipped one arm through with the bow first, and then he pulled his shoulders through. His ribs scraped along the stone opening. He could feel two jagged points cutting into his skin, but he didn't stop. Better to have a couple of minor cuts than to drown.

When he finally got his hips and buttocks through, he quickly pulled his feet up and then used the top of the stone to propel himself upward. He broke the surface of the water quietly, grabbing hold of a stone outcropping near the wall. As quietly as possible he let out his breath and sucked in new air. Then he looked around the room.

There were many braziers with great flames rising high into the air. A throne of gold and bones sat behind a large, black altar just as Ziegler had said. A wide walkway of stone led from the altar out to some tunnel. On the opposite side of the walkway was another pool of water. Behind the throne was a wall that rose up high into the arched ceiling that was beset with thousands of tiny red stones that glowed in the darkness above.

Everything was just the way he had expected, except for one thing.

The troll king was nowhere to be seen.

CHAPTER EIGHTTEEN

Jonathan pulled himself up on the handhold, lifting himself out of the water a bit. He looked around the chamber, but he saw nothing. He slid the bow over his shoulder and then dipped back into the water. He moved with slow, controlled strokes so as not to splash in the water as he swam to the stone walkway between the two pools. As he moved around the rock outcropping he looked to his left and saw a vast tunnel that ascended abruptly in a steep, wide set of stairs.

Where was the king?

He grabbed onto the walkway and was nearly about to pull himself out of the water when his left hand began to tingle. He paused, looking up the stairs. No one came. Finally he looked to his right, confused by the fact that he couldn't see anyone. Then he saw it. A glowing purple heart was approaching the back wall about ten yards away from where the throne sat. As the young archer focused on the wall itself, he saw a thin outline of a doorway in the stone.

Jonathan slipped down into the water and moved back to the outcropping. He put his hands to the rock and took a deep breath as the stone doorway swung open. The glowing heart stepped through just as Jonathan dropped below the surface of the water. The troll moved toward the altar and then lifted himself onto it.

Another figure moved in behind the first and even under the water Jonathan could hear the reverberating echo of the stone door closing. Slowly, Jonathan broke the surface of the water just enough so he could breathe through his nose as he watched his target intently. The second troll was most definitely the king. He wore the long, black hooded robes that Ziegler had talked about. He stood maybe nine feet tall, towering over the smaller troll, who himself was no feeble creature.

As the troll king turned and produced a wickedly curved knife from the folds of his robe, the blue amulet swung into view. The gem glowed brightly, and was easily the size of Jonathan's fist.

It dangled from a chain of black metal as it swung softly back and forth.

The smaller troll laid upon the altar and became motionless.

The troll king began to speak. His voice was low and hoarse, echoing off the walls and filling the room. As the large troll spoke, the fires dimmed in the chamber. It was as if the king's chant absorbed all of the light. The fires quieted down and came to be only miniscule flames that barely flickered above the braziers. Shadows swept into the great chamber, leaving only a small sphere of light around the altar itself.

Jonathan used this time to get into position. He crept along the rim of the pool until, hidden by the dense shadows, he was able to pull himself onto the walkway. He pulled his bow around and nocked an arrow. Like the previous shaman Jonathan had slain, the troll king's heart did not glow under Kigabané's enchantment. The young archer would have to aim this one all on his own.

He drew in a deep breath as he slowly pulled the string back. His shoulder blade tensed as the arrow came to rest against the corner of his mouth. Jonathan focused on the troll's chest, aiming for the creature's heart. The troll king raised his curved knife into the air and then shouted something that Jonathan could not understand. Down came the knife and the troll upon the altar died instantly, but this time the glow did not fade. As the troll convulsed in death, the purple glow from its heart rose from its body like a mist and entered the blue amulet. The amulet glowed much brighter, creating an indigo hue of light that enveloped the troll king. So entranced by the sight was he, that Jonathan nearly forgot what he was to do.

As the troll king raised his head toward the ceiling and let out a feral cry, Jonathan took his shot. The arrow flew straight and true. It buried itself into the troll king's chest and the giant creature stumbled backward a step.

The blue light swirled back into the amulet and all at once the fires in the braziers raged into full force again. The troll king lowered his head and looked directly at Jonathan. He reached up calmly and snapped the arrow shaft with one hand. He pulled it up to inspect the arrow and then tossed it to the ground.

"Kigabané," the troll king shouted. Then the giant troll ripped its robes away to reveal a long shirt of chainmail that glimmered in the firelight. "Kigabané kus do frobar!"

Jonathan didn't hesitate. "Heart or head," the young archer said as he drew another arrow. This time he aimed for the king's left eye. He let loose the arrow and it flew swift and straight.

The troll king waved his hand and the arrow veered off to the side, slamming into the stone wall and snapping the head clean off as sparks flew out.

The troll king laughed and then he chanted something that Jonathan didn't understand. A column of water emerged from the pool on the left and then it stretched out to strike Jonathan, throwing him down to the ground and nearly sweeping him into the other pool. Jonathan rolled out of the water and came up with another arrow. He fired, and then quickly grabbed a second and a third arrow. He fired all five of his remaining arrows in less than two seconds, hoping that his speed would somehow get through the troll king's spells. The first two arrows dropped to the ground, skittering across the stone but not breaking. The third and fourth were directed into walls and shattered. The fifth was redirected down and sunk deep into the troll body on the altar.

Jonathan ran forward, knowing that three of the arrows would return to him. He sprinted in closer, hoping that by decreasing the distance, he could shoot faster than the troll king could react. Walls of water rose from the pools, slamming into Jonathan as he barely managed to keep his footing and run toward the altar.

The arrows began reappearing in the quiver and Jonathan pulled them as quickly as they appeared. He fired them all and continued running. As the troll king's attention was consumed by the flying arrows, the walls of water stopped emerging from the pools. One arrow turned up, striking the ceiling and snapping in half, another turned down and sank into the water, and the third spun out to hit the wall.

Two arrows left.

Jonathan ran in close, now only twenty yards away from the giant troll. The troll king grinned wickedly and raised its curved knife in its right hand while calling forth more columns of water with his left.

The arrows reappeared and Jonathan pulled the first. A thought came to his head then, that perhaps the troll king was counting the arrows as well. If so, he would be expecting two this round. Jonathan fired the first and then went through the motions of retrieving the second arrow and pretended to pull the string back and then release his fingers.

The columns of water fell and the troll king turned his magic to divert the arrows. After the first arrow shot down and struck the altar, the troll king flicked its green eyes around the room, looking for the next arrow as he sent a wave of air up. By the time it looked back to Jonathan it was too late for the king.

It summoned forth a column of water, sending it parallel to the floor, but Jonathan dropped onto his left leg, easily sliding over the wet granite surface as he drew his final arrow and aimed for the troll king's eye. The troll king looked down in horror, snarling wildly as the arrow shot up and crossed the five yards between them much faster than the troll could react to. The arrow tore through the left eye and sunk deep into the troll king's skull.

A whoosh of air swept through as the troll king's slow attempt to block the arrow failed. The large creature fell back to land half-way in the large throne. Some of the bones cracked and the large chair broke and leaned to the side under the impact of the giant troll's body.

Jonathan slowly rose to his feet as his last arrow reappeared in his quiver. Blood oozed from the troll king's left eye socket, dripping down his ashen skin and falling to the floor below. The young archer looked to the stairs behind him, fearing that perhaps the commotion had drawn the attention of troll soldiers. For the moment, at least, the path was clear. He sighed with relief and then moved to the troll king. For good measure, he took the arrow out and shot it through the other eye. He was not about to chance anything with a creature such as this. The arrow went in easily and the head jerked to the side.

Figuring it was now safe, Jonathan took the large knife, which compared to his size was almost the size of a full sword, and climbed atop the king's body. He raised it high over his head and then came down on the troll's neck. The head dropped unceremoniously to the floor and rolled around the back of the throne. Jonathan dropped the bloodied knife and put his left hand to his mouth to ward off the stench of the blood. With his right hand, he took the amulet and then jumped down.

He thought of keeping the stone, and trying to take it back to the others. Perhaps Raven could tell him what it was used for. Then again, as he looked to the stairs, he knew the chances of him escaping at all were less than favorable. He looked to the stone altar and gripped the chain tightly in his hand. Perhaps it was better to destroy the item. Whatever it was, it was fueled by sacrifice. Jonathan couldn't imagine letting an item like that fall into the wrong hands.

With every amount of strength he could muster, he swung the chain behind him and then whirled it up over his head and down toward the altar in a mighty chop. The amulet whined and whistled as it ripped through the air, and then exploded upon contacting the obsidian altar. Shards of blue stone flew out in every direction, and even the altar itself cracked in half and fell apart. A great burst of purple and gold light erupted from the impact and Jonathan was sent flying backward to land against the dead troll king's body.

Screams and screeches filled the room, causing the entire chamber to tremble and quake. Jonathan covered his ears and fell to the floor in agony as the screams threatened to rupture his ear drums. His hair and clothes whipped in a great vortex of wind, and all the fires in the chamber were blown out.

Bits of stone and dust began to fall from the ceiling. Explosions of water lashed out at him as hunks of stone splashed down. Other pieces fell to the ground, shaking and cracking the walkway and the area around the throne.

The only saving grace for him was the fact that there was a purple and blue light pulsing from the shattered pieces of the amulet, and they were augmented by the red, glowing stones in the ceiling and in the hunks of rock that had fallen. It wasn't a lot of light, but it was enough for Jonathan to try to escape.

He got to his feet, gathered the bow, and looked to the stairs. Great hunks of stone fell all around him. There was no way he would make it, he knew. So he turned to find the hidden door behind the throne. No sooner had he gone four paces, than a gigantic slab of stone crushed the throne and squished the troll king's body. The impact caused Jonathan to stumble, but he caught himself with his hands and scrambled toward the secret door. His hands rubbed and felt all along the surface, but there was no handle that he could find. He slipped his hands into the small crack around the doorway, but couldn't get a good grip.

Stones fell all around him and the light was dimming. Dust and water filled the air, making it difficult to breath.

"Think!" Jonathan shouted to himself. He glanced over his shoulder and caught a glimpse of the troll king's knife shimmering in the faint light. He rushed toward it, dodging a stone the size of his head as it crashed into his path. He grabbed the large knife and ran back to the door. He slipped the blade into the crack half way and then pressed against the handle. Jonathan grunted and groaned as his arms and legs pushed against the heavy portal.

Finally it popped open and moved just enough that Jonathan could slip inside. He took the knife with him as he leapt into the secret tunnel.

Two seconds later, a massive pile of stone fell onto the door. Sparks shot out as the stones broke and smashed into each other, and the impact sent him tumbling into the tunnel, gasping for air against the eruption of smoke and dust.

CHAPTER NINETEEN

The sun was just breaking over the eastern horizon as Jason and the others came close to Shadowbore's entrance. The golden rays streaked out over the bleak, gray stones and refracted off the rain to create a faint rainbow that disappeared as it arced up into the dismal clouds above. The only bit of clear sky they could see was off far to the east, between the rising sun and the blanket of gray storm clouds that covered The Warrens.

"There it is," Raven said as he leaned heavily upon Miranda's staff to traverse the rocks.

"I don't see Captain Ziegler," Bull said as he scanned the area about them.

Raven shook his head. "He likely stayed behind to guard the entrance to the waterway."

"Let's move in," Jason said.

Moose reached out and seized the young man with one hand. Everyone froze as the large man turned about, scanning the area. Moose pulled his warhammer to the ready position and shook his head. "They're coming," he said.

"Now how can you know that?" Bull groused. "I don't see anything, do you, Winnie?"

Bear grimaced and drew his knives. "I never knew Moose to be wrong." Then he pulled one of his knives out and pointed it at Bull. "And call me that again, and I'll be sure to cut your tongue out and hang it on a necklace."

Bull winked.

Off in the distance a plume of smoke erupted from the ground, spraying shards of small rock up into the sky and raining them down on the area around the freshly made hole.

"What in Hammenfein was that?" Bear asked.

The Warrens shook terribly then, throwing all of them to the ground as waves of rock heaved up and down and the whole plane shook from side to side. Great gasps and screams filtered through the ground as some places sank in, collapsing underground tunnels, and spears of rock stabbed up through the surface in

215

others.

"Raven, do something!" Bull ordered.

The cracking rocks crashed around like thunder as The Warrens continued to shake and tremble violently for more than thirty seconds. The area around Moose fell into the earth about ten feet, jarring and throwing the large man against a great boulder.

Bear crawled over to check on Moose, and barely saw the big man offer a thumbs up gesture before a gust of wind and steam shot out of the ground and threw Bear four feet into the air. The man dropped onto the ground hard, tweaking his shoulder and taking a cut from a jagged rock that sliced the side of his left arm when he hit.

Bull stood to rush to his aid. Bear tried to wave the bald-headed warrior off, but Bull was too stubborn to listen. A massive spire of black rock shot up from the ground, catching Bull in the stomach and heaving him fifteen feet into the air before the jagged rock cracked and tipped precariously to one side.

Raven used his magic to buffer Bull's fall as the man slipped from the spire, cushioning him as he tumbled onto the ground. Miranda then sent a series of fireballs that managed to push the drooping rock enough out of the way that Bull was unharmed when the stone toppled over a few feet away from him. Raven shot a nod of approval toward his daughter, and then the ground opened up into a wide fissure beneath him, sucking him down feet first.

"Father!" Miranda shouted. She could see him clinging to the edge with his elbows and chin, straining not to slip on the wet stone.

Jason rose to his feet and rushed over to grab Raven and pull him up to safety.

The shaking stopped then and the earth groaned heavily.

A purple and gold mist rose from the open fissures, and screams the like of which none of them had ever heard assaulted their ears. The shrill noise was so stabbing that each of them grabbed their heads and doubled over in pain.

A great thunder rolled through The Warrens, and as the mist rose to the sky, the clouds ripped apart and the rain stopped. The screams and shrieks died down and the valley was peaceful again.

Slowly, the group picked itself up from the ground and gathered back together. They were cut and bruised, but none of them were seriously injured. Bull had a hard time breathing without a slight wheezing sound, but the rock spire had not punctured him. Moose bled from his nose and the top of his forehead, but he didn't seem to care. Bear was quick to wrap some cloth around the cut on his arm and then they all looked to the tunnel where Shadowbore had been.

Now it was a sunken depression with obvious signs of tunnel collapse. Dirt and shards of rock filled what had once been the opening. Clouds of dust that had been so fierce as to erupt and withstand the rain were now settling back down to the ground, turning to a light mud coating over the wet rocks. They looked all around them and noticed the great, bright rainbow that stretched from one end of The horizon to the other, seemingly arcing across the entire Warrens.

"Why has the rain stopped?" Bull said when he finally could breathe normally.

"Because the troll king is dead," Raven said. The mage turned to Jason and clapped the man on the shoulder. "Your brother has ended the war."

Jason looked to the collapsed entrance and tried to smile as a tear fell from his right eye. "He never did know when to give up," he said.

Bear moved in and put a hand on Jason's back, offering a nod of sympathy. "His sacrifice will not be forgotten, Boar," Bear said.

Jason turned to say something, but then his eyes turned cold and his jaw tensed. He pointed out beyond the depression. The others looked to see what had caught his attention and gasped when they saw a line of trolls emerging from the ground. The first two were whole, with spears in hand. The third had lost its arm, with only a bloody stump sticking out below the shoulder. As they watched it emerge from the ground, the stump grew a new bone. As the bone formed a new radius and ulna below a regrown humerus, the pink muscle stretched across it, and then a covering of greenish skin formed.

"Looks like some of them don't know when to give up either," Bull growled.

"Gather your weapons," Bear said.

Jason moved back to where he had fallen and picked up the bow he had taken from the tunnel when he was liberated. He took aim at the first troll and sent an arrow flying straight to the creature's heart. The arrow dropped the troll, and the others looked back at Jason and the others. They snarled and raised their weapon as they let out a battle cry.

"I guess we don't want to surprise them, then," Bear commented wryly as he glanced toward Jason.

Jason shrugged and nocked another arrow.

The battle cry echoed across The Warrens, and then it was repeated. Pockets of angry trolls emerged from the ground all around the heroes. First twenty, then thirty. They kept coming out from the ground and shouting their war cry.

"We used magic," Miranda said.

Bear shook his head. "No, this time they would have come anyway. Their whole home has collapsed."

"Then we kill every one of them," Jason snarled. "If they can survive the quake, then so can my brother."

Bear glanced to Moose. The big man grinned and took out a crumpled cigar. Moose turned to Raven and held out the cigar. The mage laughed and lit the cigar for the giant man. Moose drew in a deep drag and then blew the smoke into the sky. He then turned to Bull and smiled slyly.

"What you thinking, you big ox?" Bull asked.

Moose pulled the cigar from his mouth and pointed to the gathering trolls. "Last round?" he asked.

Bull sniggered and nodded his bald head. "I'm going to win this time," Bull said.

The group then turned as one and ran out toward the west, where the closest pocket of trolls was gathering. Miranda concentrated her fire spells on the two archers, devouring their bows and stopping them from firing their deadly arrows. Raven called down a hailstorm of ice spikes from the sky that impaled a dozen of the nasty creatures before the two groups collided.

Bear worked his knives effortlessly, slashing and slicing to distract them before thrusting his blades through their hearts. Moose worked his warhammer, crushing skulls in and then flipping his hammer backward to drive the spike into a large troll's heart.

Jason and Miranda kept their distance, using arrows and magic to slay any trolls that tried to flank the group.

When that pocket was destroyed, Raven sent a wave of roiling fire into the hole from which they had emerged. Shouts and screams rose up from the flames, but no more trolls escaped from that fissure.

Arrows plinked off of the stones around Jason and Miranda then. The two turned to see a grouping of troll archers standing on a small, rocky knoll. Jason dropped two and Miranda destroyed the last three with a fireball that incinerated them.

The others in the group turned to receive a charge of angry trolls armed with spears and swords.

Moose swung and caught three trolls with one strike, bashing all of their heads together. He then flipped his grip and bashed a fourth in the face with the spike at the base of the hammer's shaft before coming in with a chop that all but flattened the hapless creature. Bear rushed in and took down two from the side as Bull charged in wildly, screaming like a maniac as he swung his sword.

In a fit of rage, Bull severed arms and legs as he barreled into a group of seven trolls. He spun around their spear thrusts, ducked under an axe swing, and the he twirled once with his sword and seven heads hit the rocks. The bodies stood stiff for a second before toppling over onto the ground. "I have twelve!" he shouted as he rushed onward to the nearest troll. The poor creature actually turned and tried to flee, but Bull caught him with a thrust of his sword, picking the flailing troll up and letting him slide down the blade before discarding the body. "Thirteen!"

Moose broke into a run, slamming and chopping with his hammer in a way that seemed almost ethereal. The heavy weapon moved as if it were a light, well-balanced sword in the hands of a master. It twirled around and flipped directions gracefully as the giant man worked through a throng of trolls. None of them stood a chance, though one of them did graze Moose's side with the edge of his spear just enough that it left a small cut.

Bear called out over the fray, "Moose is winning!"

"Gargh!" Bull snarled as he continued to fight on.

Miranda and Jason were joined by Raven. The three of them fought from a distance, stopping smaller pockets of trolls from flanking the others, or going after troll archers, of which there were fortunately few.

The battle raged on for a few minutes before The Warrens groaned again. A great wave of stone heaved up and down from south to north, disrupting the entire fight. The trolls scampered away, falling to their knees as the stones rolled through like an ocean wave. The heroes, having already experienced one such quake, dropped to their hands and knees and waited for it to pass. After it did, they killed the few trolls close enough to strike, and then watched as perhaps one hundred of the creatures formed a long semicircle in the north.

"What are they doing?" Miranda asked.

"Maybe they know something we don't," Jason replied as he readied another shot with his arrow.

"How many arrows you have left?" Raven asked him.

"Two," Jason said without even looking. "One in the hand and one in the bag."

Raven nodded. "You may want to save them."

A great rumbling sound tore through the rocks and ground some fifty yards to the east. The trolls in the north raised their weapons overhead and began hooting and hollering.

"They definitely know something we don't," Jason commented.

Bull, Bear, and Moose hurried back to the others, arriving just as a massive spike tore through the ground. Rocks cracked and crumbled as they fell from the ivory spike rising from below.

"By Khefir's bones," Bear cursed. "What evil is this?"

The spike rose for fifteen feet before what looked like a large, leathery brown sphere pushed through. A few more feet and then three great eyes opened. They were followed by a wide, flat nose and a mouth that had a great set of yellowed teeth. The giant head shook to the side and rocks were pushed away. A pair of hands emerged and grabbed onto the surface, and then a massive beast emerged from the gaping hole.

It snarled and growled low with the force of thunder as it took in a breath and extended to its full height. It stood at least forty five feet in the air, not counting the spike on top of its head. It had two massive arms and two legs that made even the thickest of oaks look like saplings by comparison. A massive, leathery tail unfurled behind the creature and it roared again, opening its horrid mouth and spewing spittle across the rocks. The trolls to the north shouted and hollered, cheering their new champion.

"What is that?" Bull asked.

Raven shook his head. "I don't know."

"It's mortal," Jason said decisively. "Let's take it down." He took aim and fired his first arrow. It flew straight and true, piercing the middle eye that sat above the other two. The beast shied away, turning its head and swiping at the arrow. It broke the shaft and then turned back with an evil grin as the eye healed itself.

"That is one big troll," Bear grumbled.

"I think you just pissed it off," Bull said.

"How do we kill it?" Miranda asked.

The giant let out another roar and then whirled around, sweeping its tail out toward them. Rocks and boulders caught in the tail's wake were slung at the heroes. Raven created a magical shield that deflected the rocks, but then the beast turned around and took two steps forward and lunged with its massive hand. It caught Bear with its fist. Bear tried to fend the blow off with his knives, but there was no way for him to stop the massive creature. His body was crushed instantly by the blow and thrown back into the air several hundred feet, landing broken along the rocks.

"BEAR!" Bull shouted as he ran in toward the giant troll. He dove in and slashed at the beast's left leg, tearing a deep gash into the creature's foot and ankle. The giant whirled around, slinging his tail behind him at the other heroes.

All were able to dodge the tail this time, ducking low under the massive appendage. Moose even had the presence of mind to jump onto the tail, racing up on his hands and knees as he carried his hammer in his left hand.

"Use your fire, Miranda," Raven instructed. The two of them launched a fiery assault at the giant's neck. Fireball after fireball crashed into it, singing and burning away the first layer of flesh.

The beast stomped down near Bull, knocking the man to the ground as it turned and looked at Raven and Miranda. It howled and spat a large glob of slimy saliva toward them. They dodged it in time, but the splashing impact covered Raven in a layer of thick goo that he could not breathe through.

Miranda rushed to his side and tried to pull the thick, green sludge away from his face, but nothing worked. "Help!" Miranda cried out.

Jason was aiming with his bow, but he abandoned the shot and came to her aid. He pulled a small field knife and carefully sliced through the thick mess until he was able to peel the slime away from Raven's face.

"Look out!" Bull cried out.

Jason and Miranda dove to the side just as the beast swiped its left hand at them. Luckily, it caught only air. Bull then jumped up and drove his sword into the beast's right leg, hanging from the sword and trying to make the hole as large as he could.

The giant troll-beast roared and stumbled backward. It was then that Miranda and Jason could see that Moose had reached the beast's hip. He dug in sharp with his hammer's spike and then pulled a pair of knives out. He used the knives to climb up the giant's back.

The monster howled in pain, spinning around and swiping its tail and arms at its back. Still Moose climbed on, digging in his knives as well as the cleats on his boots to ascend the thick, leathery skin. Bull was shaken loose with his sword during the spinning, but he didn't stop. He turned and chopped at the leg.

The giant troll howled in rage and opened its arms out wide to the side.

A flash of an arrow flew up and struck the beast deep in the chest.

Jason and Miranda turned to see Jonathan and Captain Ziegler running toward them. They were covered in dirt and ash, but alive.

"Jonathan!" Jason cried out.

Jonathan pointed to the giant. "It's a troll-kin," he shouted. "Take the heart or the head!"

Jason turned and nodded as he drew back his bow.

The troll moved its left hand up to protect its chest. There was no clear shot. Bull hacked at the giant's legs, but the troll leapt up and away from the man, landing sixty yards away and causing a minor tremor across The Warrens. Moose nearly lost his grip, hanging on with just one hand onto a knife in the creature's back.

"What's he doing?" Miranda gasped.

"Going for the head," Ziegler said. "Come on, we have to distract it and get an open shot to its heart."

Ziegler ran out into the field, shouting and hollering at the giant. Miranda continued to send fireballs blazing at the creature to keep it distracted from Moose. Bull was already charging the creature, shouting Bear's name and running like a crazed fiend.

"Jonathan, help Raven," Jason said as he pointed with his chin to the wizard.

Jonathan ran over and continued peeling the thick sludge away from the man.

He didn't watch as the giant beast made its way closer and closer to them. He trusted the others to do their best. He heard the arrow reappear in his quiver and silently offered thanks to the gods. A few moments later, he had Raven nearly free when Miranda and Jason called out their warning.

Jonathan saw Raven's eyes go wide and caught a glimpse of a massive limb swinging toward them. Jonathan didn't budge. He pulled on the last flap of slime holding the wizard in place, grunting with his effort. It pulled free just in time for the two of them to dive out of the way. Raven landed safely behind a large boulder, but Jonathan was not so lucky.

A great stone the size of a pumpkin grazed his back and dragged him across the rocky ground several feet.

Crrrrack-snap!

Jonathan's eyes shot wide. He thought for sure his back had broken. He laid on the ground, numb and too afraid to move.

Jason was there in an instant. "Are you hurt?" Jason shouted.

Jonathan dared to move, placing a hand down and sliding it to his back. He breathed a sigh of relief, but then his eyes shot open wide as he felt a jagged, sharp edge. He jumped up and pulled Kigabané around. The magical bow was entirely broken. The top limb had snapped off and the bottom limb had a great crack running through the side. He reached for his quiver only to find that the stone had ripped it from his back. He rushed over to it and found the last arrow splintered to bits beneath the stone.

"No, no, no!" Jonathan cried out.

Jason stood and called out. "It's alright, I have a bow. I

can finish it."

Jonathan shook his head. "No, his heart is too deep. You would need several arrows, magic arrows, to pierce the beast's skin."

"How could you know that?" Jason asked. Jonathan turned around to explain, but then he saw a massive hand sweeping down.

"Look out!" Raven called to them.

The thick fingers wrapped around Jason and the young man dropped his bow and arrow to the ground as he struggled to free himself from the beast's grip.

"Jason!" Jonathan cried. He ran to the bow and picked it up as the beast slowly rose up, standing straight. It was now ignoring Bull and Ziegler. The gashes in its legs were quick to heal, and there was no sign of Moose anywhere.

Jason struggled against the crushing grip and then he caught sight of the arrow still stuck in the troll-giant's third eye. He called down to Jonathan. "Let's play centers!"

Jonathan looked up and saw the arrow shaft embedded deeply in the third eye.

"Remember..." Jason shouted as he struggled for breath. "Remember..."

Jonathan did remember. He drew Jason's final arrow back and looked to the eye. He focused on the fletching, and then when the beast stood still and was moments from putting Jason into his slime-filled mouth, Jonathan shifted his gaze and looked at the hole, pretending the arrow wasn't there at all. He let the arrow fly and then closed his eyes, praying to the gods that his aim would finally be true.

The arrow flew up toward the eye, aiming for the arrow already stuck therein. It spun gracefully as time seemed to slow. It streaked past Jason and the young man stopped struggling against the troll-giant's hand long enough to watch the missile fly. A moment later, the first arrow exploded into three as Jonathan's arrow drove down through the exact center, splitting it and driving in deeper than the first.

That was when Jonathan saw Moose. The giant man dropped down from the troll's forehead, and with a mighty roar he used his hammer to drive the arrow even farther into the beast's head. So ferocious was his swing that the hammer pushed through the torn eye and embedded itself in the cracked skull behind the eye socket. Moose dangled from the hammer for a moment before his weight propelled him downward and he lost his grip.

Jonathan held his breath as the large troll began to fall backward to the ground. It toppled over at the waist, its legs crumpling beneath it. Bull and Captain Ziegler barely managed to escape while Moose landed atop the crumpled troll and then bounced off to the side.

Jason called out in fear as the hand holding him followed the rest of the giant's torso to the ground.

Dust shot out from the side and rocks bounced away as the troll impacted the ground.

The semicircle of troll warriors shrieked and turned to flee.

The battle, and the war, was over.

CHAPTER TWENTY

By the time the others got to Jason, Moose had already pried the troll-giant's fingers loose and the two were walking back toward them. Jonathan rushed up and the two brothers embraced, sharing a laugh and tears of joy.

"How did you find me?" Jason asked. "Nobody survives in the Murkle Quags. What were you thinking?"

Jonathan pushed away and smiled. "I'm stubborn like that," he said grinning at his older brother. "Besides, you needed my help."

Jason smiled and hugged him again.

"Oh, and, I think I finally beat you at centers," Jonathan added.

Jason sniggered and pushed Jonathan away playfully. "Don't let your ego get inflated too much, little brother. I say we need a rematch."

Captain Ziegler stepped in and shook his head. "No rematches," he said. "I only fight giant trolls once in a lifetime." He turned to Jonathan and slapped a hand on the young man's shoulder. "This little boy has not only helped us take down the giant beast, but he slew the troll king that we saw in the throne room."

Raven came in then and pressed for more information. "Was there anything else there?" he asked.

Jonathan nodded. "He had that amulet Ziegler told me about. When I broke it, that's when everything started shaking."

Raven nodded grimly as he reached up and stroked his chin, which was still spotted with bits of green goo. "I see. So it appears the king was using the artifact to amplify whatever magical powers he already possessed."

Jonathan shrugged. "I don't know, but whatever it was, it was evil."

"Why do you say that?" Raven asked.

"He saw the troll king sacrifice another troll on the altar," Ziegler put in.

Jonathan nodded. "My bow helps me see a troll's heart, and its life force. When the troll king sacrificed the other troll, its life force went into the amulet."

"Was it like a purple and gold mist?" Raven asked.

"How did you know that?" Jonathan asked.

Raven arched a brow. "Because that same mist rose up through the rocks when the earthquake occurred. After it rose into the sky, the rain stopped entirely."

"So the monsoons are over then?" Jason guessed.

Raven shrugged. "There is much I don't know, and can't know until I research it out a bit more. I have some theories though. Either way, it seems that this war is over. The surviving trolls fled from the battle after this giant beast was slain."

Ziegler nodded. "It's over," he said. "We can go home."

"I would even wager that the swamps will be a bit safer now," Raven put in. "What with the king and this behemoth dead, I am sure the remaining trolls will be cowering in their holes for a long time now."

Ziegler smiled wide and tilted his head up to the warm sunlight. "Not to mention that the rain is gone. They won't dare venture northward into our kingdom now. In the dry air without the rains, they'll be too susceptible to fire and we can send them running with their tails tucked firmly between their legs." He turned and smiled to the others, but then noticed that Bull was missing. "Where's Bull?" he asked.

"Bear died," Moose said.

They all looked to see Bull rushing toward Bear's crumpled body.

Ziegler hung his head low and sighed.

Over the next few hours, the group built a fine funeral pyre out of the best stones they could find. When they had finished, Moose helped Bull place Bear on top of the pyre. Bull arranged Bear's hands over his crumpled chest, trying to make him look as though he were only sleeping. He placed the man's knives on either side of him. Bull let a couple of tears drop from his face as he whispered goodbye.

"I'm going to miss you, Winnie," he said. Bull patted the man on the arm and then bent down to give him a brotherly kiss on the forehead. "Go swift and quick to Volganor, and see if you can save a seat for me in the best mead hall they have."

Bull climbed down then and went to stand next to Ziegler.

Raven summoned a powerful fire and they watched their friend as the flames enveloped the entire pyre and a column of smoke rose up to the heavens.

As they stood there, staring into the flames silently, Miranda slipped her hand into Jonathan's and leaned her head on his shoulder.

"I was thinking," she began. "Maybe I would like to see Tirnog first."

Jonathan smiled and squeezed her hand. "I'll make sure we have a place for you when you come."

Keep your eyes open for the next adventure for Jonathan, Jason, and the Ghosts of the Quags, <u>Brothers Haymaker</u>, coming Fall 2016!

If you enjoyed this book, then join Sam Ferguson's Facebook page, sign up for alerts on his Amazon page, and by all means leave a kind review!

For more great stories presented by Dragon Scale Publishing, go to our website:

www.dragonscalebooks.com

Sign up for Dragon Scale Publishing's newsletter to receive updates on new titles being released, information about give aways and other promotions, and news about events where you can meet our authors.

Other Books by Sam Ferguson

Other Dragons Scale Books:

About the Author

Sam Ferguson is a fairly average guy.
That's it.
No, really, that's it.
Oh- you are actually reading this?

Well... the truth is that Sam is a very *lucky* guy. He juggles work in such a way that he makes sure to spend enough time with his loving wife and sons. He loves being a fulltime writer and enjoys sharing his workspace with two bearded dragons. If he can carve out an extra hour for himself during the day, he'll hit the gym to try and regain the body he used to have in his youth (but he eats too much junk food to ever accomplish that goal).

He spent nearly five years serving as a U.S. Diplomat and absolutely loved the experience, but decided to move back home. Outside of the U.S. he has lived in Latvia, Hungary, and Armenia. He speaks Russian, Hungarian, and Armenian. (He used to speak some Latvian too, but he has no one to practice with anymore...)

He also has two dogs.

He plays the Elder Scrolls series.

His favorite superhero is Wolverine, but Batman is a close second.

If the kids go to bed at a reasonable hour, he will cuddle up with his wife to watch Scrubs reruns, the Big Bang Theory, Castle, and Burn Notice.

See, really just an average guy after all.